BUSY LIZZIE

The life of Lizzie Plant
BY

ADELE WOOTTON

Published in England by:
Teckle Publishing
Ashbourne
Derbyshire
DE6 1GA

Content copyright ©Kath Eaton 2012

All rights reserved. No part of this publication may be reproduced, stored in a retrieval system, or transmitted, in any form or by any means, electronic, mechanical, photocopying, recording or otherwise, without the prior consent of the copyright owner.

Cover designed by Designwall, Sudbury, Derbyshire

ISBN 978-0-9572139-0-6

First printed in 2012

Special thanks to Mick and my lovely girls,
Loz, Jo, Dani, Leonie and Elise,
for your help and faith in me.

Grateful thanks also, to Lenny.

Enjoy!
Adele Wootton

Adele Wootton is the pen-name of the youngest daughter of Elizabeth Plant (**Busy Lizzie**).

When Lizzie died, Adele Wootton felt alone in the world – her siblings all had 'someone special' in their lives, but, she had her dog, Candy, and the connection with animals has remained with her, throughout her life.

At fifteen, she left school with no qualifications, to begin her diverse working life – she was a sales assistant, clerical worker, telephonist and finally, personal assistant to a Managing Director, prior to her marriage to Michael.

After her children were born, she helped out with the family budget by working at a local knitwear factory, became an Avon lady and even picked mushrooms. Shortly before her youngest daughter started school, she became a bus driver – this job fitted in really well with school hours and holidays.
The poverty of her own early days made her more determined to better herself, and give her own children a good standard of living. During this time she trained to be a beautician, and eventually set up a treatment room within the family home.

In 2009, out of the blue, she suffered a heart attack and was forced into retirement, giving her the time to reflect on her life, and to write this book.

She had great fun re-naming the villages and towns of this area (Staffordshire/Derbyshire borders) see if you can guess what they are.

Dedicated to Candy, Bex and Izzy.

BUSY LIZZIE

By

Adele Wootton

CHAPTER ONE

Slowly, Lizzie opened her eyes. As she came out of her deep sleep, she squeezed her eyes shut again to try to re-capture the comfort of her night time repose. But, of course, it didn't happen! Her father was calling up the stairs "Lizzie! – are you out of that bed yet? You'll be late for work!"

"Yes Father, I'm up" she called back. She stretched, luxuriating in the warmth of the soft down of the mattress, with the entire bed to herself. Then - she remembered… Her best friend, who had arrived every month, as regular as clockwork since the age of fourteen, had let her down badly. It was now in the second month of the friend's absence and Lizzie was well aware of the consequences. Tonight she would see Reggie Jenkins and tell him of their shared problem. He would sort everything out: he always knew what to do.

Oh, how she loved him. Almost a year now, she had been seeing him. Not openly, of course. Father might not approve. So they met when they were at work, innocent smiles as they passed each other in the corridor of the Pot Factory where she worked as a glazer, while Reggie worked in the general office, alongside Mr. Wirksworth, the owner of the factory. They had then progressed to chats about their work and the weather and then meeting after church on a Sunday and walking out on to the moors, laughing and enjoying each others 'company. Then, one Sunday in September, the day was so warm - they had wandered off the usual route and into a shaded copse. There, Lizzie leaned against a tree looking at Reggie. He thought she had never looked so lovely. He cupped his hands around her face and gently kissed her lips. Lizzie felt all her dreams had come true. Soon the kissing was not enough for either of them. He spread his coat down on the moss covered ground and laid Lizzie tenderly on it. Their lovemaking was all-consuming and although Lizzie had had a very strict up bringing, she could see no wrong in their actions.

A knock on her bedroom door brought Lizzie back to reality. She leapt from her bed and snatched open the faded curtains. In an instant she felt so nauseous. She grabbed her coat from the nail behind the door and ran down the stairs and out of the kitchen, into the back yard to the outside lavvy where she vomited violently. "This is it" she thought. Back indoors she was sure her step-mother Fanny, had heard her retching. However, much to her surprise nothing was said and Lizzie heaved a sigh of relief. Her sisters, Dolly, Mary and young Cissie were all eating their buttered toast and the kitchen was buzzing with the usual early morning chit chat. No-one noticed that Lizzie wasn't eating. Cissie and Lizzie worked together at Wirksworth's Factory and as well as being sisters they were also best friends.

* * *

Reg Jenkins had worked hard at school and then taken himself off to night school where he studied book-keeping and any other subject that he thought would give a better chance in life. Common factory work was not for him. Oh no! He was going places. He wanted more out of life than his factory-working twin brother Charlie, father and grandfather before him.

He wanted the sort of life that only money and position could bring. And why not? He was a good looking fellow; he had charm, wit and charisma. He loved the life that his boss, Cuthbert Wirksworth had. Lovely house, large garden, motor car, gentle wife. Oh yes. He could manage that. Then there was Flora, only daughter to the said Mr and Mrs Wirksworth. She could be his passage to the lifestyle he so deserved. Okay, she was no raving beauty or scintillating company, and about ten years his senior, but, he could live with that.

He had taken to visiting his boss at home at a week-end on the pretext of some trivial matter concerning work. Mr Wirksworth was impressed by the conscientious young clerk, who also availed himself to menial jobs around the house and garden, insisting that it was no problem for him and there was no need, as he was already there, to ask the gardener or the odd job man. This often resulted in the old man inviting Reggie to stay and eat with the family, which is exactly what Reg wanted.

Feet under the table.

Yes, indeedy!!

At the moment his home was a seedy little bed sitting room at the top of an old house in the poorer part of town. All the cooking smells seemed to rise and settle in Reggie's room. Soon, he would be moving, when he married the fragrant Flora. Only last night he had carefully broached the subject and was amazed when the Wirksworths had shown such delight at the idea, suggesting that the wedding should take place as soon as possible. The only fly in the ointment was Lizzie. Still, she would get over it. She was such a pretty girl; she wouldn't be alone for long.

Then, the thoughts of some-one else making love to her made him stop in his tracks.

CHAPTER TWO

As Lizzie and Cissie arrived at the factory gates they were surprised to see a crowd of co-workers gathered there, chatting excitedly. A notice was attached to the factory gate.

IT IS WITH GREAT PLEASURE AND PRIDE THAT MR AND MRS CUTHBERT WIRKSWORTH ANNOUNCE THAT THE MARRIAGE OF THEIR DEAR AND ONLY DAUGHTER, FLORA TO MR REGINALD JENKINS WILL TAKE PLACE ON SATURDAY 12TH DECEMBER.

"Well!!" said one of the men, "Didn't think owd Reg had it in 'im to expect to go above is station like that. Who'd 'av thort it – crafty little bugger".

Lizzie's head started to spin. Voices all around her blended in to a buzz as she fell faint on to the ground. Immediately, the chat stopped and Lizzie was carried gently into the canteen, accompanied by a very worried Cissie. There, she was laid across a table. Quickly she regained consciousness and felt embarrassed to be the centre of attention. "I am so sorry to be such a nuisance. I was late rising this morning and missed my breakfast. Thank you all for your kindness. I feel fine now." And with that she slid from the table and went to clock in for her shift with a concerned Cissie at her side.

"Don't you think you should go back home Liz? You look awful" she said.

"Thanks a lot. You don't look too ravishing yourself, our Cissie" Lizzie retorted spitefully.

"Sorry Liz, I'm just worried about you, you really scared me just now," complained Cissie.

"Well don't. I'm ok... Right?" When Lizzie used that tone Cissie knew it was time to give in. They walked together to collect the pots that were lined up ready to be glazed. Today they groaned when they saw the row of large vases – that meant not much money would be earned today as they were paid by the amount of pieces they completed, and as the vases were so large, it took ages to complete just one. Never mind, they just had to get on with it. With brushes poised, they soon began the task in hand, the first smell of the glaze threatening to make Lizzie sick and faint all over again.

Women all around were chatting about the weekend, their families and, inevitably, the forthcoming marriage of the boss's daughter to their very own wages clerk. Lizzie started to hum to herself, a little habit she had devised to drown out words she didn't want to hear.

The whistle blew to tell the workers to down tools – it was time for lunch. Lizzie and Cissie went to the cloak room to retrieve a sandwich that they had tucked into the pocket of their coats. They decided to go outdoors and sit on the wall and enjoy the fresh air whilst they had the chance. Although it was late autumn the sun was warm on their backs. A couple of friends sauntered over to join them and Lizzie spied her chance to escape for a few minutes.

On the pretence of needing the wash room she dashed inside before any of the others offered to accompany her. Inside the corridor, she knew exactly where she was going. To see Reggie! There he was, sitting at is desk – chest puffed out – looking like the cat that got the cream.

"Pssst – Reg!" she whispered. He swung round to face her and she saw the anger in his cold blue eyes.

"You know you can't come in here, you fool. Get out now, before anyone sees you." he roared.

"But I need to speak to you. It's urgent!" Lizzie replied authoritatively. He stopped.

"Come to the back of the Furnace Shed at the end of work" he said through gritted teeth.

Six o'clock…. It seemed an age before the clock went round to the appointed hour when work finished and Lizzie could get to see her beloved Reggie: there had to be some simple explanation. It would be another Reginald Jenkins that was betrothed to the mousey Flora Wirksworth. She was sure that Reggie wouldn't look twice at such a plain creature. Besides, when she told him of her plight………

At last, the whistle blew to signal the end of this working day. Lizzie half ran to the cloak room, grabbed her coat and tore off down the corridor, ramming her fingers into her gloves as she went, pushing people aside in her haste to be outside and at last in the presence of her beloved Reggie. Turning the corner at the end of the furnace shed her heart leapt as she saw him standing there, collar turned up and hands pushed deep into his pockets. She ran to him and said,

"I m so glad you've come, Reggie".

He looked down at her with eyes as cold as ice. "It's over Lizzie; you must have heard my news?"

"Reg, say it's not true – how can you marry her when you know it's me that you love?"

"You just have to believe it, Daarlin', I am to marry Flora and take over the Factory, so, we can never meet up like this again. Goodbye, Lizzie, it's been fun."

At this he turned and walked away. She stood there, eyes wide open, staring after his retreating figure, hands held out in front of her, reaching out to him, as he walked out of her life.

Another problem sorted thought Reg as he walked away. Pretty little thing was Lizzie – they'd had some good times, but she didn't come with a factory as a bonus, like Flora did. One had to do what one had to do. He did feel ever so slightly guilty at the thought of Lizzie's distraught face - but – well – she'd get over it. She would never be short of a boyfriend, but what she needed was someone of her own kind. A factory worker, who would give her a neat little house, a few babies and a lifetime of work.

Now he, Reggie, deserved more than that and intended to have more and if it meant upsetting a few people on the way – so be it!

***

Cissie knew better that to say anything about the morning's events to Fanny when they arrived home. Lizzie, as always, helped prepare the evening meal and wash the pots when they had all eaten. Along with Cissie, Lizzie, Dolly, Fanny and Father, there was Mary, Flo and Jim all living in the tiny house. Dolly was already walking out with Harry, and their wedding date was set. Mary was planning her wedding to Jack for late next year when they had saved a bit more money, so that was going to ease the space problem very slightly.

Lizzie excused herself earlier than usual, saying she was feeling rather tired, but she really needed time alone in the bedroom before the others retired. She was in turmoil. Reggie didn't want her – he was marrying someone else – and she, Lizzie was expecting his baby.

Too soon it was morning and the whole ritual started all over again. Lizzie – out of bed – down the stairs – to the outside lavvy – was sick – back indoors. But, this time, Fanny was waiting for her. Instead of the usual hustle and bustle of the early morning rush the kitchen was silent. All eyes turned to her as she entered the room.

"Well. What have you to say for yourself, Young Lady?" boomed her father's voice.

"Whaaat what aaabout" stammered Lizzie, her eyes as big as saucers, looking from one to another of her siblings, then her step mother and finally, her father. She was aware that her condition was in no doubt.

"I want you out of this house by this evening, and, what's more, I never want to set eyes on you again, Elizabeth. You have brought shame on this family –. You are no longer my daughter"

Her father roared out the last words with such vehemence that it made Lizzie shiver. Her head bowed she crossed the room and ascended the stairs, her heart in her boots.

In the solace of her shared bedroom she started to pack her meagre belongings in to a hession bag.

She didn't have very many clothes; just spare underwear, a couple of pairs of woollen socks, her Sunday best dress and a couple of 'hand me down' woollen jumpers. From under her bed she pulled her best boots. Stuffed in the toe of her right boot was her savings, eleven pounds twelve shillings and seven pence ha'penny. Her hair brush and comb, which had been a present for her 21st birthday from her father and Maude was tucked carefully down the side of the bag along with a small towel and flannel. She then lifted the latch on the bedroom door and made her way down the stairs and back into the kitchen.

It was now silent – and empty!

On the table was a brown paper bag with her name on it. Inside were two rounds of bread filled with coarsely cut cheese, an apple and a tomato. A ten shilling note was placed underneath the bag. Ahh! Fanny. *She* must have done this last thing for her.

She smiled sadly to herself – not such an old witch, after all!!

She turned and looked round the only home she had ever known, imprinting every last detail on her mind. The fire grate, set and waiting for the match to be struck and bring the room to life with its warmth. The small window sparkling and letting in the morning light. The thick red chenille table cover, the worn linoleum on the floor. The peg rug that they had all helped to make out of old coats and skirts, how they'd laughed as they worked the peg through the sacking, each one making their own patterns and making it unique. The gentle tick of the little mantle clock that had belonged to her real mother, who had passed away, oh so many years ago.

Lizzie wished so much that she was alive – her real mother wouldn't have let her father turn her away, in her hour of need, she was sure of that. She turned and stepped out into the new day, closing the door carefully behind her. The she walked briskly away from the house, head held high, shoulders squared, bracing herself for whatever else life had in store for her.

She walked for a while with a constant ache in her throat. Whatever was she to do? Whatever it was, she was on her own.

Reggie didn't want her.

Her father didn't want her.

But there was someone who would want her. This life, growing inside her. This little baby had been conceived in love, and love is what would surround it when it was born. It would never know this feeling of rejection, or her name wasn't Elizabeth Plant.

At least the weather was kind to her. A weak sun shone down as she turned the corner and realised that she had reached the railway station and what was even better, a train was there awaiting the signal from the guard to say it was time to go. She saw this as a sign and rushed to the ticket office buying a single ticket to Utchester. She leapt aboard just as the guard blew his whistle and waved his green flag. She placed her bag on the rack above her head then settled down in the seat to watch the familiar countryside fly by.

The train arrived at Utchester in the early afternoon, after numerous stops along the way. As she left the station she realised how thirsty she was. First job, a cuppa and a bite to eat she planned.

It was market day and the little town was buzzing, but Lizzie soon found a small tea room where she ordered a pot of tea and scone. She paid for them and then struggled with her tray and bulky bag containing all her worldly goods, to the only vacant table. She sat down with great relief and poured out the tea, drinking it quickly and savouring every last drop. Suddenly, the door burst open. In walked a large plump woman. She seemed to know everyone in the tea room, greeting each of them by name as she made her way to the counter.

"Afternoon, Ida. The usual please, duck" said the woman.

"Comin' up Gwen – take a seat an' I'll bring it over to ya" said Ida kindly. The only vacant seat in the place was at Lizzie's table so she pushed pots to the side to make room for Gwen. Gwen plonked herself down on the fragile looking chair and nodded thanks in Lizzie's direction.

"How's things then Gwen?" enquired Ida as she set down the tray on the other side of Lizzie's table.

"Huh. Lost another housemaid terday. Her said I worked her too hard and her's got herself another position. No notice mind. Tells me this morning and then off she goes. No thought for anyone but theirselves – young uns terday".

Lizzie's ears pricked up. This must be fate. She smiled shyly at Gwen who barely glanced at her as she continued her conversation about the youth of today with Ida, until duty called her back to her counter. Lizzie's heart was pounding in her chest, this was her chance and she mustn't miss out.

"Erm – I couldn't help but hear that you are without a maid. I, myself am looking for a living-in position. I have no references with me but I am a good worker, I'm honest and I can start immediately." She paused, amazed at what she had just said to a total stranger, and looked at Gwen to see her reaction.

"Okay, you can have a months' trial. Be outside in ten minutes".

Gwen emptied her cup and then left as noisily as she had arrived, calling 'ta-ra' to each and everyone as she blustered out of the door.

"Well" thought Lizzie, "That must be the shortest and easiest interview ever. Wonder what I've let myself in for now. Still beggars can't be choosers and no mistake".

She finished her scone, had a second cup of tea then returned her tray to the counter, asked to use the ladies' rest room, and was still outside with minutes to spare. Within a couple of minutes an old Austin Seven pulled up next to her.

"Hop in gal" called Gwen. Lizzie lifted her bag on to the back seat of the car and then slid into the front seat next to Gwen. The car immediately lurched forward scattering a group of pedestrians who were waiting to cross the road. Lizzie had to stifle a giggle.

They left the little town and the scenery soon changed. Lovely wooded areas lined the road on which they were travelling and small rolling hills appeared ahead of them.

"So! What's yer name and where yer from, gal". Asked Gwen.
"My name is Elizabeth Plant and I'm from Livingstone in the Potteries" said Lizzie truthfully.

"Well I'm pleased ta meet ya and I hope we get on well tergether. I'm Gwen Taylor and I own a little hotel in Ellswood. All I ask is a good days work and I'll give a good days pay, with yer board and lodgings thrown in. One day off a fortnight and no men in yer room".

"Sounds ok to me, Gwen" Lizzie had already warmed to the rough country woman who had already been as kind to her as anyone had ever been in her twenty two years. Likewise, Gwen had felt an instant bond with the pretty dark haired girl with the 'oh so sad' eyes. She knew there was more to the story than Lizzie wanted to tell, at the present time but that could all come later. As they trundled along Gwen started to hum a tuneless melody and once again, Lizzie had to suppress a giggle.

Suddenly, the little car swung to the right and into a drive way leading to the small hotel called the Abbots Arms.

"Here we are then, Elizabeth, out ya get". Gwen was out of the car in an instant and Lizzie felt she would struggle to keep pace with the energy of the older woman. She gathered her bag from the back seat along with a couple of boxes of groceries that Gwen had signalled her to bring with her. She followed Gwen into a huge kitchen. So warm, so welcoming, so large, yet, so cosy. Gwen filled a large kettle and placed it on the range and prepared the teapot, cups and saucers. She reached up to a shelf and lifted down a tin that contained a delicious looking chocolate cake and placed it on a plate in the middle of the huge well scrubbed table.

"I'll show yer, yer room while we're waitin' fer the kettle ter boil, gal. Bring yer stuff with yer." Gwen said, walking from the kitchen into the hallway that led to the staircase.

Obediently Lizzie followed. Up one flight of stairs and then another smaller staircase led to a tiny attic room. This was a light clean room, sparsely furnished with just a single bed pushed up against the wall, covered in a pretty lemon cover that matched the curtains. On a small table in the corner stood a jug and bowl for washing, and a chest of drawers on the other wall, but it felt cosy and peaceful to Lizzie.

"Put yer things away and then come down and we'll have a drink of tea and a chat" Gwen said kindly. It didn't take her very long to find homes for her few belongings and when her bag was empty she thought the best place to store it would underneath the little bed. Pushing it under, she discovered an enamel chamber pot.

"Yes!" she thought." That will be so necessary with two flights of stairs between me and the lavvy".

Within minutes she was back down the stairs in the warmth of the homely kitchen. Gwen nodded towards the chair and Lizzie sat down at the table as Gwen placed a steaming cup of tea and generous slice of chocolate cake in front of her. They sat eating and drinking in companionable silence, both deep in thought. Gwen was first to break the silence.
"Want ter talk about it?" she asked kindly. Lizzie could see that not much escaped the notice of her new boss.

"Felt it was time to stand on my own two feet" she fibbed. Gwen thought that was quite a good answer to her pertinent question, and decided that was as far as she needed to go at this stage. The girl would open up to her in her own time, but she could see that she was a decent girl and that was really all she needed to know for now. Lizzie rose from the table and took the two plates, cups and saucers to the huge stone sink beneath the only window.

"Don't bother washing those up now, Lizzie. It's time to prepare the evening meal for my residents. There are just four of them this evening. Enjoy my home cooking, they do. Pop into the larder and fetch out the veggies, there's a good girl. Taters, carrots and cabbage will be ok for tonight. I cooked a leg of mutton yesterday so we'll make do with that. Think there should be some apple pie left on the shelf so we'll make up a jug o'custard and that will do for their pudding. You make a start while I go and shut the hens and ducks safely inside afore Mr Fox has a chance of lickin his chops around 'em"

Lizzie found some large heavy pans and starting peeling and chopping the vegetables, glad that she could work out for herself how much they would need. Her days of helping Fanny prepare meals for her large family had stood her in good stead. Gwen didn't fail to notice this when she returned to the kitchen after tending her feathered friends and gathering their eggs in readiness for the guests breakfast the following day.

Of the four guests for the evening meal, only three of them were residents, staying from Monday evening to Friday morning. Then, when their days work ended on Friday, they would return to their respective homes and families after the working week had been spent travelling around the Utchester area selling their wares and collecting further orders. So, each week there were different guests all with different products to sell, returning every four to six weeks, thinking that of all the hotels or guest houses they had to stay in this was, by far, the homeliest with the very best meals.

The fourth guest, Bill Udall, was a local widower in his sixties, whose late wife Connie, had been a dear friend of Gwen's. He worked at Callidge Hall where he was Head Gardener, but his real love was looking after the horses. The cottage in which he lived, was in a tiny hamlet called Southwood, belonged to the Hall and was a perk of his position as Head Gardener. Gwen being the kindly soul that she was, insisted that he call in on his way home from work to have his evening meal at the hotel.

"It's now't to me, Will", she said. "I'm cookin' anyways and one more won't make much difference to me".

At Bill's insistence, he re-paid her by planting vegetables in her garden, and tending them, and also doing odd jobs for her around the hotel, when he wasn't working at the Hall. This meant he was around the Hotel quite a lot, but it worked really well for the two of them. Will suspected that, just before she passed away, Connie had asked Gwen to keep an eye on him – and she was doing a grand job. Quite often they shared a bottle of milk stout after all the chores were completed. He loved being in the company of Gwen and they often talked in to the night.

The guests were served their meal, and only when they were satisfied did Gwen and Lizzie sit down to enjoy their own meal. Lizzie made Gwen a cup of tea and saw that as she relaxed, the older lady's eyes were slowly closing as she sat in front of the range. Lizzie silently crossed the kitchen and quietly washed and wiped all the pots and pans and put them all back in the places where she had found them. She then made her way up the two flights of stairs to her room carrying a small kettle of warm water so that she could wash the days grime from her tired body. After pulling on her nightgown she dropped into the little bed and was asleep in minutes.

CHAPTER THREE

Cissie felt distraught. Lizzie wasn't only her sister; she was also her best friend and workmate. She had missed her so much today. Walking alone, to and from work just emphasised the fact that Lizzie had left home. It was ok whilst she was actually at work, as Betsy and Sarah had included her in everything, even asking her if she would like to go the picture house with them on Saturday night.

When she got home she tried to talk to Father about Lizzie, but he said, in no uncertain terms that she was not to mention her again.

On the bright side, he had said she could go to the pictures with her friends on Saturday night and also there was a little bit more space in the bed. She felt so guilty thinking these thoughts, she just wished she knew that Lizzie was alright – and if it was true that she was….. with child…. how would she manage on her own? It was early days, she was sure Lizzie would contact her as soon as she was settled.

She must miss me as much as I miss her, she consoled herself.

Saturday night arrived, although it had seemed such a long week to Cissie.

"Come on slowcoach" Sarah called to her as she headed towards the queue for the cinema. In front of them were a group of young fellows. Betsy was in easy conversation with a couple of them as they had all been to school together. One member of the group stood slightly back from the rest. Cissie looked up at the tall quiet young fellow and into the bluest, most twinkling eyes she had ever seen. She smiled, blushing ever so slightly, as her heart raced at his smile. Betsy introduced her to the group leaving the quiet man until last.

"This here is Ted Bentley; he's George's cousin and lives over in Endown."

"Pleased to meet you all" Cissie said – still looking into Ted's blue eyes that were smiling back into hers. She hoped against hope that they would be sitting next to each other once they were inside the picture house, but Sarah chivvied her along and Cissie ended up sitting between her two friends. Her mind was not on the film and at the end of the evening, when they all called a cheery goodnight to each other and went off to their respective homes; she couldn't help but feel a little disappointed. Still, Endown was not the other side of the county and Ted may visit his cousin again soon and she soon drifted off to sleep in a more optimistic state of mind.

All too soon it was Monday morning, and the rush in the little cottage started all over again. Cissie grabbed her work coat, and her cheese sandwich, and dashed out of the door calling cheerio to all. Betsy and Sarah were at the end of her road, so ran even faster to catch up with them, and they all chatted amiably about their night out at the picture house, and their opinions of the film. As usual, their day was busy with little time to chat and the time seemed to fly by. Betsy and Sarah had an errand to attend to before they went home so Cissie made her way, alone, towards the factory gate. Head bent and deep in thought she suddenly bumped into a young man standing outside the gate.

"Oops, sorry" she said. "Oh. It's you"! Of all the people, in all the world! There stood the one person who had occupied her thoughts for the last forty-eight hours, in fact, ever since she had been introduced to him. Ted Bentley!!

"I hope you don't mind me turning up like this, Cissie. I've been waiting for you" he said. "I was wondering if you would like to come out with me some time" he added shyly.

"I will have to ask Father, but I hope he says yes, as I would like to very much, Ted" Cissie replied, her hazel eyes shining to match the twinkling of Ted's blue ones. They walked along the road together chatting about their mutual friends until they reached her home.

"I'll call for you at 2.30.on Saturday, Cissie" he promised, and then turned round and walked back down the road. Cissie stood and watched until he reached the corner. There he turned to see her still standing there watching him and raised his hand and smiled the smile that lit up his entire face. Cissie smiled and waved back but stayed where she was until she could no longer see him. Only then, did she turn and enter the house with a warm glow within her soul.

The days until Saturday seemed to drag by, each one similar to the last. Work and missing Lizzie. But soon it was time to clock out, as the whistle had blown to say that was the very end of the working week. Cissie arrived home, helped to prepare the evening meal and wash the pots and re-place them neatly on the shelves. It was strange how she seemed to have taken over all of the chores that were once done by her beloved Lizzie. She then boiled the kettle and washed her lovely nut brown hair and sponged her body from top to toe to make sure she smelt fresh for her date with Ted, tomorrow. She didn't want any trace of the smell of the factory on her hair or body.

Saturday night was usually bath night in their house, which was when they brought in the zinc bath from the back yard and placed it on the kitchen floor, filling it with kettle after kettle of boiling water, then taking it in turns to bathe themselves until the water was either too cold or too dirty.

Cissie could hardly contain her excitement. Once in bed she struggled to get to sleep, and when she did, she dreamt that Father had said no she couldn't go out walking with Ted, and woke relieved to discover it was only a dream.

Cissie had never known a day pass so slowly.

She rose early to do her chores, starting with washing her work clothes. The smell of the glaze was ever present in the fabric, no matter how hard she rubbed with the bar of soap. She rinsed her dress, cardigan, over-all, stockings and under-wear and squeezed as much water out of them as she could before putting them through the mangle, and then hung them to dry on the make-shift clothes line strung across the back scullery.

She then went upstairs into her shared bedroom and stripped the sheets, pillow slips and bolster cases from the bed, and replaced them with clean ones Fanny had left for her at the bedroom door.

They didn't have much money, and so very few luxuries, but the house was always clean and fresh, and Fanny prided herself that her 'whites' were the whitest in the row of washing lines, on a Monday morning.

Lunch, on a Saturday was usually a pan of lobby that Fanny had set simmering straight after breakfast. The comforting smell of carrots, potatoes, turnip and onions cooking permeated the entire house. Cissie was surprised how hungry she felt and ate a good dish full before helping to clear the table and wash the pots.

But, it was still only one o'clock!

She went back to her bedroom and pulled out a little note pad which served as her diary and began to write down her innermost thoughts and feelings. She wrote about her excitement of seeing Ted again, how she was looking forward to the Christmas break which was only a couple of weeks away, and also her concern for her absent sister. She wrote of her hopes that Lizzie would be in touch, very soon.

At two o'clock, she again brushed her hair and took her coat from the small shared wardrobe, put on her best shoes, picked up her handbag and went down the stairs. At precisely two thirty, the knock came that she had waited all week for. With pounding heart she opened the door, to a smiling Ted.

"Hello, Cissie. You look nice" he beamed. She stood to the side so that he could enter the house where she introduced him proudly to the family; Father, Fanny and all of her siblings.

Once that was out of the way, they quickly said their goodbyes and were on their way. They chatted about mundane things as the made their way down the street and towards the town centre, stealing admiring glances in each other's direction. They looked in shop windows, marvelling in each others company and all the things they found they had in common.

After about an hour of meandering, they found a small tea shop and decided it must be time for some afternoon refreshment. Cissie sat at the table and watched as Ted went to the counter. He smiled at the girl as she took his order – his whole persona was so lovely and he was there with HER, Cissie Plant – she tingled with happiness. She just knew that today was just the start of something very special.

Something so special that it lasted their entire lifetime.

CHAPTER FOUR

"Well, Reg! How are ya feelin?" Joe Stokes, foreman from the factory had agreed to be Reg's best man, although Reg had a twin brother somewhere out there, he wanted to leave his former life where it belonged – in the past - Reg smiled back at Joe like the cat that got the cream.

"I'm feelin great" he exclaimed. His few belongings were packed and Joe was helping him to carry them over to his new home, which was a small lodge in the grounds of the home of his future in-laws. The idea being, when the old man retired, he and his good lady would move into the Lodge and Reg and Flora would fill the big house with their off-spring and make Cuthbert and Grace very happy grandparents.

Reg didn't even bother to take a last look at the scruffy bed sitting room and closed the door and walked down the stairway, pausing only to smooth down his auburn hair as he passed by the mottled mirror in the hallway, to start his new life.

After depositing his worldly goods at the Lodge, Reg and Joe walked up the sweeping drive to the big house. The maid showed them into the sitting room and was back in a flash with a tea tray and after placing it on a small table in front of the two young men; she bobbed a little curtsey and excused herself. Joe looked in awe then glanced in Reg's direction and saw he had a permanent smirk on his face. Joe thought it was fitting for him to pour the tea and as they enjoying the warmth and comfort of their opulent surroundings the door was flung open and in breezed Mr Wirksworth.

"Ahh Gents! This is no time for tea," and strode purposefully across the room and poured three large glasses of port from a beautiful crystal decanter.

Reg and Joe stood up as he passed the drinks to them. Jo thought, "Well – Reg has certainly done well for himself. From today onwards, he'll have it all!"

"Right – let the celebrations begin."

Cuthbert led the way to the west drawing room where the wedding ceremony was going to take place. The room was tastefully decorated, a beautiful Christmas tree stood in the corner, a huge fire blazed in the grate and the natural light cast a calming amber glow. Not that Reg was nervous. No, he knew exactly what he was doing and couldn't wait to get on with it. The parson stood by the french doors, so Reg and Joe took their places in front of him.

The next minute Flora entered the room on her father's arm and the afternoon sped by in a blur.

The vows were made the brash Jenkins, promising to love, cherish etc., in a loud baritone voice. Poor Flora's voice was a mere whisper.

In no time at all it was over.

Mrs. Flora Jenkins ascended the stairs in the little lodge with her handsome husband. He went into the bathroom and by the time he came out, Flora had quickly removed her bridal gown, donned her chaste nightdress and was already in the bed. Reg slowly undressed and climbed in beside his wife. He gently took her in his arms and kissed her lips – they were thin – and dry! And it was like holding a piece of wood. He coaxed and cajoled to try and put her at ease but nothing seemed to work. Feeling hurt and then angry at her lack of response he threw himself on top of her and performed better than he had ever done, or so he thought. When he rolled back on to the bed, he was furious to hear her softly sobbing. His usual magic obviously hadn't worked – in no time at all he was fast asleep and snoring.

Flora was horrified at what had just taken place, she hadn't been forewarned how awful it all was,

"Let's just hope we've made a baby" she thought and crossed her fingers.

CHAPTER FIVE

Lizzie was settling well into life at the hotel. She soon learned the likes and dislikes of the guests and was very popular with them as she had such a ready smile, and the will to please.

On the 12th of December she was so busy and it wasn't until she fell into bed exhausted that she realised that the man of her dreams was now the husband of another woman.

Christmas came and went.

Winter turned into spring and the countryside came alive with colour.

First the brave little snowdrops appeared through the smattering of snow and then the pussy willow – followed by the purple and the yellow of the crocuses. Then the daffodils burst forth in all their golden glory.

Lizzie noticed that her waist-line was also bursting forth. It was just a matter of time before it was noticed. She tried not to think what would happen when Gwen found out she was pregnant. She had spent some of the happiest days of her life here, living simply, working hard but at peace with herself. She didn't have to wait long....

The following day she was out in the orchard, feeding the hens and encouraging them to go into the hen-house for safekeeping over night, when she slipped. Her ankle was so painful that, when she tried to put her weight on it, she fell again.

Tears of frustration welled in her eyes, as she shuffled on her bottom towards the gate. Just at that moment, Bill Udall turned the corner and saw poor Lizzie struggling. He ran to help and lifted her with ease and carried her into the kitchen. Gwen fussed over her as Lizzie told her what had happened, she was sat in Gwen's chair next to the range and her ever swelling foot was gently placed on a small stool and covered with a cold wet towel.

"Can you just pop up the road to Dr. Clayton's, I think he should be finished surgery by now" she said to Bill, as she glanced at the clock.

"Ask him if could pop and have a look – it may be broken".

Bill was out of the kitchen before Gwen had finished speaking and was back with the doctor within minutes.

Fortunately, the doctor was taking his evening constitutional, after surgery, and before his evening meal, so Bill caught up with him and told him the story of Lizzie's accident.

"Now young Lizzie, what's happened?" asked the kindly doctor. He took the swollen ankle and pressed it, and looked this way and that, and then ummmmed and arrrrrred, as doctors do. Then he said,

"No bones broken, Miss. Just a bad sprain – a couple of days rest and you'll be as good as new."

With that he took a bandage from his black bag, and quickly and deftly had the ankle swathed in no time at all.

"Thank you Doctor Clayton, so much" Lizzie said gratefully.

But, as she raised her eyes from the puffy ankle to the doctor's face, she caught him looking at her spreading girth. The way she was sitting in the chair accentuated the swelling of her belly.

The doctor knew!

Gwen made them all a cup of strong tea and after exchanging a few snippets of village gossip, the old gentleman went on his way, and Gwen saw him out.

Bill was standing, looking embarrassed and not knowing what to do next.

"Thanks for helping me Bill, I really don't know how I would have managed if you hadn't come along when you did", Lizzie said gratefully.

"That's ok", he replied self consciously, "Let me know if there's anything you need". With that he went off into the dining room to eat his meal.

Lizzie thought, "What a lovely man Bill is".

When Gwen returned to the kitchen Lizzie half expected her to make some reference to her condition, but when nothing was said, she inwardly heaved a sigh of relief.

Gwen then helped her to the table where, she surprisingly discovered she was starving and really enjoyed her meal. Then, Gwen fussed over her, bringing her blankets and pillows, and made up a bed for her on the large sofa in the warm kitchen, to save the girl having to manoeuvre the two flights of stairs, to her own little room.

The next morning Bill called in on his way to work, to see how the invalid was feeling, and to bring her a book to read, to save her being bored. It was 'Little Women' and Lizzie couldn't wait to start it, and thought it was a kind thing for Bill to do. Next it was the turn of Dr. Clayton to call in and see his patient. Gwen was busy clearing the breakfast pots from the dining room and it was only the two of them the doctor boldly said,
"You need to tell Gwen – and soon".

"I will" promised Lizzie.

Gwen bustled in just as the doctor was leaving.

"See ya Doc – thanks a lot" Gwen called out to his retreating figure.

"See you tomorrow, Lizzie. 'Bye Gwen", he called.

Lizzie watched as Gwen methodically brought the pots through and began the arduous task of washing, wiping, putting away, a task that they had normally shared over the last few months.

When the chores were completed, Gwen took a short break to enjoy a well earned cuppa with Lizzie.

Lizzie was feeling guilty that the older woman was looking worn out already, so she suggested that Gwen brought the vegetables to her and she could peel and chop, whilst sitting in her chair. Then, in a quiet moment, Lizzie decided that the time was NOW. With heart thumping, she opened her mouth to reveal something that she was sure was going to change her life, forever.

At that moment Bill came into the kitchen with another book for Lizzie to read. This time it was Anne of Green Gables.

Gwen was so pleased to see the two of them getting on so well – she often worried about Bill and his loneliness. She also sensed that Bill was becoming fond of Lizzie, but it was obvious to her, that Lizzie was oblivious to the fact.

When Bill finally left Lizzie knew that she could put off the dreaded deed no longer.

"Gwen" she started to say. The anguish in her voice made Gwen stop in her tracks. "What is it Lass?"

"I need to talk to you and tell you…….." Lizzie's confidence faltered, as if, by not saying the words out loud, she could somehow, make the problem go away.

"You tryin' to tell me you're in the fam'ly way"

Gwen made it as easy as she could for Lizzie. She had been waiting weeks for this conversation and had it all worked out, already in her head. But her heart went out to poor Lizzie.

"How do you know – did the doctor tell you?", stuttered an astonished Lizzie.

"Nah! course not. He wouldn't do that. Nah – that first day I metcha I guessed, and then as time went by, I could see fer meeself. I knew you'd have to tell me evencherly." Gwen said matter of factly.

"Oh Gwen, You took me in – knowing all this. You really are an amazing person. But what am I going to do?"

"Do ya want the bairn?", asked Gwen.

"I don't see how I can" cried Lizzie.

"I asked – Do yer want this babby?"

"Yes I do. But……"

"Then we'll work something out, doncha worry. We're always full these days and I've been thinking of takin' on a bit more help. Eva Finney, down the village could do with a bit of cash and I've been thinking of askin' her ta come a few hours a week. We'll manage between us, gal. You've proved to be a good little worker, honest, reliable and friendly, I don't want ta letchya go".

Gwen was amazed at herself. That must have been the longest speech she had ever made, and all in one breath.

"Oh Gwen, I don't know what to say. You are so kind; I'll not let you down, Thank you, thank you so much." Then the tears that had been brimming in her eyes spilled over and coursed down her cheeks in gratitude.

Lizzie could not believe how different Gwen's re-action had been to that of her Father. Thinking of him made her think of home, but no, this was her home now.

But she decided she must write to Cissie and let her know where she was living, and that she was going to be alright.

CHAPTER SIX

"What have you planned for today, Flora Dear" enquired Reg, the loving husband, more out of duty than genuine interest.

"Oh, I'm going to see Mummy this morning. Then we are lunching with Mrs Gerrard and Mrs Myatt from the Embroidery Circle," Flora replied softly.

Humph! Never done a days work in her life, and never likely to either, thought Reg, ungraciously.

"That's nice but don't go over-doing things, now," he replied.

Flora had just mis-carried their third child in the last six months and was looking even more fragile than usual. Her attempt at a smile made him feel like shaking her and telling her to lighten up. Having a baby was important to him too, but you didn't see him mooching around the place with a long face.

Yes, Cuthbert was anxious for them to make him a Grandpa and he wasn't afraid to express his desires, no matter who was around. It was beginning to get a bit embarrassing, to say the least, but Reggie knew that it was no failing on his part.

He was putting them there alright, and with Mrs 'Prim and Proper' that sometimes took some doing, it was Flora that couldn't keep them in place.

"Right, see you this evening then", he said, anxious to get away as soon as he could. He loved the lifestyle and status that being married to Flora brought about, but she was such a boring and cold person; nothing like Lizzie Plant.

"Now what made me think of her?" he puzzled. But then, Lizzie was a lovely warm, and oh, so passionate girl – woman – all woman, quite the opposite of his lady wife. Then he wondered what had happened to Lizzie, he hadn't seen her around the factory lately, come to think of it, but he had really wanted her to keep out of his way, and told her so in no uncertain terms the last time they had spoken.

He could make some discreet enquiries.

Maybe they could take over where they left off, just before his marriage. That would be good………

Just as he arrived at the factory gates he couldn't believe his luck. Cissie Plant, Lizzie's younger sister, if he wasn't very much mistaken, was about to enter the factory. He hurried along to catch her up before she joined the queue waiting to clock in.

"Cissie, isn't it"? He asked.

"Yes sir", she replied, wondering why he had spoken to her – he never had before – surprised that he even knew her name.

"Everything ok?"

"Yes sir".

"Has Lizzie changed her job? I haven't seen her lately". Cissie was even more surprised to hear him speak of her sister. A lump rose in her throat as she thought of Lizzie and spoke without realising it.

"She's moved to the country to take care of an aged Aunt", she repeated this, in parrot fashion, as her father had ordered her to do, when anyone asked of his wayward daughter, to save bringing shame on the family by admitting what had really happened.

Every day she hoped that there would be a letter waiting for her, when she returned home from work, and every day her heart dropped, as time fled by with still no word from her.

Reggie walked away, furious.

Another of his brilliant ideas gone wrong. Cissie stood watching him stride towards his office, a puzzled look on her face.

Just then Sarah and Betsy caught up with her and linked her arms.

"Dreamin' about someone we shouldn't ay Cis? He's spoken for, yer too late, Love" they teased.

Then, together they went and clocked in, and prepared to start another busy shift, their conversation soon forgotten.

When she returned home from work, she could not believe her eyes.

On the mantle shelf was a letter propped up, in front of the clock, addressed to her, Cissie Plant, in Lizzie's neat handwriting, she had thought of Lizzie, and wished all day to hear from her soon, it must have been telepathy. She snatched the letter down from the mantle shelf and ran up the stairs, to the privacy of her bedroom. She knew that if Father returned home and saw it, he would 'back the fire' with it, straight away.

With trembling hands she tore open the envelope and read:

Dearest Cissie,
I just wanted to let you know that I am well. I have a living-in position in a small hotel in Ellswood and my employer now knows about the baby, so please don't worry about me. I hope that

you and all the family are well. I think of you all the time. Please write back and tell me all of your news. Your loving sister, Lizzie'.

Cissie was so happy even with so few words; they were words she needed to hear.

She ran back down the stairs to help with the evening meal, her heart lighter than it had been for weeks. As soon as the chores were completed she took a page out of her diary notebook and sat on her bed to reply to the brief note, telling Lizzie everything that was happening at home:

Dolly and Harry were now married and had taken over a little shop.

At the factory: Betsy and Joe are now going out together.

In the street: the births, marriages and deaths:

And finally all about Ted.

As an afterthought she related the strange conversation that had taken place, only that morning, with the even stranger, Mr Jenkins.

She carefully folded the page and placed it in an envelope and then skipped down the stairs grabbing her coat from behind the door and dashing down the street to the post office, on the corner, purchased a stamp and posted her reply to Lizzie. It would soon be winging its way to Ellswood.

CHAPTER SEVEN

Lizzie was in the kitchen when the postman delivered Cissie's letter. Her eyes scanned the pages, hungry for the news from home. By the end of the letter she had developed a huge lump in her throat. How Lizzie missed them all, but particularly young Cissie – how wonderful to hear that she now had Ted in her life, she sounded so excited about her friendship with him. He was obviously someone very special. Someone who Cissie deserved because she, herself was such a warm, generous loving girl. She couldn't wait to meet this Ted, and told this to Cissie in her reply.

Her ankle was almost better, and she was now able to get up the stairs to her room, and she was also managing to do more and more of her chores. However, when she could, she sat and rested it. True to her word, Gwen had contacted Eva, and she was soon established as a willing member of the team. Bill played his part by clearing the pots from the dining room and stacking them ready for washing – sometimes he even did that too! This meant that he was spending more and more time in Lizzie's company. She soon realised what a kind and caring man he was, but, so painfully shy.

Spring turned into summer and the weather turned hot and sultry. Lizzie constantly felt so tired. Her weak ankle swelled with the extra weight she had gained. Gwen saw how exhausted she was, and gave her as many of the easier tasks as she could, without putting too much on to Eva, who was such a slightly built, little soul. Lizzie could see what was happening, and vowed to herself that she would repay Gwen's kindness, as soon as she was over the pregnancy.

By the third week in June the heat was oppressive. Lizzie's small room at the top of the hotel was airless. She had thrown the tiny window wide open but there was no breeze to cool the air.

She lay on top of the bed looking down at the mound that used to be her belly. Now it was home to her unborn baby. She sighed as she hauled her bulky body up. Once again she needed to empty her bladder so, as it was almost six o'clock, she thought she may as well go downstairs and then she could brew a pot of tea as a treat for Gwen. But, as she rose, a searing pain overtook her entire body.

She fell back on the bed in a faint.

On the floor below Gwen was woken by the thud. She knew only too well that Lizzie was at the very end of her pregnancy, and each night, when she fell into bed her last thought would be 'Tonight could be the night'. It looked as though this was it. She rushed up the staircase that led to Lizzie's room where she discovered Lizzie coming out of her faint. Just at that moment her waters broke and Gwen, in her calm way, took charge, and comforted and encouraged her to push her baby into the world. Lizzie put her faith in Gwen and pushed and pushed, and baby Margaret entered their lives. Gwen laid the little girl across her mother's stomach and then dashed back down the stairs to ask someone, anyone, to fetch Mrs Tideswell, the midwife. As she entered the kitchen she found Eva there cooking breakfast for the residents. 'What a treasure' thought Gwen? With an armful of clean soft towels she made her way back up the stairs to find Lizzie in agony. Her face was distorted with pain.

"What's wrong gal" she asked.

The next minute Lizzie gave an almighty groan, and yet another baby's head appeared. Just at that moment the midwife arrived, much to Gwen's relief. She backed out of the little room and left her to do her job, whilst she went back down the stairs to collect more towels and hot water. On her return she was met with the sight of Lizzie propped up in bed with a baby in each arm.

"Is that it then?" she asked grinning.

"Two not enough for you then, Gwen?" gasped Lizzie.

Half an hour later Mrs. Tideswell came back down the stairs, most of her work had been done for her, before she arrived. She and Gwen looked at each other.

Then they both started to laugh.

"Who would have thought it? Twins!" Gwen cried delighted. "I don't know how we'll manage but, somehow, we will"
.
Upstairs, Lizzie was unwrapping the babies that the midwife had so carefully swathed. She needed to look at their perfect little bodies; to check that everything was there that should be there, she was just like every other new mother under the sun. Eight little fingers and two thumbs each. Wonderful! Ten toes each, fantastic! But then she noticed that on both babies there was an extra nail on the second toe on the left foot.

What a bond they shared.

She smiled to herself – that makes them even more unique. The little boy, her son, also had a large, very dark freckle on his left big toe.

Ahh, a beauty spot, she thought.

That evening Bill arrived carrying something really bulky wrapped in an old sack. He, as a family friend, always used the back entrance where the residents all entered by the front door.

The residents were not encouraged to come into the kitchen, as Gwen felt this was her inner sanctum, and they all respected that.

He laid the sack carefully on the kitchen floor and the ladies watched, as he unwrapped the sweetest little baby's crib that they had ever seen. It was made of rosewood and set on rockers, and a varnished finish that you could almost see your reflection in.

"I've heard that we have another little helper in the house", he said.

Word had obviously got round that the midwife had been seen at the hotel and Bill had put two and two together.

Gwen started to laugh.

"Don't you like it?" asked Bill feeling hurt at this reaction.

"It's loverly, Bill, but…" then she proceeded to tell him and Eva all about the two babies; gilding over the gory bits; a little girl called Margaret and a little boy, who, as yet, didn't have a name. Bill realised then, that another crib was necessary.

The following morning Dr Clayton arrived to offer his congratulations to Lizzie and to check her over, along with her babies.

Lizzie pointed out the unusual toe nails and also the baby boy's large black freckle that seemed to have darkened over-night.

He assured her, that although the extra nails were quite unusual, they were nothing to worry about and the freckle was just a birth mark that would grow and darken as the baby grew – again, nothing to worry about, she had two beautiful, normal babies.

Lizzie was soon up and about after the double delivery. They were all still in shock, and life seemed to be a round of feeding, changing nappies, sleeping, but not necessarily in that order.

Lizzie knew that, to keep a roof over their heads, she had to pull her weight with the chores in the hotel, and she also wanted to show her gratitude to Gwen. They soon had a good rota in place, and fortunately, the babies were really placid, so life was good. Lizzie felt more contented than she had ever done in her life.

Margaret was a pretty baby with a shock of black hair and dark brown eyes. The little boy had a small tuft of auburn hair and blue eyes. They didn't even look like brother and sister, let alone twins.

Letters between Cissie and Lizzie usually flew back and forth, on a regular basis but the twins were three weeks old before Lizzie had time to write and tell her the news. Almost by return of post she received the reply.

Cissie was thrilled to learn that she was auntie twice over, but then astounded Lizzie by informing her, that, on the same day as she gave birth to the twins, Fanny had also produced a little girl. They had named her Marjorie, and Fanny and Father were as surprised as everyone else. They had thought that Fanny was experiencing the 'change of life' and a bit of 'middle age spread'.

Lizzie decided there and then she needed to pay them all a visit as soon as possible.

She mentioned it to Gwen and Eva, first telling them about her new step-sister, and her desire to see Cissie, as they were all enjoying an afternoon cup of tea.

Immediately, Eva offered to look after the babies for the day.

"It will be much easier for you to travel on your own, and I will love looking after them – and it's not as if they don't know me", she pleaded. "Please say yes, Liz. I'll take such good care of em, honestly I will".

"How can I refuse" laughed Lizzie, thinking to herself 'But I know you'll be ready to give them back to me, when I return'.

That evening, when Bill arrived for his meal, he came to the back door and called to Lizzie. She wiped her floury hands on her apron and followed his voice.

In the back yard stood a beautiful grey coach-built pram, all trimmed with gleaming chrome. Bill stood along side it with a self conscious grin on his face.

"This was at the back of the barn at the Hall and I asked the Mistress and she said yes and I cleaned it….. And here it is…." he rambled, looking at Lizzie, to judge her reaction.   His words hadn't made an awful lot of sense to her so she just looked at him.

"The Mistress has given you the pram for the babies. Don't you like it?"

He sounded so disappointed.

"It's for me? Lizzie asked incredulously. "It's the most beautiful pram I have ever seen".

And she dashed towards it running her hands over the shiny metal and peering inside, then standing at the handle, to check for size.

"It's just the right size, as though it was made for me" she was almost squealing with delight.

Gwen and Eva had come out into the yard to see what all the fuss was about.

They all decided it was just the best pram ever.

"How can I ever thank you, Bill – And you, Gwen, and you too Eva". These good people really were the salt of the earth. It was then she came to the decision -"I will call my son Robert **William** and my daughter Margaret **Eva Gwendoline**, and they will be known as Meg and Bobby".

CHAPTER EIGHT

Reggie and Flora sat across the breakfast table from one another.

Neither of them had much to say - they didn't seem to have anything in common.

If only they had a little baby, it would give them a shared interest...

And, maybe, the old man would retire and want to move into the Lodge.

It was Reggie's main aim in life; he knew that once he was ensconced in the big house, he would have the status and respect he had worked so hard for.

He also knew that Flora was dull and boring, but that was a small price to pay.

Today, at Cuthbert's recommendation, she was going to see a specialist in gynaecology to try and establish the reason why she kept losing their babies.

Of course, Mummy would accompany her.

Reg rose to his feet and placed a perfunctory kiss on his wife's pallid cheek. Even this chaste action caused an automatic flinch from Flora; she would prefer to have no bodily contact with him. She found the whole baby-making process totally distasteful. However, she had an obligation to her father to fulfil, and if nothing else, she was dutiful...

"See you this evening then, dear" Reg said as he walked out of the door and headed towards the factory, glancing over his shoulder towards the big house.

Not long now, he hoped.

The coldness between the couple had not gone un-missed by Flora's doting parents. They thought, hoped, that a child would bring them closer together and looked forward to a positive outcome from the forth-coming appointment. Money well spent thought Cuthbert. He was more than ready to retire from his challenging position at the factory.

He intended spending his days wandering the moors with his gun, taking a pot shot at anything that moved; then, there were days to be spent at the local race track.

Oh, and of course, he had promised Grace a holiday. They would take the train to Europe and spend a few weeks in the south of France.

So much to do – so little time!

His high opinion of Reg Jenkins had faltered slightly but he still wanted to give him the benefit of the doubt. Besides, divorce was totally out of the question. Far too scandalous for this small close knit community – he couldn't even think about that.

After today, he was sure that all would be well.

Flora paled at the very thought of having to see a doctor on such intimate terms.

Her mother was sat upright with her hands clasped together in her lap in a corner of the consulting room as the gynaecologist poked and prodded at poor Flora's tense and trembling body.

Soon it was over and the doctor left the room and a kindly nurse appeared and helped Flora from the treatment couch. As she dressed herself, her hands were shaking so much that she could barely fasten her buttons. The doctor returned, and, with a smile, said that he felt that there was no apparent problem, only, maybe her age was against them. With another smile he told her to go home and keep trying. Flora thought she would die on the spot of embarrassment at this remark – particularly said in front of Mummy.

CHAPTER NINE

Cissie was so excited to be auntie to twins as well big sister to Majorie. Each evening she rushed home from work and took over from her stepmother, cooing and singing to the baby as she bathed her and gave her her feed. Fanny was very frail after the late pregnancy and difficult delivery, and was only too pleased to let Cissie take the baby girl off her hands, if only for a while.

Mary was about to be married but helped with the chores so Cissie had a bit more free time once she had settled Marjorie.

She knew better than to say anything about the twins in front of Father but was bursting with excitement and longing to tell someone... anyone! So, it was no wonder that the following day, during her lunch break she let it slip to Sarah, without even realising what she had said.

Sarah had just started to meet up with Joe Stokes, the factory foreman and they often met up with Cissie and Ted on a Saturday. Consequently, the girls had formed a close friendship and Sarah seemed to help fill the gap in Cissie's life that had been left by Lizzie's departure.

Cissie wrote asking Lizzie to visit the following Saturday. They wouldn't be able to go back to the house, of course, but Cissie always took the baby out at a week-end, so no-one would suspect anything.

***

Saturday came round all too soon, and Lizzie rose early to complete her tasks.

Gwen had to go into Utchester that day to buy provisions that couldn't be bought at the village shop, so she had timed her trip to coincide with the train times.

But first Lizzie had to prepare the formula milk for the babies, for the day, so that Eva had one less job to do during Lizzie's absence.

At 10.30 Lizzie said goodbye to her friend and her babies and then leapt into the car next to Gwen. The car lurched forward, Gwen certainly wasn't a natural when it came to driving, but she, as she said, managed to get from *A* to *B*.

When they reached the town it was still a bit early for the train, so Lizzie went into a little shop in the market square, and bought a tiny brown bear as a gift for her new baby sister, and some pretty, lace-trimmed hankies for her other sisters.

Then, she went into the tea room where she had first met Gwen, and, together they shared a pot of tea. Gwen pushed a brown paper bag across the table to her. She had kindly asked Ida to make a couple of sandwiches for Lizzie to take with her. Ida had also put in two generous slices of her famous Victoria sponge cake as well, plus a bottle of home- made lemonade. She was fond of Gwen, and so, any friend of Gwen's, was also a friend of Ida's.

The kindness of these new people in her life still amazed Lizzie.

She looked at the clock and realised if she didn't run she would miss her train, so she gathered together all her belongings, shouted a hasty 'Tara' to Gwen and ran as fast as she could to the station. Gwen watched her retreating figure and hoped with all her heart that it would be a successful day for her.

Gwen still had a few more things to buy and then she would travel back to Ellswood alone, to see how Eva was fairing with her two small charges.

Lizzie bought her return ticket and couldn't help thinking how different her life had become since her last train journey.

How she blessed the day she decided to travel in this direction. The countryside flashed by and she was soon looking out at familiar buildings. The train slowed down as it entered the station.

Bags in hand, she stood ready to leave the train as soon as it came to a halt. She and Cissie saw each other through the crowd and rushed into each other's arms. Laughing, crying, holding each other at arms length to see how the other had changed, hugging each other, causing other travellers to step around them, smiling indulgently at the sister's obvious fondness for each other.

When they finally let go of each other, Cissie turned towards the pram and introduced Lizzie to their baby step-sister.

Lizzie smiled at the pale quiet baby, thinking how different she looked to her own two robust offspring.

They headed towards the park, chatting every inch of the way. They had so much to talk about and catch up on. They soon found a vacant seat near to the duck pond, and there they enjoyed the little picnic that Ida had prepared for them. Then Lizzie gave the little gifts to her sister and step sister and they were so engrossed in conversation, that they didn't notice Sarah and Joe approaching them.

The couple stopped and chatted for a while and then arranged a time for later when they would meet up with Cissie and Ted, as was their usual practice on a Saturday evening.

Cissie had asked Ted to come along in the afternoon to meet Lizzie, but he refused, knowing that the girls would have lots to talk about, and he didn't want to intrude on this special day.

As they walked out of earshot, Joe asked Sarah

"Is that the reason Lizzie went away, has she had a baby"?

"Oh no! That baby's her step sister. Lizzie has had twins – a boy and a girl", she informed him.

"Well….." Joe was surprised to hear this as he didn't think it was that long since she'd left the area.

After a lovely day, Lizzie returned to the hotel.

She and Cissie had agreed to meet up in a months' time when Cissie would travel to Ellswood and meet up with her niece and nephew.

CHAPTER TEN

Reg and Flora were getting ready to attend the Hunt Ball.

They did the rounds of all the local society functions, and were invited to everything, along with Cuthbert and Grace, being the next best thing to gentry in the area.

In public, Reggie always appeared to be the doting husband.

However, in the privacy of their own home, he was cold and distant.

Flora knew deep in her heart the real reason he had married her....

She came to dread bedtime, often feigning a headache or extreme tiredness so that she could go to bed before him, pretending to be asleep when he finally got into bed beside her. But lately even that hadn't put him off, he would just force himself on to her regardless – so determined was he for them to produce an heir. But still nothing happened, despite the Gynaecologist confirming that there was no obvious reason.

The music was already playing when they arrived.

Since Reg had joined the family, he contrived that they arrived late so that they could make a grand entrance. He loved the way the 'commoners' watched their every move – it made him feel so important.

Yes, this was where he belonged.

He and Flora took to the floor and woodenly saw their way through a couple of dances, then, he had a perfunctory waltz with his mother-in-law, after which he and Cuthbert went to fetch some liquid refreshment for them all.

On their way to the bar, Cuthbert stopped to chat to a retired associate called Archie Frith who shared an interest in horse racing.

"When are you going to retire and come and join us at the track then, Bert" he enquired.

"As soon as this Chappie makes me a grandfather" replied Cuthbert, nudging Reg.

Inside Reggie fumed.

"Maybe he's firing blanks" smirked Archie.

Behind his back Reg clenched his fist, he was furious. They were speaking of him as if he wasn't there. Goodness knows what they said behind his back. He excused himself and went out to the lavatory to calm down.

As he came back into the room he bumped into his best man, Joe Stokes, who was there with his new love, Sarah, from the factory.

Reg was in no rush to return to Flora and her parents so made small talk with the couple. Reg's eyes wandered around the room as Joe was talking to him, he was totally bored by all this 'nobody' was saying to him, but tried to appear interested. However, when the name Lizzie Plant was mentioned his ears pricked up, but he was careful not to let Joe see, so kept the same nonchalant look on his face whilst inside his heart was pounding.

"Yes, she not only has a baby sister but also twins of her own, a boy and a girl", said Joe knowingly.

At that moment Cuthbert caught his eye and beckoned him to return to the group, so he quickly said,
"We must meet up for a drink sometime soon" to Joe and with that he left to re-join his family.

Reggie's mind was working overtime.

The more he thought of Lizzie the more confused he became.

He couldn't believe that she had forgotten him so easily. And then, got herself involved with someone else, so quickly.

Now he couldn't wait for the evening to end he needed peace and quiet to try and work things out in his head. Flora was amazed and relieved to hear him say that she looked tired and should get off to bed as soon as they returned home.

"I shall have a small port and be up shortly" he said.

Flora couldn't believe her luck and didn't need telling twice.

Reg sat, glass in hand, staring at the dying embers of the fire.

Suddenly, it came to him.

He had worked it out – they *must* be his babies, that was what she had wanted to tell him, the last time she saw him, and he hadn't given her the chance.

"So, Archie Frith, whose firing blanks now".

His mind was racing.

He would go and see Lizzie – demand that she let him have his children…..no, that wouldn't work.

Cuthbert would never let him bring his bastard children into this family.

He rose from the chair and poured himself another drink.

He knew he had to be very careful and very clever, to get round this problem but, it could be the answer to his prayers. Very soon the drink took over and he was fast asleep.

When he finally awoke he was cold and uncomfortable.

CHAPTER ELEVEN

The following day, being Sunday, saw Cuthbert and Grace calling for Reg and Flora, to take them to church, in the Rolls-Royce.

Cuthbert employed a chauffeur but preferred to drive himself as often as he could.

"What's the point of working hard and affording a car like this only to let someone else have the joy and pleasure of driving it?" he would say.

On the journey they made comfortable small talk.

Cuthbert informed Reg that he wanted him to deliver a very special order the following day. It was a sample of a dinner service for Sir Richard Fitzwilliam of Tushingham Hall, which was over in the next county. Cuthbert was aware that it was an important consignment, which could bring forth lots of orders from other stately homes, all over the country. Reg was very professional, and Cuthbert had no qualms about him taking over this task, knowing that he would create exactly the right impression.

Reg assured him that he would carry out Cuthbert's wishes to the letter, then went on to say that, as soon as possible, he would like to take some time off from his position at the factory, to take Flora away, on a belated honeymoon.

This came as a big surprise to Flora, as he had mentioned nothing to her.

Grace thought that this was a wonderful idea, and was full of enthusiasm.

After the church service was over, they always went up to the vicarage where Grace, who was Chairman of the Parochial Committee, and Mrs Smith, the vicar's wife, discussed the forthcoming week's fund raising events, whilst Cuthbert and the Vicar enjoyed a glass of sherry together.

Reg's head felt as though it was splitting in two, because of the amount of port he had consumed well into the night, so the last thing he needed was to make more small talk.

As they left the church he excused himself saying, as he wouldn't be at the office the following day, he had a few urgent tasks to complete.

Again, Cuthbert was impressed by his conscientious son-in-law. But, once he was away from the family Reg's mind was working fast. He had a plan….

So deep in thought was he, that he didn't notice anything, or anyone, around him. He turned the corner and literally, bumped into Cissie Plant. She was in the process of posting a letter as he barged into her, knocking her off balance and causing her to drop her letter.

"I'm so sorry" he apologised, as he instinctively put out his hands to save her from falling over, then bent down to retrieve the letter.

A quick glance was all it took, as he handed back to Cissie, who popped in straight into the letter box, not realising that Reg's photographic memory had taken in all the details, and stored them for future use.

To: Lizzie Plant, c/o The Abbotts Arms Hotel, Ellswood, Nr. Utchester.

After checking that Cissie was ok, he raced off to the factory to look at the large map of Britain that was hanging on his office wall. Tomorrow he was going to Tushingham, and by his reckoning, Ellswood was about fifteen miles from there. It would make him very late getting home, but he had lots of time, between now and then, to think of a good excuse.

This was meant to be!

When he returned home to the Lodge, Flora informed him that they were invited to the Big House for Sunday lunch so they walked together up the long sweeping drive.

Reggie's mind was racing ahead; he couldn't wait for Monday morning to come. During the lunch, it was agreed that Reg would take a week or so off from the factory, starting on Tuesday, to enable him and Flora to enjoy their honeymoon.

"Shall I use the Rolls for the delivery to Tushingham", he asked expectantly.

"No, I think not" said Cuthbert. "The Austin Seven is more than adequate for that job. Besides, we don't want his lordship thinking that we are too well off now, do we? We could really do with this order, and other orders that this will most certainly lead to".

Reg could hardly conceal his disappointment; he had never been given the opportunity to drive the beautiful beast. When that day finally arrived he would know that he was well and truly accepted.

But, he could see the sense in Cuthbert's words, no point in antagonising customers by showing off in a Rolls-Royce.

Another lesson learned.

CHAPTER TWELVE

Monday dawned, a beautiful, mid-summers day.

Reg was up with the lark with no after effects of the previous day's bad headache. The delicate pottery was stored and well protected on the back seat of the little Austin.

He bade farewell to Flora and slid behind the wheel, (wishing it was the Rolls-Royce), glancing in the interior mirror he smoothed down his auburn hair, before setting off.

After an uneventful journey, he arrived at the Hall much earlier than he had anticipated. When he had completed the business with Sir Richard, (who was very impressed with the quality of goods) he was invited to take morning coffee with him.

Reg was desperate to be on his way but knew it would seem churlish to refuse. His polite and professional manner enamoured him to the Lord, and Reg was sure that plenty more orders would be forthcoming.

At long last, he thought as he sat behind the wheel, the important part of his journey was about to begin.

Within half an hour he had reached Ellswood. He drove past the Abbots Arms and stopped the car outside a small public house, a few yards down the road.

How glad he was, now, that he hadn't got the Rolls; no-one would look twice at the little Austin, but a Rolls, in a small place like this, would have caused much unwanted attention.

He walked slowly back towards the hotel and looked over a small wall, into a neat back yard. A small, slightly built young woman was just taking a baby out of a pram. She didn't notice Reg as she was talking all the time to the child, who was obviously a little boy, as he was dressed all in blue. It was a good thing that she was so engrossed in the baby and didn't see the look on Reg's face.

When he had seen the baby's tuft of auburn hair, he knew, without a shadow of a doubt, that this was his son.

0-0-0-0-0-0-0-0-0-0-0

Eva took Bobby into the kitchen to change his nappy, chatting to him as she did so. Lizzie smiled indulgently at the sight. What a lucky little boy he was, to have 'two mummies'. And what a lucky lady she herself was, to have such lovely friends in her life.

Unexpectedly, she shivered. She walked over to where Eva had expertly replaced the soiled napkin with a soft fluffy clean one.

"I'll take him back to his pram whilst you have your lunch", she told Eva. As she tucked him up in the pram, alongside his sister, she had the strangest feeling that she was being watched.

Again she shivered and glanced all around her. Everything looked perfectly normal; there was no-one around, but she had this feeling of foreboding.

"Oh, pull yourself together, Lizzie" she told herself crossly.

CHAPTER THIRTEEN

As Reg travelled away from Ellswood, his mind was working fast and furious. A plot was forming, but could he pull it off? And, would Flora go along with this plan?

On his return, he went straight to see his father-in-law, proud to tell him all about his successful visit to the Hall, and the unspoken promise of future orders.

Cuthbert shook him by the hand and said, "Well done, Reg. I knew if anyone could pull this off, you could. I'm proud of you. Now, get off on this honeymoon and have a good time, but take great care of my girl, or else." he said laughing.

Reg didn't need telling twice. As soon as he arrived in the Lodge he asked Flora if she had packed and she nodded, smiling expectantly.

"We leave for Derbyshire first thing in the morning" he informed her. Flora did her best to hide her disappointment.

Derbyshire?

She hadn't been to Derbyshire, and whilst it was probably very nice, she had been hoping to go somewhere a bit more exotic than Derbyshire, for her honeymoon.

She'd been hoping to go to the coast at the very least. Paris or Rome would have been wonderful.

But Derbyshire…

They set off straight after breakfast. Reg seemed more animated and excited than she had ever seen him, this, in turn made her feel more relaxed, and she had a good feeling that they were going to enjoy themselves, tremendously.

They soon arrived at a lovely secluded hotel called the Fishermans' Friend in the heart of the lush Derbyshire countryside. Flora had to admit to herself that it was very beautiful and looked forward to pleasant, romantic walks with her husband, along the river bank.

However, as soon as the bell boy had delivered their cases and deposited them on the floor of their luxurious room, Reg said he had to go out for a short while. Flora hid her disappointment, yet again, and started to unpack their belongings.

This only took her a very short time, so she rang room service and ordered afternoon tea – for one.

Some honeymoon this was turning out to be.

***

Reg leapt back into the car and left the hotel at speed, towards the village of Ellswood.

His mind was totally focused on what he was about to do.

He parked the car on the car park of the pub, and walked nonchalantly back to the Abbots Arms Hotel.

Again, the pram was in the yard.

His eyes were drawn to the orchard where he could see Lizzie with a basket over her arm; she was obviously collecting eggs and was intent on what she was doing.

"It's now, or never, Reg" a small voice inside his head was telling him.

He moved stealthily towards the pram.

An insect net was covering the front of the pram.

Damn.

His clumsy fingers unhooked it and he lifted out the baby in blue. Thinking quickly, he hooked the net back in place and walked briskly back to the car. With trembling hands he gently placed the baby on the front seat, next to him and started the engine.

It misfired……

He tried again………. this time it burst into life.

He was expecting someone to snatch open the car door, and demand to know what on earth he was doing.

But, nothing happened.

He carefully reversed the car from the space, and drove away.

His breathing was heavy, and his heart pounding.

He'd done it!!

He looked down at his son. What a handsome little chap.

Just like his dad.

Back at the hotel, he quickly parked the car and got out, removed his jacket, and placed it carefully over the little boy, so that when he walked through the foyer, no-one was aware of what he was carrying. He hurried into their room and placed the baby and jacket on the bed.

Flora's eyes widened in amazement.

"Whose is that"? she asked.

"It's my twin brother's baby. He and his wife were killed in a car accident earlier today. There is no-one else to care for him. It must have been twin telepathy that sent me out this afternoon, don't you think"?

His eyes were filling with unshed tears for extra effect.

Flora looked at him incredulously.

Twin telepathy?

She'd never heard of that, but the baby did look very much like Reg, with his auburn hair and blue eyes and Reg did look very sad, and the baby was so tiny and sweet. She picked him up and it was obvious he was trying to suckle.

"Where's his bottle"?

'Damn and double damn' thought Reg, 'Why didn't I stop off in that small town on the way here and buy a bottle'.

"Tell you what, dear, why don't we leave here immediately and go on to the coast, to Scarborough. We can stop off at the first town that we come to, and buy a bottle and still be there by teatime." Reggie suggested.

"But we don't *just* need a bottle – we need milk to put in it, and napkins, and nightwear, and more day clothes, and towels, and baby soap, and talcum powder, and maybe a dummy – and a cot for him to sleep in……….!

Reg was amazed at how she had just accepted what he'd told her, and how easy it had been. The next part of his plan may not go as smoothly.

Together, they packed their clothes back into the suitcases that Flora had so recently emptied. Reg told her to wait in the room whilst he took the luggage to the car.

On his return he called the manager, and explained that they'd had a family bereavement, and must return home immediately. He generously offered to pay the bill in full but the manager wouldn't hear of it. He then went back to collect Flora, again draping his jacket over the baby and hurried out of the hotel.

***

The first town that they came to, en-route to the coast was a bustling little place. They found a shop that sold all of the necessities for a new baby and soon had all the things that Flora had reeled off, in the boot of the little car, including a small pram.

Flora looked so excited, her usual pale cheeks were flushed and her eyes were bright and sparkling.

She could pass for being pretty.

As Reg had predicted, they were in Scarborough by teatime, and had soon found a lovely hotel on the promenade, looking out over the North Sea.

They had their dinner and a kettle sent up to the room and after they had eaten Flora boiled the water and prepared a bottle of milk, ready to give to the little boy after she had bathed him, and put on his new nightclothes. He smelt so sweet and fresh as she held him in her arms, whilst he drank the milk. She laid him in the pram and he was soon asleep.

Flora looked at Reg across the pram and realised that this was what had been missing from their lives. She had no interest in the factory, but now, this was a shared interest.

"What's his name?" she asked. Reg looked at her, aghast. He hadn't thought about that, either.

"David" he said the first name that came into his head.

"Ahh, that's nice" she replied.

Now for it!

"Flora, Dear, I've been thinking….. Why don't we say that he is ours? We could say that you felt unwell and we went to the hospital and you suddenly gave birth. He's still so tiny – poor little orphan – people would believe us, I'm sure. Then he would never have to know about this dreadful accident. We don't seem to be able to have our own child, so this could the solution. What do you say, Flora? Please say yes," he begged.

"I don't think that can be right, Reg. It's lying at the end of the day" she replied.

"But Flora, it's lying with good intentions. How can that be wrong? Can you imagine, in a few years time having to tell…David…that his real parents died when he was so young. It's too sad. I'm only thinking of….David…." he filled his eyes with tears for good measure.

"Besides, think how thrilled your parents will be".

He'd played his trump card.

"Oh Reg, you have such a good heart. How lucky I am to be your wife."

Again he thought, 'That was so easy. I am such a clever bugger'.

Now, all they had to do was inform his in-laws and then, he was on his way to the 'Big House', at long last.

CHAPTER FOURTEEN

Grace and Cuthbert could not believe their ears when they received the telephone call telling them that they were the proud grandparents to a little boy called David Cuthbert.

Reg thought that this added name would go down a treat with his father-in-law.

Which, of course, it did.

Grace wanted to go straight over to Scarborough to see Flora in the nursing hospital. It took a lot of persuading to get her to stay at home as Flora was 'doing well' and would much prefer Mummy to stay there, and get things ready for their return. Put this way, Grace could see that this was the sensible thing to do. Cuthbert was over the moon and immediately started to contact all of his friends, and business associates, with the wonderful news.

At the factory gates the following morning the notice was displayed for all the workers to see.

MR AND MRS CUTHBERT WIRKSWORTH ALONG WITH MR AND MRS REGINALD JENKINS ARE DELIGHTED TO ANNOUNCE THE BIRTH OF DAVID CUTHBERT WIRKSWORTH-JENKINS.

When Cissie, Betsy and Sarah arrived and saw the message they agreed it was a wonderful piece of news, and how happy they were for the couple. Flora had always had their sympathy, as she always looked so unhappy and didn't seem to have any friends, despite her privileged lifestyle, and doting parents.

On his return from the factory that evening, Cuthbert could see that Grace was eager to discuss something with him. And he sensed that his life, as he knew it, would never be the same again.

"You are always saying that you will be glad to retire, Bertie – well – why not do it now. – or, at least, when Flora and Reginald return. Let's move into the Lodge and when they get home, they can move straight in here. Reg is more than capable of running the factory: you have said yourself how competent he is: and we can take that much needed holiday, in France. What do you say, Darling Bertie – please let it be yes".

Her face was filled with happy expectancy; he hardly ever refused her anything.

She had been a lovely wife and he was so proud of her. She was beautiful and dignified – the only regret he had was the fact they had never produced a son. Now, though, they had a grandson, someone to carry on the family name – so strange that the gynaecologist had failed to notice that Flora was very pregnant when he had examined her……..

"Yes My Love. Let's do it" he answered.

The following day Grace set to; packing all of her and Bertie's belongings and ferrying them down to the Lodge. It had always felt such a homely place to her, and she knew she would have no problems settling in there. Once she'd had some favourite pieces of furniture transported over from the big house, it would soon feel like home.

Each time she returned to the big house, she took with her boxes and bags of Flora and Reggie's possessions. By the end of the third day, the moves were completed and although she was tired and her body ached all over, she was so pleased with what she had achieved.

The first night they slept at the Lodge felt like they were on a second honeymoon. And within a couple of days they felt so at home they wished they had made the move years ago.

***

Reg phoned regularly with updates of Flora's 'progress' and informed his 'in-laws' that the 'hospital' was happy to release mother and baby and they would be home the following week-end.

Bertie thought it best to be there for the next few weeks and help them settle into their new home and to supervise the change over at the factory.

He also knew that Grace would want to help out with the baby and get to know him before they went on holiday. Knowing Flora, as they did, she would need all the help she could get, if past actions were anything to go by.

With that in mind, they booked the train to take them to France for the much awaited holiday, for six weeks on.

How surprised they were when the little family returned home.

Flora looked a picture of health; tanned, relaxed, in fact, radiant. So hard to believe that she had only given birth to her baby only two weeks ago. And how surprised Flora and Reg were – Reg particularly – to find that they were now the residents of the Big House.

Reg soon showed that he was more than capable of running the factory efficiently and realised what a lucky man he was.

Occasionally, he thought of Lizzie and felt a little guilty – but she did have another baby – why should she have been blessed with two, and he and Flora with none.

No – this was a fair way of doing it. A fair man was Reg – he had only taken one of his children.

He could see no wrong in what he had done.

CHAPTER FIFTEEN

Lizzie carried the basket of eggs back into the kitchen, tiptoeing past the pram that held her sleeping babies. She washed and dried the eggs and placed them carefully inside the big brown dish, with the hen shaped lid that always stood on the dresser. Then, she started to prepare the evening meal. Gwen was sitting in her chair, reading the evening newspaper, making comments from time to time, to Lizzie, of snippets of news that caught her eye.

"I'll have to go to Utchester on Saturday," she said. "We're almost out of hen corn. It's a pity ya can't drive; Liz, then yer cud go for me".

"I'll put it on my list of 'things to do'," grinned Lizzie.

"Well, it wouldn't be a bad idea, yer know, gal. P'raps Bill could teach yer. I would meself but I could av picked up a few bad abits, over the years and I wouldn't want ta pass 'em on to yer," she said seriously.

"We'll see," replied Lizzie, grinning even more, at the thoughts of Gwen's bad driving 'abits.

"I've prepared the meal and Eva will be here in a minute to take over, so I'm going to fetch the twins in and take them upstairs."

They had recently opened up another room on the top floor, next to Lizzie's, and now the babies had a room of their own.

Gwen rose from her chair and went over to the range to check on the vegetables, and stir the gravy, when she heard Lizzie give the most piercing scream. It was a scream that she knew she would remember, until her dying day – it sounded like a wounded animal. She dropped the spoon and ran out into the yard.

Lizzie had reached the pram and unhooked the net to discover only one baby inside. Ridiculously, she bent down and looked under the pram, and then all around the yard, as if a tiny baby could get out of a pram, and go wandering around a yard!

It was when she realised that her son was missing, that she let out the blood curdling scream. At that moment, Eva came through the gate.

"Whatever's wrong, Lizzie, Love?" she asked.

"Oh Eva – you've got him – I thought I'd lost him," Lizzie said with great relief.

"Do you mean Bobby, I've only just arrived."

Lizzie started to panic.

Gwen came out to see what the problem was.

Baby Meg started to cry.

Bill arrived.

Pandemonium reigned.

They all searched the yard, the garage, the vegetable garden, the orchard.

Nothing.

Lizzie was running back and forth, clutching Meg close to her. When they had searched the immediate area, Lizzie climbed on to the wall and jumped down into the adjacent field. A hopeless feeling washed over her.

Where could he be?

Gwen had followed her into the field, and, after searching every bit of the field, and under the hedgerows, it became obvious that they were not going to find him there. Together, they walked back to the hotel in silence – each wrapped up in their own thoughts.

In the kitchen, Eva was trying to save the remains of the vegetables that had boiled dry, during the mayhem. The residents were waiting for their evening meal, and Eva was endeavouring to maintain some normality.

"Bill's gone to fetch P. C. Stanway" she informed the distraught pair. The policeman was a family man himself and to see the anguish on poor Lizzie's face was almost too much for him to bear. He went and sat next to her, on the sofa, and took out his notebook.

"I know this is so distressing for you, Lizzie, but I need you to tell me exactly what happened, then I'm sure we'll find him in no time at all" he told her comfortingly.

Slowly, Lizzie related to him the events of the last hour. Her heart felt like lead. Where could Bobby be?

P. C. Stanway wasted no time. Soon it would be dark. He gathered together a dozen or so willing helpers from the village and together they searched the area immediate to the hotel. They searched diligently, leaving nothing unturned; each and every one of them hoping against hope that they would be the one to be able to shout 'he's here, I've found him'. But, of course, it was a fruitless task. Dusk fell and night sounds surrounded them. Reluctantly, P. C. Stanway called off the search and said,
"Any of you that are able, please come back at first light and we'll resume the search and go a bit further field."

Then he returned to the kitchen where all eyes turned to him, with eager expectancy, as he opened the door. He just shook his head to the unspoken question. Lizzie's pretty face was pure white; her eyes were wide and staring in disbelief. He accepted a mug of tea from Gwen and said very quietly, just to her,

"I remember an incident like this a few years back. It appeared that a fox had taken the baby, cunning animals, foxes. I'm beginning to think that this is what's happened to Bobby".

Gwen shook her head to let him know that Lizzie wasn't ready to hear this sort of information.

Gwen, Lizzie and Meg spent the night together in the kitchen; talking, making tea, talking, dozing, talking and talking. Gwen couldn't bear to think of the girl being on her own, with her thoughts. Never had there been such a long night. Baby Meg was restless. She was missing the presence of her twin brother, whose body fitted so snugly next to hers. At first light, as the birds were singing their dawn chorus, a posse of locals returned, to quietly resume their search.

By lunchtime, almost all of the male villagers were taking part, whilst the women were calling at the hotel to re-assure Lizzie with words of comfort and support.

One brought along a sponge cake, someone else brought a pan of stew while another lady brought a freshly baked apple pie. As the searchers returned, empty handed, Gwen was constantly brewing tea and offering them a bite to eat. Lizzie sat holding

Meg, saying nothing but watching each new arrival with hope in her eyes. In her heart she felt numb. Where could her baby be?

By evening, it was obvious that their search was futile.
P. C. Stanway walked into the kitchen and again sat next to Lizzie on the sofa and gently took her by the hand.

"We've searched every inch of the village and there's no trace of him. I don't know what else we can do."

"You mean you're giving up?" she asked incredulously. "I'll go and find him myself – he'll be so hungry – I must find him," her voice was barely a whisper.

Just then, Dr. Clayton walked in and realised that the situation hadn't changed and the baby boy was still missing.

"Can we have a bit of privacy here, please?" he asked. Immediately, the kitchen emptied.

He place his bag on the table and flicked it open, filling a syringe with a strong sedative deep within the cavernous bag, so that Lizzie was unaware of what he was doing. He crossed the kitchen and took the seat that P. C. Stanway had just vacated, next to Lizzie. Gently he took hold of her arm and injected her with the sedative.

Child-like, Lizzie made no objection.

"This will make you feel better," he assured her.

"It won't find him, though," she stated, more to herself.

"They'll all return tomorrow and keep looking until they do find him," he comforted.

The sedative took effect very quickly. Lizzie felt someone take Meg from her arms and her brain was screaming "No – don't take her" but her mouth was unable to form the words.

She felt she was drifting down and down, into a bottomless pit and unable to stop herself.

Once she was asleep, the doctor took Meg over to the open door and beckoned Gwen to return to the kitchen. He handed the baby over to her and she, in turn placed the baby girl into the pram.

"She'll sleep 'til morning hopefully, on that dose," Dr. Clayton said, nodding towards Lizzie.

"Thanks Doc. That's just what she needs," said Gwen. Eva came into the kitchen and said,
"I'm taking Meg home with me – you look all in. You need to get some sleep and you won't get any if I leave her here, I know you. You'll be watching over her all night. I'll be back first thing, before Lizzie wakes, so don't worry."

She sounded so assertive; it was almost comical, coming from one so small.

Gwen didn't argue. She was just so tired; she was almost asleep on her feet. She gave Eva a wan smile of appreciation and then helped her to pack a bag with all Meg's necessities.

The residents had made do with some cold meat for their evening meal, and, as it was Friday the following day, Gwen had only the breakfasts to cook, so she told Eva just to turn up whenever she could.

Then it was just Gwen and Lizzie. Gwen took a couple of blankets from the chest in the hall, and, after lifting Lizzie's legs up and on to the sofa, she made her comfortable and placed the blanket over her sleeping form. The other one she draped over herself and settled down to sleep in the armchair.

CHAPTER SIXTEEN

Gwen woke with a start. Lizzie was sobbing in her sleep. Gwen crossed the kitchen and gathered the weeping girl into her arms. Gwen felt as close to her as she would, if she had given birth to her. She was the child that Gwen had never had, and she thanked God daily, that he had sent Lizzie into her life. Although Lizzie didn't wake up, the words of comfort that Gwen was murmuring seemed to calm her down. Gwen tucked the blanket around her and went back to her chair.

Exhausted though she was, sleep, second time around didn't come as easily. It was starting to come light and soon the villagers would be out and about again. She hoped, with all her heart that today, someone would discover the little boy, fit and well.

The church clock struck five o'clock and Gwen knew that she may as well get up, as the chances of going back to sleep now, were very slim.

Very quietly, she crossed the kitchen and unlocked the back door. Picking up the egg basket she strolled over to the orchard and opened the hatch on the hen-house, before scattering the last of the corn on the ground.

As the hens clucked their gratitude to her for giving them their freedom, they strutted down the ramp and immediately started scratching the ground, and breaking their fast. Gwen entered the hen-house by the tall side door, and although she was gathering the eggs she was looking in the least likely of places for little Bobby, hoping that the searchers had over-looked that area.

But, to no avail.

When she left the hen-house, she looked out across the field. Already there were a dozen or more villagers combing the area once again. As she returned to the kitchen door she saw Eva turning the pram into the drive and so she waited for her and together with baby Meg, they entered the kitchen.

Next to arrive was Dr. Clayton.

"I think it best if we keep her sedated for a little while longer" he said, preparing the syringe. Gwen agreed that it was for the best, but knew that if it was her baby that was missing; she would want to be out there looking for him, not locked in some drug induced stupor. But Dr. Clayton knew what he was doing. Gwen thanked him for his kindness, knowing that he had come out early before he started his regular surgery, and he went on his way with the promise that he would call again, the following day.

Usually, Eva only worked at a week-end when Lizzie had a day off, as there were no residents to tend to, so Gwen was very grateful to the girl for stepping in, and looking after the baby. Now she had another favour to ask of her.

"I really need to go to Utchester today, Eva. I just wondered if you could stay here until I return, as someone needs to be here in case they find Bobby. Also, there's Meg to be taken care of. I'm so sorry to ask so much of you."

"I can stay as long as you like, Gwen" she said accommodatingly.

"I'll get off first thing, and then you can have the rest of the day to yourself" said Gwen gratefully.

After she'd had her breakfast Eva encouraged Gwen to leave the kitchen chores and set off on her journey at once, stating that if she was quiet, she would be glad to have something to keep her occupied. Gwen knew that Eva hated to be idle; she was always looking for jobs, without being asked. Gwen knew how much little Bobby meant to Eva, too, and appreciated the fact that if she had lots to keep her busy it would, perhaps, help take her mind off the desperate situation.

Gwen crossed the kitchen, picked up her purse and shopping basket and turned to go out of the door, then, hesitated and turned to Eva and gave the tiny girl a rib-breaking hug. Not normally a tactile person, Eva was so surprised by this action. Gwen said gruffly

"Thanks, gal. don't know what we'd 'av done without yer".

Touched, Eva replied that anyone would have done the same. With this, Gwen left the room and minutes later Eva heard the engine start and chug off down the road.

Right, she thought. First I'll check on Meg. She had fed and washed the baby before she left home so Meg was sleeping well from the motion of the pram being wheeled through the village. She was keeping the pram inside the kitchen, where she could keep a close eye on it – she was taking no chances.

She then peeled and chopped a load of vegetables and set a pan of soup simmering on the range. She made a couple of cakes and some jam tarts and then washed all the pots and pans and tidied the kitchen.

She knew that Gwen wouldn't have had chance the previous day to change the sheets on the resident's beds and they would all be back on Monday, so she went to the first room, stripped the bed and then rushed back to the kitchen to check on Lizzie and Meg. She carried on this way, running back and forth until all the beds were changed.

Then she prepared a sandwich for herself and Gwen. Meg started stirring; she was ready for her lunch, too. Eva lifted her from the pram and whispered endearments to the lovely little girl, so that she didn't get distressed and cry, and disturb her mummy.

She gave her the bottle of milk, winded her, changed her nappy like an expert and laid her back in the pram. She was such a placid baby, but Eva knew that she missed the little body that had lain next to her since the day she was born – and even before that.

Lizzie murmured in her sleep and moved her body to a more comfortable position but still she didn't wake. Gwen should be back any time, thought Eva and placed the kettle on the range in readiness for the cuppa that her employer would expect, when she walked through the door.

Bill appeared at the back door and beckoned Eva outside so that they could talk more freely.

"We've been over the entire village with a fine tooth comb" he said shaking his head. "There's no sign of him – nothing. Where ever can he be"?

"It's a dreadful thing to have happened, Bill", Eva replied.

At that moment PC Stanway tore round the corner on his bike. "I've just heard that there's been an incident at the bottom of Quixhill, so I'll leave the search to you, and find out what's happened there. I'll be back as soon as I can".

With that, he pedalled off down the road. Eva felt torn. She wanted to join in the search, she felt so useless, but realised she was needed here, in case they brought Bobby back.

By tea-time Eva had completed all of the tasks she had set herself.

The kitchen was sparkling, the baking done, the beds changed, the baby fed, bathed and ready for bed – and still no sign of Gwen.

Eva smiled to herself as she thought of her rough and ready employer with the heart of gold.

"I'll bet she's chatting to one of her many friends in Utchester and lost all track of time. Either that or there's some lame dog who's attracted her attention."

Suddenly, her thoughts were interrupted by PC Stanway crashing through the door. His helmet was missing and his hair was wild and windblown.

"Oh"! Shrieked Eva. "You've found Bobby".

"No Love, we've still not found him. It's Gwen. She's crashed the car. She's dead, Eva, I'm so sorry".

CHAPTER SEVENTEEN

Eva just stood and stared at P C Stanway, unable to comprehend the words he had uttered.

"Eva –did you hear what I said" he begged. He couldn't bear to repeat the awful words. Gwen had been a true friend of his, his wife and his son Brian, since they'd come to live in the village, more than eight years ago, to take on the task of village bobby. Gwen was always ready to lend a hand, or an ear, to anyone who needed a bit of support. Along with, Dr Clayton and Rev Smilie she was the mainstay of the village.

Think of Ellswood – think of Gwen.

Now she was gone.

Eva still stared at him.

"Yes, I heard you. How did it happen?"

"I don't know for sure, as yet." He replied. "She came down Quixhill and went straight across the road, instead of turning the corner at the bottom and crashed into that big oak tree. Nasty stretch of road, that. Dr Clayton thinks she could have had a heart attack, but Dick Ratcliffe's there at the moment, and he's checking the brakes." (Dick was the local motor mechanic, and also a good friend of Gwen's).

"Always knew no good would come of her driving – you couldn't say she was a natural, now could you?" Eva gave him a weak smile at the thoughts of Gwen chugging along in her little car – always at her own speed – but she knew just what he meant.

Just then Bill walked in with a box of fresh vegetables, which he placed on the table. His eyes went from Eva to PC Stanway, and back to Eva, aware that something life-changing had taken place. Before either of them had the chance to say anything Dr Clayton arrived.

"The ambulance has taken her off to Bardy. I've just called in to give Lizzie another shot. She can't cope with this at the moment, so we'll keep her under until tomorrow."

"Have they found Bobby then?" asked Bill, not really wanting to know the answer as he was fearing the worst.

"No Bill, not yet. But I'm sure they will soon," said the Doctor, and then gently went on to tell him of the awful occurrence that would affect so many lives. Bill flopped down on Lizzie's armchair next to the range, and put his head in his hands.

"Oh my God – how much more can she take". All present knew that he was referring to Lizzie. "I'm just going to give her another dose of the sleeping draught, I will have to let her come round tomorrow, but for now, I think it's for the best," the Doctor informed him. Turning to Eva, he asked

"Eva, are you ok to take over here? I'll contact the relatives and notify them of the accident? I know she has a cousin in Trenton"

"Yes, of course. Do you think we ought to close the hotel next week? If we ring the guests now it will give them time to find somewhere else to stay." The doctor agreed that they had enough to think about at the moment without the added concern for the residents.

"Do you know where she keeps the reservations book"? At this she nodded and took the book from a drawer, in the dresser.

"I'll take it with me and ring everyone, from the surgery", he said, hoping that everyone he needed to contact, had a telephone.

With that he took up his bag and started towards the door, as he was leaving he turned to Eva and said,

"I'll be back first thing in the morning to waken Lizzie up."

"Thank you, Doctor she replied, gratefully. She had been dreading the thought of breaking the awful news to Lizzie, so it was such a relief to hear that the Doctor intended to the do the job for her.

"It would be better for her, if you were here, too," he added. She just nodded, as he and PC Stanway, took their leave. Bill rose to his feet.

"I suppose you've been here all day, have you?" Eva nodded again, not really trusting herself not to burst into tears.

"Go home for a while, Love. I'll stay with Lizzie."

"Oh thank you, I won't be long, Bill. I need a bit of fresh air. I'll take Meg with me as it's such a warm evening."

When she was outside she realised how badly she needed the comfort and support that only her parents could give her, she was, after all, little more than a child herself. She felt so grateful to Bill for recognising this, even before she had herself.

When she left, Bill stood looking down at Lizzie's sleeping form, wondering how she could cope with what was ahead of her. He looked at the pan of soup on the range but he had no appetite. He sat down again, thinking of all the kindnesses Gwen had shown him over the years he had known her.

True to her word, Eva was back within a short time. Her heart was so heavy but her spirits were lifted, by her loving parents.

At 8.30 the next morning Dr Clayton arrived and administered the antidote to bring Lizzie out of her sleep. As they waited for her to waken, Eva and the Doctor shared a cup of tea in a strained silence. Eva had bathed and fed Meg, and dressed her in a pretty white dress, which enhanced her lovely dark hair and eyes.

Within a few minutes, Lizzie was stirring. Eva felt so afraid. Lizzie opened her eyes and the first thing she saw was Meg. She smiled and held out her arms. Eva placed the baby on Lizzie's knee, and crossed over to the other side of the kitchen. Now was the time for the doctor to do his part. He went and sat opposite her, and gently asked,

"Lizzie – do you remember what happened before you went to sleep?"

Lizzie looked at him vacantly, holding on to Meg so tightly that the baby became distressed.
"Lizzie – can you hear what I'm saying?" he begged.

Lizzie then started to laugh... a loud raucous, hysterical sound, and at the same time huge tears were rolling down her cheeks.

For a second time that week-end, the Doctor was obliged to summon an ambulance.

He knew the signs.

Lizzie had suffered a total breakdown, and he could do no more for her. Whilst they were waiting for it to arrive and take Lizzie for the specialized treatment, he decided she needed sedating again. She was soon calmed and sat quietly, nursing Meg and stroking her hair and cheeks, as though she knew that it would be the last time, for a while, that she could caress her little daughter.

Eva whispered to the doctor that he could count on her to take care of the baby, for however long it took, to get Lizzie better.

He went on to say that he had contacted the cousin in Trenton. Alice and Leo Guthrie had agreed to come to Ellswood the following day to arrange the funeral with Rev Smilie.

For some reason Eva was filled with trepidation at this thought.

When the ambulance arrived Lizzie went off as quiet as a lamb, handing Meg over to Eva.

The following day Alice and Leo arrived in time to take part in the morning church service, and then followed the Rev. Smilie into the vicarage next door, and arranged for Gwen's funeral to take place the following Wednesday.
The couple were in their forties, and childless. Alice was quite the opposite of her cousin Gwen, with cold eyes and totally lacking a sense of humour.

Then they went on to the Abbotts Arms where they found Eva feeding little Meg. Gwen had told her cousin all about her 'lodgers' with great pride, and Eva then brought her up to date with Bobby's disappearance, and Lizzie's illness. Alice was very taken with Meg and could barely tear her eyes away from the baby. She then asked Eva to make them a pot of tea, and helped herself to a large slice of cake.

Afterwards, she went over to the dresser and started to rummage through the drawers. She obviously, found just what she was looking for and slipped a couple of envelopes into her handbag, offering no explanation. Gwen had promised her, years ago, that she would be the sole beneficiary of her will, and Alice was looking for the name of the solicitor so that she could inform him of her cousins' death, and hopefully, he would be able to read out the will, after the funeral.

Once she had the necessary information she was anxious to be on her way, with no concern for Eva or the running of the hotel.

Later Dr. Clayton called in to let Eva know that Lizzie had settled in and would, hopefully, respond well to the treatment. He also discussed with her, the idea that maybe the village hall would be a more fitting venue for Gwen's Wake, than the hotel. He knew that the whole village would turn out for the sad occasion, and how right he was.

***

On the day of the funeral, his insight was rewarded. The village hall was packed with locals, hotel guests, business associates, along with several 'lame dogs' who Gwen had helped, and taken under her wing.
Early that morning, the men in the village had set up all the trestle tables that they could find, then, the wives had arrived with white table cloths to

cover them with. Each and every villager arrived early for the funeral, all bearing a cake, a plate of sandwiches, a dish of pickles, a plate of scones, until all the tables were laden with food. A large water urn was switched on, so that after the service, the refreshments would be all ready, without anyone having to miss the service.

Alice and Leo left the Wake as soon as they could, inviting Eva to return to the hotel with them, for the reading of the will.

True to her word Gwen had left everything to Alice – Eva couldn't help but think that had she lived a bit longer, she may have changed it, to favour Lizzie who was, after all, more like a daughter to her, and could have run the hotel single handed – but, it was too late now!

Eva was astounded to hear Alice instruct the solicitor to put the hotel on the market.

"I have no desire to live in Ellswood, and I have better things to do with my life than fetch and carry for other people," she stated sourly.

With that, the solicitor snapped shut his briefcase, shook Alice and Leo by the hand, and said he would be in touch.

As soon as he had left, Alice prepared for her departure, donning her coat, hat and gloves. She turned to Eva and said,
"Pack Meg's clothes and napkins for me. We will be taking her home with us".

"I..I..I....don't think...." Eva stammered.

"Don't waste time, girl. Just do as I say," the bossy Alice replied. With trembling hands Eva packed a small valise with the pretty dresses that Lizzie had so lovingly made for Meg, along with a stack of fluffy napkins. Leo picked up the case and took it out to the car. Alice lifted Meg from the pram and picked up the baby's bottle of milk from the table. Meg's huge brown eyes looked over to Eva.

Then they were gone......

Eva was rooted to the spot, hardly able to believe what had just taken place.

What now?

She may as well go home.

Bill just missed Eva. He arrived at the hotel to find it deserted. He went and checked on the hens and then decided he would call in at Eva's home – he was sure she wouldn't mind.

When he arrived, Eva's parents welcomed him, and Eva, who had only just finished telling them of the events of the late afternoon, felt obliged to repeat it all again, to Bill. When he heard that they'd taken Meg, he was livid.
"They never bothered that much with Gwen when she was alive; all they're concerned with is feathering their nest. But they had no rights, whatsoever, to take Meg. She is nothing to do with them," he ranted.

113

"I'm so sorry, Bill." Eva was distraught.

"I'm not blaming you Eva. You've had to shoulder so much responsibility during this dreadful time, and they've taken advantage of you."

"Tomorrow, I'm going to the hospital to see Lizzie," Eva informed him.
"Oh my goodness – please Eva – don't tell her."

"Of course I won't," she retorted. "She can't take any more bad news, even I can see that."

Bill looked so relieved and then apologetic, he should have known Eva would do nothing to hurt Lizzie.

"Tell you what, I'll see if I can borrow Mr. Duncombe's car and I'll come with you."

"Bill – don't you trust me not to tell her – is that why you're offering to come with me," she asked.

"Of course I trust you, you silly girl. No! I need to see Lizzie for myself," he admitted.

"Ok then, we'll go together" she finally agreed: she would be glad of the company as she hated hospitals and was not too sure how to get there from the bus station.

So, the following day, as soon as he arrived at the Hall, his first job was to find his boss, Mr Duncombe, and ask him for the favour.

Mr. Duncombe was always impressed by Bill's amenable attitude, and his willingness to tackle any task that they asked of him. Therefore, he was only too happy to grant him this request.

Eva and Bill travelled to the hospital in companionable silence, both wrapped up in their own private thoughts and expectations of Lizzie's state of health and mind.

At the information desk, they were directed to a separate area of the hospital and when they arrived at the door to the ward, they were alarmed to see the nurse take out a key from her pocket. They watched as she unlocked the door, and summoned them to enter, and then proceeded to re-lock the door behind them.

Eva looked terrified.

Bill squeezed her arm and said,
"It's ok. It's only for the safety of the patients," he assured her.

They were taken to Lizzie's bed. She lay on her side and showed no re-action when they spoke to her. Her eyes were vacant, her mouth unsmiling. Eva stood back, not knowing what to say or do.

Bill fetched two chairs and Eva sat down quickly. Bill placed his chair within Lizzie's line of vision. He sat down and took her hand, stroking it gently, and telling her, in little more than a whisper, that everything was going to be alright, he would always be there for her.

Eva felt inadequate. Why couldn't she have said and done all that. Lizzie was her dearest friend, and she didn't want to let her down.

But there was no re-action from Lizzie, to Bill's words – her eyes showed no signs of recognition.

They realised that they were not reaching her, so after a very short time, decided that they may as well leave.

They travelled back to Ellswood in even deeper thought. Bill was aware that he needed to visit Lizzie on a very regular basis and as he couldn't keep asking his boss to lend him the car, it was with this thought, after her had dropped Eva off at her home; he went to see the local mechanic, Dick.

Unfortunately, Dick couldn't help him with a motor car but, as an after thought he said he had an old motor bike and Bill was welcome to it, if he could ride it. Bill thought this was an excellent idea as it would be a very economical way of travelling. Dick went on to tell him, with great relief, Gwen's car had been announced in tip-top condition and the cause of the accident was either health problems or, maybe, lack of attention.

CHAPTER EIGHTEEN

Lizzie woke to the autumn sun shining through the hospital window and on to her face. For the first time, since she had been there, she had woken up of her own accord, and not by the nurse asking her to sit up and take her medication.

Her mind was alert now. She was aware that she had been to a deep dark place, a living hell, and she'd had no desire, at the time, to try and get out.

But now she felt different. She'd travelled through a long black tunnel, and now with her own determination and encouragement from some other, unknown source, she had finally emerged. She was aware that something or someone had urged her on; unaware that Bill had been at her bedside almost every day, talking, cajoling, begging, and even insisting that she came back to him.

The nurse arrived at the end of her bed and scrutinized the chart hanging there. She looked at Lizzie and was surprised to see her awake and smiling, watching the nurse's every move with interest.

"Hello, Love", the nurse said brightly. "You're feeling better today, I can see."

"I feel wonderful," Lizzie replied.

The nurse was surprised at this response; she realized that Lizzie had no memory of the devastating events that had caused her to have the break-down. This was probably due to the gruelling treatment she'd had to endure, over the last few weeks. The nurse watched as Lizzie obediently swallowed the tablets, and then she plumped up the pillows before going to report the breakthrough, to the ward sister.

At visiting time Bill was thrilled to see the change in Lizzie that he had longed for. She smiled at him as he walked down the ward.

"Bill – how lovely to see you. Thank you so much for coming," she said.

Bill realised that she had no idea that he had been so many times before, but decided to let her lead the conversation. He was delighted to be talking to the old Lizzie, the one he had come to know so well. But, he also became aware that she had no recollection of losing Bobby, and Gwen's untimely death.

The doctor had been summoned, to see for himself the amazing progress that Lizzie was making. He arrived at the bedside during Bill's visit and closed the curtains around the area, giving them a modicum of privacy. He introduced himself as Dr Scott, and assumed that Bill was Lizzie's father. Embarrassed, Bill declined to put him right.

Dr Scott knew that it was imperative that Lizzie was told the truth, as soon as possible. If left until a later date, the knowledge of the heart breaking events could cause her to have a relapse. So, very gently, he started to reveal the harsh facts that had contributed to Lizzie's illness. Lizzie's eyes brimmed with tears as he told her of her little boy's demise that they were now sure that he had been taken from his pram by a fox. Moving on to Gwen, he told her that she had, without a doubt suffered a heart attack and had no knowledge of the crash, and therefore, suffered no pain.

As the Doctor was speaking, she had reached for Bill's hand. Her finger nails were digging into his flesh, but he didn't flinch. The Doctor then suggested that a mild sedative might help to keep her calm, and she nodded in agreement. It soon took effect, and the ache that was within her heart, dulled, a little. She was drifting off to sleep when Bill left her, telling the nurse to let Lizzie know that he would be back tomorrow.

Lizzie drifted in and out of sleep and when the sedation began to lose its effectiveness, the nurse returned to administer a second dose.

Lizzie begged her not to,

"I have to deal with this, without drugs," she said." I have a little girl and I must get back to her, and cope with the knowledge that I have lost my little boy, and my best friend."

Tears now coursed down her face as she spoke the sad words of acceptance of the situation, but the nurse knew that she had just taken yet another step closer to her recovery. She held Lizzie, and let her cry, murmuring gentle words of pacification.

When the tears stopped Lizzie fell into a deep natural sleep and awoke the following day, sad, but determined to accept what had happened, and get back to little Meg, as soon as she possibly could.

Bill arrived to find her sitting in a chair next to her bed, staring through the window. He stood for a minute, feeling her sadness, then she must have felt his presence and turned and gave him such a sad, weak smile that it tore at his heartstrings.

"Hello Bill, how are you?" she asked. He said he was well, and that the doctor had given him the good news that she could now, go home.

This was obviously going to be a problem, as she no longer had a home to go to, but this was a fact that they had still to break to her. Bill promised her that he would come for her the following day and bring her day clothes, which he needed to collect from Eva's house. There was no way he was going to allow her to ride pillion on his motor bike so, again, he would ask Mr Duncombe for the loan of his car.

As soon as he returned to Ellswood, he called on Eva and told her the good news of Lizzie's recovery.

Eva had taken all of Lizzie's possessions that had been left at the hotel, and stacked them in the pram, which was, in turn, stored in the shed, as her parent's home was very tiny. Bill could see for himself that there really was no room for Lizzie and Meg to stay in this small house, not even for a short time.

Well, he thought – I have a spare bedroom – they will have to come and stay with me, regardless of what people may say.

So, the following day, with great trepidation, he set off in the Duncombe's car to bring Lizzie back to Ellswood. The return journey was a delight to Bill, all of Lizzie's former enthusiasm for life was back. She pointed out landmarks, animals, birds, trees, and flowers en-route, and asked a million questions, it was as though she had been re-born. Then she said,
"Eva will miss Meg so much; I expect they have become very close. She is such a true friend to me I do hope that she stays on at the Hotel, we work so well together."

Bill gently drew the car to a standstill and took a very deep breath.

"The hotel's just been sold. Gwen's cousin, Alice, who was the sole beneficiary of her will, didn't want to take it on. It's she who's been looking after Meg for you, as Eva was offered a job at the dairy. So, we'll get Alice's address and fetch Meg back immediately – and as I have a spare bedroom, you and Meg are very welcome to stay with me for the time being".

"Oh Bill, what can I say. You've already been so kind to me. I'll accept your offer but will find another position and somewhere to live as soon as I can, I promise," she said.

Bill was racking his brains to think who would know whereabouts in Trenton, Alice and Leo lived. First of all he called on Dr. Clayton, who only had a telephone number for them. However, he said he could ring the solicitor, who was sure to have their address. Which, of course, he had, and was quite happy to divulge this information to the Doctor.

For some reason, Bill thought it would be better to arrive unannounced, rather than ring and forewarn them, so they left the village immediately.

Trenton was only half an hour's drive away, and soon they were walking together, down the garden path, of a neat semi-detached house - with a For Sale sign in the garden.

Bill rang the bell and instantly the door was opened by Leo.

"May we come inside?" asked Bill assertively. Leo stood to the side to allow the two of them to enter the hall. Alice was just walking down the stairs and looked enquiringly at the two strangers. Bill held out his hand to Leo as he introduced himself,
"My name is Bill Udall and this is Lizzie Plant", he heard a loud intake of breath from Alice. She quickly scuttled past them and ran into the lounge, with Bill and Lizzie right behind her.

There, in a playpen sat Meg. Lizzie ran to her, arms outstretched, beaming from ear to ear.

"Oh my little Love, how you've grown," she sang. Then, turning to Alice, she said
"I can never thank you enough for taking such good care of her." Alice scowled.

"Who are you?" she asked.

"I'm Meg's mother," Lizzie replied.

"And how do I know that? You could just be saying that to take Meg away from me. This is now her home and this is where she belongs. Now, go away."

Alice was very agitated by this time. Lizzie was left speechless. It was Bill who took control of the situation and answered for her.

"No! Mrs. Guthrie – Meg's home is with her mother. I can vouch that Lizzie is indeed Meg's mother, so now, if you'll kindly gather together her belongings, it's getting late and we need to take her home." Lizzie looked at him, so grateful for his support.

"Never" snarled Alice. Leo walked over to his wife and said,
"Let her go Alice. The adoption will never go through, now *she's* out of hospital."

Bill and Lizzie looked at each other – if they had left it much longer, it may have been too late, ever to get Meg back.

The house was for sale, and they could have moved anywhere; anywhere in the world, with Meg, without leaving a forwarding address.

They were only just in time!

Lizzie lifted Meg from the play-pen or cage as she was thinking. The little girl was unsure, at first, of this strange lady, but her mother spoke to her in a quiet comforting way, and Meg soon relaxed.

The first few weeks in Alice's care had not been filled love and fun. Yes, she was clean, well fed and warm, but love and fun was both alien to Alice.

Whilst all this was taking place in the parlour, Leo was packing Meg's belongings and brought the bag down into the hall.

Alice knew she was beaten and walked out of the room, and up the stairs. Bill picked up the bag and held the door open to allow Lizzie to take Meg out first. Leo didn't speak as they left the house. Bill placed the bags on the back seat of the car and held Meg whilst Lizzie settled herself comfortably in the seat.

He then placed Meg on Lizzie's lap, where she belonged. He raced round to the driver's side and quickly started the engine. Lizzie took one last look at the house and saw the net curtain twitch, as they set off.

With the motion of the car, and the late hour of the day, Meg's little eyes were soon closing, and by the time they reached the cottage in Southwood she was fast asleep.

Once in the house, Bill took out a drawer from the chest in the living room, padded it with blankets and placed Meg inside it. They looked at each other and started to smile – thinking, this is how her little life began. He showed Lizzie to her room and as she looked so tired he suggested that she went straight to bed – she was still very fragile.

It was work, as usual, for Bill the following day, so on the way he called in on Eva and told her the story. Eva said, as she was on a late shift at the dairy, she could wheel the pram and the rest of Lizzie's belongings over to the cottage. Bill was glad to hear this as he was a little concerned as to how Lizzie would cope on her own. Eva's company was just what she needed. But he needn't have worried as Lizzie was in her element. By the time Eva arrived, she had bathed and fed the baby, laid her back in her drawer and cleaned the house from top to bottom. She had also prepared some soup for Bill's tea and was sitting writing a letter to Cissie. The two friends hugged each other and then felt a mutual sadness as they thought of their dear departed friend.

Excitedly, Lizzie unpacked the pram and carefully transferred the sleeping baby into it, from her drawer. Then together they went for a stroll around the hamlet.

When Bill arrived home from work, he was delighted with the way Lizzie had settled into his little home.

They sat in companionable silence whilst eating their evening meal. Then Lizzie prepared the weary baby for her bed whilst Bill washed the pots, then together they sat and enjoyed listening to a short play on the radio before retiring to their respective bedrooms.

Their lives soon entered into this pattern, with Eva a very regular visitor, depending on her work shifts.

Everything appeared satisfactory, apart from, during the long nights, when Bill could hear Lizzie weeping softly. It tore at his heart-strings, as he knew he was powerless to ease her pain.

During the day she put on such a brave face, but, just occasionally, he would catch her looking at Meg, or just staring through the kitchen window, with a far-away look in her eyes – her thoughts with little Bobby. He knew that she would never get over her loss but hoped, in time, the hurt would ease, and he, along with Eva would do all they could to help her over this difficult time. Between them they encouraged her to invite Cissie to visit, as she needed to feel the family bond.

CHAPTER NINETEEN

Cissie tore open the letter from Lizzie –

"Oh my goodness" – "Oh no" – "Oh noooo" she cried, tears coursing down her face as she looked towards Fanny.

"Whatever's wrong" asked her step-mother, half-heartedly. She was still weak from Marjorie's birth and didn't really have the strength, or even the inclination to cope with anyone else's problems. But Cissie had been such a treasure, taking the baby over the minute she arrived home from work, sometimes having her in her bedroom over-night, so that Fanny could get full night's sleep.

"Lizzie has lost her little boy and her boss has died in a car accident. She has no baby boy, no job and no home" said Cissie in an uncharacteristically dramatic way.

"Well – I'm sorry to hear that, dear, but there's no room for her here – even if Father was to agree, which, of course, he wouldn't", said Fanny defeatedly.

"What happened to the boy – and is the girl alright?"

"Well, apparently, the babies were in their pram in the yard, and when Lizzie went to fetch them indoors, little Bobby wasn't there – just disappeared – they searched the area but couldn't find hide nor hair of him – they assume that a fox has taken him. I was reading only last week of a similar case in Wales. Oh! how awful, Fanny, for our poor Lizzie. I must go and see her. Can you manage with Marjorie on Saturday, and I'll see to her on Sunday and cook the lunch as well, if you like."

"I suppose so" Fanny answered tiredly. "Lizzie will need some support. Tell her we'll ask around for a living in post, perhaps in Footly."

Cissie agreed with Fanny that Lizzie should come and live closer to the family so that they could give her the support she desperately needed at this awful time.

Cissie had prepared the evening meal before leaving for work that morning, and Fanny had set everything cooking, later in the day, and laid the table in readiness for their return. She prepared Marjorie's bottle then passed the baby and bottle over to Fanny whilst she, Cissie, strained the vegetables and served out the meal.

When all the chores were completed, Cissie went to her room and wrote a very brief note to

Lizzie, saying that she would visit her at the weekend and would Lizzie kindly meet her off the bus. She quickly folded the page and was stuffing it into an envelope as she was leaving the house to be sure she caught the last post. She was glad of this time out of the house, away from all the pressing chores and responsibilities that rested heavily on her young shoulders.

Her heart was heavy for her sister's sadness and also for the little nephew that she had never met. She would spend Saturday with Lizzie and Meg and travel back in time to meet up with Ted, her one shining light, as was usual on a Saturday night. She was longing to see Lizzie but at the same time she was dreading it.

Lizzie's reply was waiting for her when she arrived home from work on Friday evening. Her instructions were clear and concise and Cissie was sure that she would cope easily with the journey – on her own.

CHAPTER TWENTY

Cissie woke early on Saturday morning and quietly left the warmth of her bed. She pulled on her clothes and tip-toed down the stairs and into the back scullery. She lit the gas then placed the large kettle over it and whilst it was coming to the boil she went through to the living room and gently raked the dead ash out of the grate, scrunched up yesterdays newspaper, placed on some sticks that had been drying out in the bottom oven and struck a match. Immediately the room felt cosier. She then placed on a few of the bigger cinders that hadn't burnt through last night, and then at the very top she placed new nuggets of shiny coal. By the time the kettle was boiling the fire was crackling merrily in the hearth.

One by one the family emerged from upstairs, yawning and mumbling their morning greetings.

Cissie felt a little guilty when she saw Fanny's pale and tired looking face. But, she did have Mary there to give her hand, thought Cissie.

However, she was well aware that Mary didn't like to have to change her plans. Her Saturdays were usually spent looking round the shops with her friends or Jack, picking up items for their 'bottom drawer'.

Cissie shook her head – she couldn't take on everyone's problems and try to solve them –but today she would concentrate on Lizzie and Meg, and tomorrow, well……..tomorrow was another day.

She went upstairs and took her good coat from the shared wardrobe, she also added a woollen scarf as the autumnal days were becoming decidedly chilly, then dashed through the door calling cheerio to all as she went, making her way to the station.

The countryside sped by and soon the train was slowing down as it approached the station in Utchester. Lizzie's instruction were clear in Cissie's mind, - turn left out of the station – up into the market place – left again, and there, would be waiting a maroon and cream bus with Ashtown on the front. She was to pay for a return ticket and ask the conductor to tell her when they arrived at Ellswood. The journey was interesting as Cissie had never travelled to this area before – in fact – when she thought about it she hadn't really travelled anywhere before!

As the bus trundled along, stopping to pick up more passengers, then stopping to let others get off with their bags of shopping, Cissie couldn't help but think of Lizzie travelling along this same road just about a year ago, all alone, and pregnant, how scared she must have felt.

"Ellswood comin up, Young Lady" called the jovial conductor. "We have three stops in the village, first one is Dove Street".

Cissie raised herself up in her seat and, as she couldn't see Lizzie waiting for her, she shook her head.

A couple of minutes later he called, "Abbott's Hotel". Again, Cissie looked ahead – no Lizzie –so again, she shook her head. Just a minute later he called "Southwood Lane End". Cissie could now see Lizzie waiting expectantly for the bus. Her eyes lit up and nodded to the conductor who pressed the bell once to advise the driver to stop. She gathered up her bag and held on tight to the backs of the seats as she edged her way to the front of the bus. The conductor slid open the door and gave her a cheeky wink as she alighted.

In an instant Cissie and Lizzie were hugging each other. This time though, they were more reserved. So much had happened to Lizzie since their last meeting. The bus pulled away from the stop in a cloud of smoke, making the girls cough and laugh at the same time.

Cissie, at last, met little Meg.

The bus stop was only a ten minute walk from Bill's house, so they chatted amiably as they walked along the narrow lane.

Bill was waiting for them at the gate and he took hold of the pram and manoeuvred it up the garden path and in through the door.

Once they were all indoors Lizzie introduced Cissie to Bill. Cissie warmed immediately to the old man, who insisted that she take a seat at the table where he would serve the lunch that Lizzie and prepared for them earlier. He enquired about her journey and made her feel very welcome and very much at home.

As soon as lunch was over Bill tactfully said he had chores to see to outside and would they please excuse him, then left the girls to converse as only close sisters know how!

"It's so good to see you Cissie. Thank you so much for coming so promptly" Lizzie said sincerely.

"That's ok. Fanny says to tell you that she is asking around to see if anyone needs some live-in help in our area. She really is concerned about you, you know, Liz, and she still looks so poorly - she still isn't over Marjorie's birth."

"The only way I'll get a live-in post is if I give up Meg for adoption – and there is no chance that will happen. It's me and my daughter from now on. Nothing and no-one will ever come between us.

Don't worry Cis, Bill says we can stay here as long as we like, he's been such a good friend".

She looked fondly through the window where Bill was pulling a dead plant out of the ground – unaware that he was being scrutinized by the two sisters.

"Are you happy here? Don't you feel you'd like to be back in Livingstone, where all your family are?" Cissie enquired.

"Think about it Cissie. Father would never give me the time of day, now would he? And just supposing it became public knowledge that I'd had, not one, but two illegitimate babies, my life would be unbearable. No...I'll take advantage of Bill's kindness and stay here until something else turns up"
.

"If you're sure…..said Cissie uncertainly.

"Yes!! I'm sure! Now tell me all of your news. How is dear Ted" she teased, lightening the mood and lessening the tension.

Once they had started there was no stopping them – Cissie relating funny tales of things that had happened at the factory, of people they both knew. Births, marriages and deaths in the Livingstone and surrounding areas. Bill could hear their undulating voices intermingled with giggles and the occasional shriek as he found jobs to do in the garden to give them this time on their own.

At 3.30 he popped his head round the door and said that as the bus went back to Utchester at 4 o'clock, perhaps Cissie had better prepare herself for her journey home.

Cissie leapt to her feet, alarmed that she may miss the bus, which meant she would miss the last train home.

"Calm down, Our Cissie" said Lizzie, not unkindly. "It's only ten minutes walk down the road and we'll come with you".

They donned their warm coats and scarves and tucked little Meg snugly into her pram. Bill raised his hand as they walked down the path.

The next minute Cissie was standing in front of him. She stood on tip-toe and kissed his cheek, "Thank you for making me so welcome and thank you, from the bottom of my heart for what you're doing for Lizzie and Meg" she gushed.

Bill tried not to show his embarrassment, but, as he was not in the habit of being kissed, even chastely, by pretty young women – he couldn't help blushing at her naïve spontaneity. She skipped back down the path and fell into step with Lizzie. At the corner, they both turned and waved to Bill, who was watching their retreating figures.

After just a couple of minutes the bus arrived and they realised how finely they had timed Cissie's departure. She leapt on to the bus and quickly found a seat and peered through the murky window to see Lizzie waving vigorously at her. She waved back and mouthed "see you soon". The conductor took her return ticket from and punched a hole in it then gave it back to her.

Cissie was deep in thought for the entire journey and soon she realised that the train was pulling into Livingstone station. She glanced down the platform and was delighted to see Ted waiting for her. She rushed up to him, her delight at him being there to meet her evident in her sparkling eyes. As they left the station she took his arm and began to relate to him the events of the day and her concerns for Lizzie and Meg's future.

Ted could see how worried she was and voiced his thoughts that he wished there was some way in which he could be of help.

Cissie replied "She is so independent – and she is adamant that she won't come back to this area, mainly because of Father. Bill seems very kind and has said that they can stay there as long as they want to but I don't think that it's really appropriate – a young woman and and an older man living under the same roof – and a very small roof at that. Lizzie said that one or two comments have already been made within her ear-shot".

"Well", replied Ted, "You are being supportive – she knows that you will always do what you can for her – so just keep going to see her, when you can. I'm sure things will sort themselves out".

Just then, Reggie and Flora Jenkins appeared, pushing their baby boy in a beautiful navy and white Silver Cross pram.

"Oh hallo, Mr. Jenkins, Mrs Jenkins", said Cissie respectfully. "May I have a quick peek at the baby, please"? Flora proudly eased back the soft downy blanket so that they could see what a beautiful baby they had. A shock of auburn hair and a pair of striking blue eyes was all that Cissie had time to see before Reg rudely pushed the pram away.

"Time for his feed", he muttered. Flora looked at the couple and smiled apologetically and followed he husband.

"How ignorant", said the usually easy-going Ted.

"Well, I'm sorry now that I asked to see him" said an embarrassed Cissie.

CHAPTER TWENTY ONE

"Wasn't that a little rude?" Flora simpered to Reggie as they walked back to the big house. She had to say something but was loathe to create an argument with her husband – he had been so different, so amenable, towards her since David had come into their lives. There were times when she had to remind herself that she hadn't actually given birth to the little boy as she felt such an overwhelming love for him. Reg too, was so happy and she didn't want to jeopardise this contentment for the sake of the two people that Reg had dismissed so impolitely.

"It was getting near to his feed time" he replied. "No knowing how long they would have kept us talking".

With that, they both hurried home to where Flora was immediately involved in David's feed and bath time routine that she never gave another thought to the brief, uncomfortable incident.

Whilst Flora was busy in the nursery, Reggie went into the sitting room and poured himself a large glass of port.

Taking it over to the French doors he gulped down a large amount as he gazed across the beautifully manicured lawns and surrounding borders. He appreciated how his life had changed; - beyond recognition – he couldn't let anything spoil what he had achieved. He had felt un-nerved by the presence of Cissie Bentley in such close proximity to her nephew – as if some family bond would manifest itself in that moment.

His heart had finally stopped racing – he realised he should have prepared himself for this eventuality. It was inevitable that they would meet up again and again as they lived in such a small community.

Yes – he must have a plan – he mustn't appear rude again – if Flora had noticed then chances were that Cissie Plant and Ted Bentley had too.

No – he didn't want to attract unnecessary attention to himself, or more importantly, his little 'son'. The next time he saw any of the Plant family he would go out of his way to be more than pleasant to each and every one of them – or he would just go out of his way!

He puffed out his chest – what an amazing chap I am, he thought, and poured himself another generous glass of port.

***

The factory continued to thrive under Mr Jenkin's watchful eye.

Orders poured in from stately homes all over the country following his highly successful meeting with the honourable Sir Richard FitzWilliam. True to his word, Sir Richard had recommended the Wirksworth factory to all who had complimented him on his fine china. Reggie went on to remember that meeting and of the days that had followed it –

Yes, I am a truly amazing chap.

Flora let the nursemaid, Ellen bath David and prepare his bottle, then, as usual, she held him and gave him his final feed of the day. She treasured this time with her 'son'.

And occasionally, Reg would come into the nursery and join them. This evening there was nowhere else in the world that he would rather be. Flora looked almost pretty as she clucked like a mother hen at the baby as he suckled on his bottle. Yes, he was a proud father indeed. Ellen used this time to go and visit her family, making sure she was back by bed-time, as Reg didn't want his nights sleep disturbed by a crying baby, but really, David was so contented that he rarely woke during the night.

Their peace was disturbed by a sharp rap on the front door. They looked at each other, puzzled. They were not expecting guests and Flora's parents were still in the south of France. Adams, the butler, stood in the doorway of the nursery and gave a slight cough to attract their attention.

"Sorry to disturb you, Sir, Ma'am", he said softly. Reg nodded for his to enter the room.

"What is it, Adams?"

"It's Ellen. She's had a fall on the way to see her parents; the doctor has confirmed that her leg is broken and obviously won't be able to work for quite a while. She thought she should let you know as soon as possible so that perhaps you can get someone in temporarily to look after Master David."

"Humph" said Reg.

"The poor girl", said Flora. "I will go and see her tomorrow and tell her not to worry, her job is safe.

"We will have to get a replacement", said Reg. "You can't possible manage David on your own, day and night for the next couple of months".

"That's true, Dear. I will have to have some help. I need to be tending to my charity work and attending my lunches. I won't be able to take David with me…"

Turning to Adams she asked, "Do you know of anyone who would be suitable, Adams?".

"As a matter of fact, I do, Ma'am. My niece, Lucille, is staying in the village for a few days before taking up a new position as Governess to a family in Somerset. I'm sure she would agree to help out for the immediate future, until you find a replacement for Ellen."

"Oh Adams, that would be perfect, thank you. Perhaps you could go and tell her of the situation and maybe she could return with you" said Flora.

Malcolm Adams went into the village, to his brother Sam's house and related the story to the rest of the family.
"Lucille's not here at the moment, she's just gone to see Mary Plant. I'll pop down the lane and get her to come back with me," said Sam's wife Annie.

"We'll not see her for a couple of hours", said Sam grinning. "Once she and Fanny Plant get chatting.... And then there's Marjorie to coo over – it may even be three hours" he said good-humouredly.

Annie rapped on the door and opened and called "It's only me", then went to great lengths to explain the quandary that Mr and Mrs Jenkins were in. Lucille said she would be more than happy to help out for a couple of days but really needed to be in Somerset by the week-end to get settled in before starting her new job the following Monday morning.

Fanny and Cissie looked at each other, their minds working in unison. "Lizzie"

A perfect job for Lizzie! Cissie fled up the stairs and quickly scribbled a few lines, telling Lizzie of the amazing chance for her to come back to her roots, and be nursemaid to Reg and Flora Jenkins's baby son.

CHAPTER TWENTY TWO

Lizzie's eyes were like saucers. She couldn't believe what she was reading.

Cissie - was suggesting that she, Lizzie, take up a position in the home of the man who had let her down so badly. But then, Cissie had no idea of her association with Reg Jenkins. No one had. She wouldn't realise the pain, the salt in her ever open wound that looking this man's son would cause her. Although she was aware that the idea came to her with the very best intention in the world, and Lizzie knew that she must reply immediately, it rankled that they would never know the truth behind her refusal to work for a man, they so highly respected. She just hoped that her hurt and anger weren't revealed in the brief reply.

Lizzie was walking back along the lane when Bill caught up with her on is way back from work.

"I've just been to Ellswood to post a letter to Cissie", she explained.

"It's a shame there's no letter-box in Southwood, it's a long walk for you, just to post a letter" he said.

"Oh, I bought a few groceries, whilst I was there" she added. "Besides, I may as well get out when I can, before the weather turns bad."

Bill had warned her that the narrow lane was often blocked with snow during the winter months, and with this in mind, she was determined to get out as much as she could, while she could.

Bill sensed that she was tense and asked if everything was ok.

"It was" she replied. "Until I received a letter from Cissie - telling me of a vacant post just outside of Livingstone. She is determined to get me back there. But I've told her that I'm not interested – there's no going back".

Then suddenly she realised what she had said.

"I mean…. if it's alright with you, for us to stay a bit longer, that is". Bill was a man of few words and just said,
"Course it is".

What Lizzie didn't tell him was, that she had overheard two ladies in the village shop talking about the rights and wrongs of two people living in the same house, and not being married to each other, looking blatantly at Lizzie.

145

She knew it would upset him if she repeated the conversation to him, so kept that bit to herself, letting him believe that it was only Cissie's letter that was distressing her.

Unbeknown to Lizzie, Bill himself, had suffered the same fate on several occasions, and likewise, thought it would upset Lizzie, to tell her of the dour comments.

***

Christmas this year was very different for both Lizzie and Bill, compared to the previous year. Meg was now sitting up and taking notice of all that was going on around her, much to Lizzie's joy and Bill's amusement.

During the morning, they walked together to St. Peter's Church in Ellswood to attend the service. As they were walking through the lych-gate on their way home, two spinsters of the parish were just behind them, speaking in unusually loud voices.

"Should be ashamed, flaunting themselves in the house of God. Connie Udall must be turning in her grave."

The normally quiet retiring Bill turned.
"Call yourselves Christians?" he said angrily. "You have such evil minds to think as you do. All I have done is given Mrs Plant and her child a home. No more – no less".

"Humph" said the spinster. "You expect us to believe that – we weren't born yesterday, you know" with that she turned on her heel and strutted away before Lizzie or Bill had the chance to reply.

Bill looked at Lizzie apologetically. Lizzie said, "We can't do anything about the way people think, Bill. Just forget it". She could see how angry and frustrated he was.
"But we could do something to stop them talking – let's get back to the cottage and we'll see what you think of my plan".

On their return Lizzie served out the Christmas lunch, a plump little goose, courtesy of Bill's kind employers. When they had both eaten a portion of plum pudding, Meg became unusually fractious and demanding Lizzies's undivided attention.

All the time she was tending to her baby, Lizzie was wondering just what Bill was going to suggest. Perhaps he had heard of someone locally who was prepared to employ her, baby and all, – perhaps – surely he wouldn't just throw her out?

But then, why not? Her father had!!

Her father had known her all her life – Bill had only known he a year or so …….oh dear, dear dear.

With a feeling of doom, she eventually went back into the small sitting room where Bill had cleared all the pots from the table, and stoked up the fire. How cosy it looked – how she would miss all of this.

"Sit down, Lass" said Bill kindly. He handed her a small glass of sherry, another Christmas gift from his employers, which she accepted gratefully. She hoped he would get it over and done with as quickly as possible.

"Thank you, Bill" she said calmly, not daring to look him in the eye.

"What I'm going to suggest is going to be a bit of a shock, Lizzie. I've given it a great deal of thought and it is the best way, I believe. I don't want you to answer straight away – just give my proposition a bit of thought, please."

Lizzie waited. Nothing more was said. Lizzie slowly lifted her eyes to look at him across the hearth and could see the hand that was holding his glass of sherry was shaking. This doesn't look good, thought Lizzie. Bill cleared his throat.

"I think we should get married" he blurted.

Lizzie sat looking at him. This was the last thing she had expected.
"Oh Bill", she said. "You don't have to do this. I really appreciate your offer, but I don't expect you to do this for me. If you feel so uncomfortable with the gossip, I will accept the offer of the post in Livingstone…."

"As I just said – don't give me an answer, right now. Think about it for a few days. There's no rush".

With that he walked out of the room, donned his coat and hat and left the house.

Lizzie's mind was in a whirl.

What a shock!!

CHAPTER TWENTY THREE

Lizzie's letter arrived by return of post and Cissie tore eagerly at the envelope, hoping against hope that her sister would agree to come back to the area. Cissie had already confided in her friend, Sarah of the plan, so it was a dreadful disappointment to read of Lizzie's refusal.

Unbeknown to Cissie, Sarah had also mentioned the possibility of Lizzie's new post to Joe Stokes – who, just at that moment in time, was in Reg Jenkins' office, reporting that a consignment of clay, ordered days ago still hadn't been delivered. As stock was getting dangerously low, he knew that it was imperative for Reg to sort the problem out.

Reg picked up the phone, immediately and told the supplier, in no uncertain terms that if the clay hadn't arrived before the end of the working day, he would take his custom elsewhere. Joe was so in awe of Reggie, who had risen through the ranks and emerged as 'the boss'.

So, when all the business talk was completed, he turned the conversation to a more personal level, enquiring after Flora, her parents and finally, David, adding that it would be nice to see Lizzie Plant back in Livingstone. He said he was sure she would make an excellent nursemaid to Reg and Flora's son.

Just at that moment someone rapped on the door of the office calling,
"Clay's 'ere, Joe", so before Reg could make any reply, Joe had disappeared to over-see the unloading of the precious clay.

Reg's heart was pounding. There was no way he could allow Lizzie to even see the baby boy, let alone care for him. One look at his left foot would verify that this was her very own baby!

He had to think fast!

***

Lucille, Adams's niece, was an excellent nurse-maid – she had been caring for David for a few days now, and Flora was full of praise for the girl. She told Reg that it was going to be difficult to find someone to beat Lucille's high standards.

Right – he thought – I have the answer!

He would make Lucille an offer she couldn't refuse. Whatever the salary the family in Somerset was offering her, he would double it, if she would become David's full-time nanny. Whoever had said that money wasn't everything, didn't know what they were talking about. Having money certainly made things much easier to attain and in his opinion, money talked. Time, now, was of the essence, he realised. With this in mind, he quickly grabbed his coat and, on his way out, called to Joe that he would be back shortly, and made his way home.

Flora looked up in surprise, when he entered the sitting room.

"Hello Reg, are you feeling ill, Dear"? Her voice full of concern.

"I'm fine, Flora. I was just thinking about Lucille, and how pleased we both have been with the way she cares for David. I was thinking of asking her to stay on here on a permanent basis, instead of going to Somerset. What do you think?"

"Oh Reg – I think it's a wonderful idea – but – do you think she'll agree to it at such a late date?"

"I'm sure I can persuade her" Reg replied confidently.

"But, we can't, can we? What about Ellen? I promised her that her job was safe. I really can't go back on my word".

Flora was distraught.

"Leave it to me" Reg said with his usual authority.

He left the room and went into the nursery, where Lucille was busy folding napkins, whilst David slept soundly, in his crib.

"Hello, Mr Jenkins" she said, smiling up at him.

"Hello to you, young Lucille. Everything seems to be running smoothly in here. You have done really well to take over as you have".

Lucille replied,
"Well, David is such a contented baby – it has all been so easy. Ellen had a really good routine in place and I have just carried it on".

"I have a proposition to put to you, my dear" Reg continued. "Mrs Jenkins and I have discussed this at length, and we would like to make you an offer. We would like you to consider staying on here, as David's full time nanny, for now, and, governess as he gets older. I'll match the salary that your new employers have offered you, and, as we promised Ellen we would keep her job for her, she will be your assistant".

Lucille looked amazed. She was aware that Mrs. Jenkins-Wirksworth was happy with her work, but this was so unexpected. When she didn't reply immediately, the usually impatient Reg decided to change his tactics.

"Don't decide right now, you can have until the morning, to make up your mind".

He'd also changed his tactics on doubling her salary. He'd made the rash promise to employ Ellen as her assistant, so felt that to match her salary would be an adequate offer.

Lucille was secretly thrilled. She had lived in the Midlands all her life. All of her family were close by, and as the time drew closer to her moving south, the more she wondered if she was doing the right thing. Now, however, she was being offered the opportunity to remain on familiar ground, with a top position, with a top family. There was also the bonus that she could develop her new-found friendship with Joe Stokes's younger brother, Matthew.

Reg went back to join Flora in the sitting room, a smug smile on his face.

"You look pleased with yourself, Dear" she said.

"I think you will have a nice surprise, in the morning" was all that he would say – then he took himself back to the factory.

Whilst David continued his afternoon nap, Lucille made her decision. She would accept Mr. Jenkins kind offer. She quickly wrote an apologetic letter to the family, in Somerset, stressing how badly she felt at letting them down at this late date, then dashed into the kitchen with the envelope, and asked Uncle Malcolm if he would kindly post for her, on his way home.

CHAPTER TWENTY FOUR

Bill returned to the house with some trepidation. He closed the door quietly behind him and slowly removed his coat and hung it behind the door. When he entered the sitting room Lizzie was just pouring water from the kettle into the teapot.

"Tea's almost ready" she said, not looking at him. He pulled out a chair and sat down at the table, looking apprehensively at her, as she passed him the cup. She drew out the chair and down opposite him. He slowly raised his eyes to meet hers. She was smiling.
"Bill, if you really mean it, I would be honoured to become your wife" she said.

"Of course I mean it" he answered. "I know I am an old man but I promise you this, Lizzie, I'll be a good husband to you, and the best father that I can be to Meg – not that I've not had any practice in that role".

She smiled again.

"Thank you, Lizzie, you've made me the happiest man in Southwood".
This remark caused Lizzie to laugh out loud. Southwood was such a small hamlet, there couldn't have been more than half a dozen men living there! She was sure, then, that she had made the right decision, they would be very happy together.

Bill said as he had to travel into Ashtown within the next few days, he would call in at the Registry Office and make all the necessary arrangements. He couldn't see why they shouldn't be married as soon as possible. Lizzie thought this was a splendid idea; as soon as the Christmas holiday period was over, Bill caught a bus to the nearby town.

As he boarded the vehicle and passed the time of day with other passengers from the village, he spotted Eva sitting alone. He also saw that she making room for him to sit with her and he hurried down the aisle and took his place.

"You're out bright and early" she jested.

"Yes, Eva. I'm on a very special mission" he confided. "I know Lizzie won't mind me telling you. I've asked her to marry me and she's accepted my proposal – I'm now on my way to see the Registrar".

"Ohh Bill, that's wonderful" she sighed.

"It's going to be a very quiet affair, obviously, but I would like it if you would say you'll be a witness for us".

"Of course, I will" said a delighted Eva.

When they arrived in the town, they went their separate ways, knowing full well that they would be travelling back to Ellswood together.

Bill strode off the Registry Office, thinking the last time he had been there was to register the death of his beloved Connie. He knew she would have approved of Lizzie and he entered the room with a heart lighter than it had been for many a year.

Between them they came up with the date of March 8th, 1932. Bill left the office with all the essential documentation tucked carefully in his inside pocket and made his way up the market place to buy a new handle for his garden rake at the Hall. As he came out of the door of Woodissee's Iron mongers shop, he was surprised to see Eva waiting outside.

"Have you sorted everything, then, Bill" she asked him, excitedly.
"Indeed I have".he replied.

"Well, there's something I want you to take a look at" she said mysteriously, and catching him by the arm hurried him back down the market place and on towards the bus station.

En-route was a small ladies wear shop called 'Miss Desborough's' and Eva came to an abrupt stop and stood looking into the shop window. A head-less model in the window was displaying a lovely pale blue knitted two piece.

Eva looked at it, looked at Bill and then back at the outfit, willing him to respond.

After a minute, the penny dropped in Bill's masculine mind.

"Ahhhh, I see. An outfit fit for a bride?" he asked. Eva nodded furiously, and quickly opened the shop door. The little bell above it tinkled as they entered and Miss Desborough herself appeared from the room at the back of the shop. Eva took the lead as she could see that Bill was way out of his depth in the situation. Miss Desborough agreed that it was a perfect choice for a wedding and folded it expertly, with layers of tissue paper between each fold, and then placed it all inside a box. Bill took out his wallet and counted the money, as Miss Desborough brought out another smaller box, from under the counter.

She opened the lid to reveal the prettiest pale blue hat with a tiny veil across the front. Eva gasped in amazement. This re-action convinced Bill that he must also buy the matching hat, although no words had been exchanged.

Miss Desborough smiled and said" You have very good taste – the lady will be so pleased, I'm sure."

Together, Eva and Bill left the shop and sped on to the bus station. If they missed this one, they would have a two hour wait for the next one and it was already turning very cold and going dusk. They journeyed back to Ellswood in comparative silence, both wrapped up in their own thoughts.

Lizzie saw Bill coming up the garden path and poured out a cup of tea in readiness for him coming through the door. A tasty stew was simmering in the oven at the side of the fireplace, and the appetizing smell permeated the room. As Bill entered the room, he sniffed the air appreciatively.

"That smells so good. I'm starving" he said.

"That's good. Did you sort everything out?"

"I certainly did" he said grinning. 8th March, you become Mrs Bill Udall – is that ok?"

Lizzie nodded with an equally wide grin on her face.

After they had eaten, he went back into the porch and returned, carrying the two boxes and placed them on the table in front of Lizzie. She looked at him uncertainly.

"Open the big one first" he ordered. She carefully removed the lid and lifted the first layer of tissue paper, revealing the lovely outfit.
She couldn't speak.

Again, she realised how lucky she was to have Bill in her life. When she opened the second box and took out the pretty hat, she thought she would cry with happiness.

The only thing wrong in her life was that her little boy was no longer with her.

CHAPTER TWENTY FIVE

Once again, a letter was winging its way from Lizzie, this time, informing Cissie of her forthcoming marriage.

Cissie read the words with deep concern, Yes, Bill was a kind and thoughtful man, but husband and wife? – with a forty year span between them?

Would it work?

Could it work?

Lizzie wasn't her only concern either. There was little Meg to consider, too. But, she thought, they must have thought it through and talked about all the pitfalls before making their decision.

In the letter, Lizzie asked if Cissie and Ted would come to the wedding, but omitted to include Father and Fanny in the invitation, much to Cissie's relief. Father still wouldn't tolerate Lizzie's name being mentioned in his presence.

As soon as her chores were completed and Marjorie settled down for the night, Cissie sat in her room and wrote out her reply. She said how thrilled she was to hear their wonderful news, and that 'wild horses' wouldn't stop her and Ted from joining them on their special day, with not a hint of criticism, just genuine gladness that Lizzie, had now found the happiness that had previously eluded her.

The following morning she posted her letter as she met up with Sarah and Betsy, on the way to work.

"Mornin' Cis. You look happy" said Sarah. "Had some good news, have you"?

"Indeed I have" she replied, excitedly, and proceeded to tell them both about the imminent marriage.

"But…… I thought you said Lizzie was coming back to look after Reg Jenkins' baby" said a puzzled Sarah.

"Change of plan" said Cissie, smiling broadly.

They arrived at the factory gate at the same time as Mr Jenkins – he looked across at the three of them and they thought he was going to speak, but then he just turned and walked on. The girls looked at each other, shrugged their shoulders, and then went to clock in, soon forgetting their boss's strange behaviour.

Reg stormed into his office. Why was that family haunting him? He sat at his desk with his head in his hands. After a few minutes, when his heart rate had returned to normal, he realised he was over re-acting. He really had to control his attitude to the Plant family – or arouse suspicion. Deep down he knew it was conscience that was affecting him. But then, he thought, why shouldn't he have the little boy? – who would never want for anything, *and* who was as much his flesh and blood as he was Lizzie's, and *she* still had their daughter, after all.

With his inner-self comforted, he decided the best way was to face his demons, and took himself into the Glazing Shed, where he went over to speak to Joe. As they were talking, he looked casually around until his eyes rested on Cissie and her colleagues. He abruptly ended his conversation and left the Shed, purposely passing through the girls work area: he nodded and smiled to all as he passed.

Back in his own domain he thought, that's what I'll do, meet her regularly on *my territory*, and then, when I meet her in the village, or anywhere else, it will just get easier and easier. Yes, Reg! Another problem solved - well - almost. Only time would tell.

As Reg predicted, Flora was very pleasantly surprised when Lucille announced that, after her conversation with Mr Jenkins, the previous evening, she had decided to accept his offer and decline the post in Somerset. Flora was thrilled, and relieved to hear that Reg had affirmed that they would honour the promise made to Ellen.

This knowledge pacified her and by the time Reg appeared that evening, she was feeling very happy.

CHAPTER TWENTY SIX

The winter progressed with little disruption, small scatterings of snow appeared, and disappeared just as quickly. Eva's visits to Lizzie and Meg were frequent, and the main topic of conversation was, obviously, the wedding.

A couple of weeks before the big day, Lizzie took kitchen scissors to her lovely, thick, dark hair and trimmed it in what she believed to be quite a fashionable bob. When Eva saws it for the first time she had to suppress a giggle – it looked as though a pudding basin had been placed on her head and someone had cut round it.

"What do you think?" asked Lizzie. "Is it a little bit too short?"

"Well" started Eva diplomatically. "Not too short, no…..I think maybe it could do with a bit of curl. When I go to Ashtown tomorrow, I'll call in at Osborne and Beeby's Chemist and see if they have a Tweenie Twink perm. I can wind it on to the curlers for you – I've done my mum's a few times".

"Ooh thanks so much Eva, I really want to look my best and do my lovely outfit justice".

The following day, Eva alighted from the bus at the Southwood stop on her way back from Ashtown, and hurried up the lane to the cottage, full of intent and purpose.

That evening, when Bill returned from work, instead of being met by the usual appetising aroma of tea cooking, all he could smell was ammonia, and shrieks of laughter coming from the kitchen.

"Hello Bill" Eva said, as he put his head round the door. "Just attempting to turn this young lady into a beautiful bride", she quipped.

Bill smiled and went to greet Meg as she was beaming at him. Already he had such a fondness for the sweet-natured baby.

Lizzie came into the sitting room with towels around her shoulders and hair dripping in the neutralizer – the perming session was almost complete. She went into the larder and brought out a tureen of winter vegetable soup and proceeded to heat it up on the fire. Whilst it was warming through, she set three places at the table and insisted that Eva dine with them. They just had time for the final hair rinse before sitting down together and enjoying the comforting, warming soup.

When the meal was over, Eva set Lizzie's hair in the curlers, stressing to her that they must stay in place until the morning when the hair would be completely dry. Only then could she remove them, otherwise she would have a frizzy mass of hair for her wedding. Lizzie realised that there would be very little sleep for her that night.

Bill insisted on walking Eva back home as the winter's night sky was as black as ink with no hint of a moon.

***

The morning of March 8th dawned. The winter sun shone weakly, with very little warmth in it.

Earlier, when Bill had informed Mr Duncombe of his forthcoming nuptials, true to form, the kindly squire had insisted on lending Bill his car, yet again.

As Lizzie was dressing herself in all her finery, Bill went to fetch the car and then, together they took Meg to stay with Eva's parents for the day. Eva jumped in the car and they drove to the end of Dove Street to await the bus that was bringing Cissie and Ted, and due to arrive in Ellswood at 11.30. The wedding was to take place at 12.30 so that would give them ample time to get to the town with, hopefully, a few minutes to spare.

The car journey from Ellwsood to Ashtown was full of good humoured banter, with the usually quiet Ted joining in, although he had never met Lizzie, Bill or Eva before – Cissie was surprised and thrilled that he was so at ease in their company.

At the door of the Registry Office, Cissie produced a bunch of daffodils, tied with pretty pale blue ribbon, from her bag. Lizzie hugged her sister and looked every inch the blushing bride.

After the ceremony was over, as a post-wedding treat, they all filed into the Green Man Hotel, where Bill ordered five glasses of sherry, then they drank a toast to the future happiness of Mr and Mrs William Udall.

Later, together, they travelled back to Ellswood where Lizzie had prepared a tea of sandwiches and scones and jam. After they had eaten and chatted, they took Cissie and Ted to catch the bus for their return journey, delivered Eva back home and picked up Meg, who, they were assured, had been a perfect little angel.

Then they began their married life.

***

On their journey home from the wedding Cissie and Ted were both wrapped up in their own private thoughts.

Cissie was concerned about the age gap, although she would never have voiced her thoughts to her sister.

Ted, on the other had, was thinking how he would love to marry Cissie. They had been seeing each other for almost two years now and the simple wedding ceremony had touched on his romantic nature and he wished, so much that he could propose to her, here and now. But, he realised, this was not the time. He was supporting his invalid mother, as his father died many years ago, which left Ted the head of the household. He had two teenage brothers, coming up to school leaving age and two younger sisters. Ted's job, as farm labourer didn't bring in very much money but their cottage was part of his salary, so whilst he had a job they had a roof over their heads.

However, it was a small roof covering six heads already. The time wasn't right for him to take a wife. When the lads were working and bringing in a wage, then....he would be in a position to look for a little house and beg Cissie to be his bride.

CHAPTER TWENTY SEVEN

EASTER 1934

Lizzie woke with a feeling of sublime happiness surging through her body. It was just over two years since her marriage to Bill, and not a not a day had passed when she didn't thank God for sending this wonderful man into her life.

The rift between Lizzie and her father was healing. She and Bill had visited her family home on numerous occasions, where her father, who was several years younger than Bill, had really taken to the man who had shown untold kindness to his wayward daughter.

Lizzie still had no desire to move back to the Potteries permanently. Southwood was home. And it was going to be more so, in a few months time, for Lizzie suspected that she was carrying Bill's child.

She had been feeling off-colour for a few weeks now, and last night it had suddenly occurred to her that maybe, yes, maybe, she could be pregnant. She wasn't sure how Bill would re-act to the news, but just at that moment in time she felt this overwhelming happiness – a feeling she had never experienced before. So, for the immediate future, she would keep the secret to herself - just until she was one hundred per cent positive.

Bill had taken his role as Lizzie's husband and Meg's father very seriously. He was constantly checking that they were ok and had everything that they needed... Meg adored him, watching each day for him coming home from work. As she saw him coming through the gate she would yell "Daddy" – Lizzie would open the door and she would run as fast as her little legs would carry her down the path, where Bill would sweep her up in arms, causing shrieks of delight. Lizzie would smile fondly as she watched the two of them and, again, count her blessings.

Only occasionally, Bill would see a distant look in her eyes, and he knew that at that moment, her thoughts were with Bobby.

Tomorrow, she had decided, she would see Dr Clayton, and once he had confirmed the pregnancy, she could tell Bill. Then together they would tell Eva and their respective families. But for now, it was her little secret – just between her and the new life growing inside her body. She hugged herself, with just a ghost of a smile on her lips – an emotion that didn't go un-noticed by her husband.

After Bill had left for work the following day, Lizzie was washing and dressing Meg when she was over-come with nausea. When the feeling had passed she tucked Meg into the pram and began the walk to Ellswood. The birds were singing and the sun in her eyes as she trundled down the lane. The newness of the grass, and the trees and hedgerows lifted her spirits, and, out in the fresh clean air, her sickness was soon forgotten.

She had no qualms about going to see the doctor as Bill had stressed that any time she or Meg were in need of medical attention she was not to worry about his fees. He said that he and the doctor had an understanding. What he meant was, every week during the spring and summer months, Bill provided the doctor and his wife and daughter, Saxone, with vegetables from his own garden and tomatoes and cucumbers from his own greenhouse. In the autumn, it was potatoes and apples and pears from his orchard. Therefore, the doctor was more than happy to treat Bill, who was healthier than most twenty year olds; and when he married Lizzie, the doctor insisted that she and Meg be included in the 'deal'.

Most of the villagers had a similar understanding: Mr Evans, the butcher, provided most of his meat: Dick Ratcliff serviced his car and Fred Goodhall supplied his milk. It was only the local gentry that actually paid him in money.

When it was Lizzie's turn to be seen by the doctor, Mrs Clayton took Meg into their private sitting room where she played ring-a-roses with her, to give Lizzie the opportunity to describe her symptoms.

Dr Clayton smiled, as did Lizzie.

"Well – do you think Bill will be pleased?" he asked.

"I do hope so. He's wonderful with Meg; he can't seem to do enough for her. I'm hoping that he will be as happy as I am," she replied.

"As far as I can tell you, this one should arrive in the autumn, towards the end of October. Come and see me again in a couple of months – before if you need to – oh, and tell Bill to come and see me if he needs something for the shock!" he said laughing.
Lizzie laughed at that, thanked him and made her way out, through the waiting room, where the very people who had once ostracized her and Bill, before their marriage, were now nodding and smiling and wishing her "Good morning, Mrs Udall".

Lizzie smiled back at them, whispering to herself, 'Two-faced sods', as she went and rescued Mrs Clayton from the wiles of her small daughter.

As Lizzie was serving out their tea, she came over all nauseous yet again. This time, however, she wasn't sure if was caused by the pregnancy, or thoughts of telling Bill and him being horrified.

She needn't have worried at all. As the words left her lips, a grin spread across his face –. He rose from the table and took her in his arms.

He was a man of very few words, but just at that moment in time, no words were necessary.

CHAPTER TWENTY EIGHT

The summer passed in a haze of semi-contentment. Meg learned to do something new every week, much to Bill's pride and delight.

However, Lizzie had this small section of her heart locked away – only opening it when she was alone. This belonged to her and to Bobby - and no-one else. Only occasionally did she allow herself to venture into this sad, dark area, but knew that she must go through this pain to keep the memory of her baby boy alive.

Lizzie's pregnancy progressed with comparative ease. Eva was still a frequent visitor, even though she now had a young gentleman friend, Jim, in her life. She would often call in at the cottage and take Meg for a walk, so that Lizzie could rest for a while, in an afternoon, as her ankles were swelling. But, on their return she would smell the cakes baking as they walked up the path, or the path itself would be newly swept – so, Lizzie's ankles kept on swelling.

Talk about Busy Lizzie, thought Eva.

Cissie and Ted were also regular visitors, particularly towards the end of the pregnancy, as they insisted the journey was too gruelling for her.

The morning of 20th October had not dawned when Lizzie was awoken by racking pains in her back, in her front, in her head and even in her feet.

"Oh Gwen – I wish you were here right now, my dear friend" she cried.
Bill woke with a start at the sound of her voice.

"Is it time, Duck" he asked, gently. The pains had temporarily subsided and Lizzie nodded her head.

"Yes, I'm sure it is, but there's no rush. But I could murder a cuppa."
Bill was straight out of bed and whilst he was waiting for the kettle to boil, he scrambled into his clothes.

"I'll go and fetch Mrs Tideswell, and then pop down and tell Eva".

"You'll do no such thing, Bill Udall. It's not five o'clock yet, we'll wait another hour, at least".

Bill, who had had no dealings in this sort of thing, took her at her word and went back down the stairs to fetch her tea. When he re-entered the bedroom he could see that she was in the throes of having another contraction. He set the cup down on the chest of drawers at the side of the bed and disappeared, in a flash, back down the stairs, out of the door, on to his motor bike and was knocking on Mrs Tideswell's door, in Church Lane within minutes.

It didn't take long for her to prepare herself; she was a light sleeper and always had everything to hand well in advance, when a birth in the area was imminent. She was a powerfully built woman and it was quite a comical sight to see her hanging on to Bill's waist, as he and his trusted motor bike took the corners at speed.

Lizzie was sipping her tea as the two of them entered the bedroom. She smiled apologetically at the midwife.
"I'm so sorry that he fetched you here at this time of day. I told him there was no rush...."

The words were barely out of her mouth when her face contorted - again she was experiencing the excruciating pain.   Bill looked terrified.

Mrs Tideswell looked at him and saw that he wasn't going to be of much use, so she ushered out of the room, telling him to go and boil the kettle.

Fortunately, Meg slept through this first stage, so Bill spied his chance to be useful and went off to fetch Eva, who had generously offered to help out, when the time arrived.

Lizzie heard the engine start up again and smiled to herself at the thought of Bill's face – the look of blind panic – she realised where he would be going and just hoped that he would drive carefully……..another contraction overtook her body, pushing all thoughts of everything and everyone else from her mind. Mrs Tideswell saw this and said "What a good job that man of yours came and fetched me when he did. Push, Lizzie, push, my Duck. It won't be long now".

So Lizzie pushed and pushed and pushed for all she was worth. Then the pain subsided. Almost immediately it all started all over again, and Lizzie delivered her baby, just as the bike came to a halt at the gate.

"My word – you are such a lucky young lady" said the midwife. "A couple of pushes and you've got your baby. There's some of the poor buggers pushing all of the day and into the night."

Lizzie was exhausted and couldn't really believe that anyone could go through that agony, for that length of time and survive, but when Mrs Tideswell placed her baby in her arms, everything else was forgotten.

She had a son.

She cried……and cried.

Mrs Tideswell gently took back the baby, bathed him and dressed him in the little winceyette nightgown that was draped over the back of the chair, then swaddled him in a shawl and laid him on the foot of the bed. She then set to work cleaning up the new mummy, and on completion of her task, bade Lizzie goodbye and took herself off down the stairs, where Eva was waiting with a welcome cup of tea.

"You can go up now" she said to the apprehensive father. Bill took the stairs two at a time. He opened the door to see Lizzie, smiling, and holding out the baby for him to hold. He thought his heart would burst.

"What do you think of William for his name?" she laughed.

"Well – it was good enough for my dad; it's always been good enough for me, so – yes! Bill it is".

***

Young Bill was a contented and happy baby. Meg felt very much the big sister when they went to the village. She now walked at the side of the pram holding on to the handle, until her little legs could go no more. Then Lizzie would pick her up and sit her on the end of the pram where she could turn and check that her little brother was ok, often giving a running commentary on his actions.

"He's asleep – he's awake – he's blowing bubble – he's smiling – oh no! I think he's going to cry" etc.

For Lizzie, life was good; very, very good. Bill, too, was incredibly happy. Marrying Lizzie so late on was a bonus to what had been a pleasant life, but to become a father too, had exceeded his wildest dreams.

So, when Lizzie started to look pale and tired, just after Baby Bill's second Christmas, he was convinced that his luck was running out and he was going to lose Lizzie, as he had lost Connie.

As they sat together, one evening, when the children were tucked up in bed, he decided he could no longer sit back and say nothing.

"Lizzie, my Duck, you really don't look too good, and it's gone on for while now. Would you just pay Dr Clayton a visit, just for me, just to set my daft old mind at rest?" he begged.

"Of course I will, Love" she replied, matter-of-factly. I'm going to see him next week, when Eva can come and look after the little 'uns".

Bill looked at her, she seemed so unconcerned, where as he was quite beside himself. But she had agreed to do as he had asked, so there was no more to be said. Just keep his fingers crossed.

At the appointment, the following week, Dr Clayton confirmed what Lizzie had expected. She was having another baby! Later, when she gave Bill the news, she thought he would cry with relief. He confessed to her what he had been thinking and she chided him for not sharing his concern with her – she could so easily set his mind at rest, as she had recognised the symptoms very early on – being an old hand at this pregnancy malarkey.

Dr Clayton had predicted that this would be summer baby, possibly July.

Again the confinement was a healthy one, the morning sickness lasting only a few weeks.

Meg was coming up to five years old and would be starting the village school in September, and Lizzie realised her days were going to be very busy when the new baby arrived.

July was hot and oppressive. Lizzie's lumbering body was constantly tired and was ready to be relieved of its burden. When the month was out and she still hadn't produced her off-spring, she felt she couldn't go on much longer.

On the 3rd August she was up early, as she was too uncomfortable to sleep. As she was just about to waken Bill, she felt the now familiar pain.

"Bill – wake up, duck" she said. "I think it's started". He was out of bed, dressed and down the stairs in an instant. If Lizzie hadn't been in so much pain she would have laughed at his antics.

Once again, he was tearing along the lane on his trusted bike and, very soon, heading back with Mrs Tideswell riding pillion, and hanging on for dear life. As she entered the house, he was already driving back to fetch Eva.

This time, however, the labour was more prolonged, despite the encouragement from the midwife, Lizzie struggled to bring this little one into the world. It was tea-time before it was all over. Bill was thrilled to gently hold his second daughter – he didn't think of Meg as anything but his very own.

"Well, what are we going to call her?" he asked.

"I quite like Dorothy – but please say if there's another name that you'd prefer".

"Dorothy it is, my duck" said Bill generously. Then his face clouded over as he looked at baby Dorothy.

"This must be the last one, Lizzie! I know I won't live to see them grown up, but while I'm here, they'll want for nothing – the three of them".

CHAPTER TWENTY NINE

Lucille continued to enjoy her job looking after David Wirksworth-Jenkins and her relationship with Matthew Stokes blossomed, while Ellen also enjoyed her less demanding role as nursery assistant. The break in her leg had been quite drastic and as David grew, she was glad that she wasn't the one picking him up and therefore putting more pressure on her damaged limb.

Reg was a superb business-man, who commanded ultimate respect from his workers. Cuthbert visited the factory less and less as he could see at a glance that it was running even more smoothly than when he was in charge.

With orders flooding in from all over the country, Reg had to introduce night shifts just a couple of nights a week to avoid disappointing any of his valued customers.

His proudest moment, ever, came when he asked his father-in-law to accompany him to Bowd's Car Show Room to order his very own Rolls-Royce. Cuthbert was as delighted as Reg and slapped him soundly on his back when the deal was completed.

"I'm proud of yer, Lad" he said. "Yer've not let us down". Reg puffed out his chest, as he usually did when he was offered praise.

"Thanks, Sir" he said respectfully. He was still a little in awe of Flora's father and had always had a sneaking suspicion that the old fellow didn't totally trust him.

However, today, he felt on top of the world.

He drove the long way home, enjoying every second that he was behind the wheel of the beautiful machine. Finally, he turned into the drive and slowed down as he passed the Lodge – there he could see Cuthbert and Grace standing by the door, watching for his return. They waved and he waved back, but didn't stop. He wanted to show the car to Flora and David.

His son was growing up fast and was also doing really well in his lessons with Lucille. He had a quick brain and an alert mind, and was constantly asking questions.

Also, he was fascinated with the workings of the factory – he loved to watch the potters throwing the clay and forming magical shapes at the wheel. Reg was convinced that there would be no problems when the time came for him to choose his career – it was in his blood after all!

Flora and David rushed outside as they heard the car come to a halt. Flora, of course, had grown up being driven around in cars like this one, but she was aware just what it meant to Reg – and she was happy for him.

The following day, the delivery van driver, Norman, called in at the office, before he set out on his journey. He had a patch over one eye.

"What's appened to you, Mate?"asked Joe. "'As her belted yer one?"

"Shurrup yer daft sod" said Norman. "I were choppin' sticks last nait and one shot up an 'it me straight inth eye. Bloody hurt – I can tell yer". Reg entered the office just then and said, "Not started your deliveries yet, – Oh my goodness – what's happened to you?"

"Nowt t'worry about Boss, I'll be owrait."

But when Reg heard what had happened he advised Norman to pay a visit to the Cottage Hospital, just to be on the safe side.

"Doug's on 'oliday, and there's no bugger else to take th'van out" he argued. "I'll be ok, this's only one t'day and that's Tushin'ham 'All".

When Reg heard this, he was even more insistent that his driver get checked at the hospital; then he had a couple of men transfer the china from the van to the boot of his new car. This was a heaven sent opportunity for him to road test his pride and joy. Of course, the back of his mind was imprinted with his first visit to Tushingham Hall, and the ulterior motive behind that journey.

As he was leaving, the day shift was just arriving. A group of girls stood back as he drove through the factory gates. His eyes locked with those of Cissie Plant. Sarah and Betsy could fail to notice.

"I think he's got a thing for you, Cis" she joked.
"That's his look-out. I'm more than happy with my Ted – thank you very much" Cissie retorted.

"I know that. You know that. But I don't think our Reggie knows it, Duck".

"He gives me the creeps when he looks at me like that" Cissie shivered.

Reg drove sedately towards Ashtown, the only way to drive a Rolls-Royce, in is opinion, and when he arrived at the Hall he was disappointed to discover that Sir Richard was away on holiday. So, now he was at a bit of a loss. He was expecting to have coffee with his Lordship – and yes, he was invited to have a coffee in the kitchen, with the housekeeper, but that wasn't quite as appealing to *Mr Jenkins*.

He left the Hall and instead of heading back towards the Potteries – he made a detour, and re-traced the route he'd made five years ago.

He coasted down Callidge Bank and glided over Ansons Bridge, driving past the Abbott's Hotel, which now looked deserted, and came to a halt outside the Overbrush Arms.

He sat for a moment, wondering if he should go inside and have a glass of beer, but immediately dismissed that idea – he had a factory to run. His thoughts went back to the last time he was here in Ellswood – not for one moment had he ever regretted his actions of that fateful day.

Turning the car round, he headed back the way he had come. As he rounded the corner he almost collided with a young woman, heading in the same direction, pushing a pram with a small child sat on it and another small child, walking at her side. Expertly, he swung the car around the family and glanced in his interior mirror as he over-took them and left them behind. For a second, his heart stopped beating.

That was Lizzie.

He was so sure it was Lizzie. But he couldn't stop as another car had just come up behind him, and, as he approached the bridge, the driver of a lorry coming in the opposite direction had beckoned to him to come across the bridge first, as it was too narrow to take the two vehicles.

So, he continued up the hill, his mind racing. It wasn't Lizzie – it was too much of coincidence that she would be on that stretch of road, at exactly the same time as he was. Even as he was trying to convince himself that it wasn't Lizzie, he found himself slowing the car down and looking for convenient place to turn it around, and go back and have another look.

But, by the time he had completed the manoeuvre, and driven back down the hill, the woman had disappeared. She could have gone into any one of the few houses dotted around the vicinity, or even walked up the lane to the right, signposted to Southwood. Wherever she had gone, she was lost to him right now.

So he admitted defeat, turned the car round, yet again, and headed back to his factory.

CHAPTER THIRTY

Meg started Ellswood Village School shortly after her fifth birthday and settled in really well, taking an avid interest in her numbers and her letters, which she had no problem remembering and was apt to chant them to Lizzie during their walk back home. She also tried her hardest to get young Bill to join in with her but, at only two years old, he had no concept of such things and carried on in his own quiet way, building up his bricks and knocking them down again.

Lizzie had anticipated that her days were going to be hectic once Meg started school – and she wasn't wrong! She got up at six o'clock each morning, feeding and dressing baby Dorothy, after she had washed and dressed herself.

At seven o'clock she roused Meg and Bill and together with husband Bill they all sat down to a steaming bowl of porridge. Bill then cleared the table and washed the pots, whilst Lizzie washed and dressed the older children. Bill left for work around seven forty-five and Lizzie set off at eight fifteen, to allow time for Meg's little legs to carry her to school for nine o'clock. Sometimes, on the return journey, Meg would be so tired from her intensive learning, Lizzie would sit her and Bill, one behind the other in the pram and carry the baby Dorothy in her arms.

She was constantly tired, but it was a 'happy' tired.

A new family came to live in Southwood, a Mr and Mrs Bailey and their son Michael took up the tenancy of one of the few farms in the hamlet. At eleven years old, Michael was quite mature. Mrs Bailey had witnessed Lizzie's gruelling schedule and suggested that Michael would be happy to call for Meg and accompany her to and from school. Lizzie was delighted with the kind offer but said she must discuss it first with her husband, and then let them know. Bill thought it was an excellent idea, as, without the pram, they would be able to cut across Church Fields, thus, halving the journey.

On the first day, Mrs Bailey kindly offered to sit with the little ones, so that Lizzie could supervise them on this first occasion, and also, be aware of the actual route they would use.

Mrs Bailey was a homely lady, who looked older than her years. It had always been her desire to have a large family but, sadly, after Michael's difficult birth she was told that he would have to be her only one. She doted on him, and he was a charming, bright young fellow.

Lizzie's life became much easier and she was soon looking and feeling so much better – much to Bill's relief. Her days were still busy but so much pressure had been taken from her shoulders. She couldn't thank the Baileys enough. Again, she knew she had been blessed with friendship.

When Lizzie discovered that Mrs Bailey, for all her motherly ways, was an absolutely awful cook – in her own words 'I could burn water' – Lizzie started to double up the amount of vegetables when she was making soup and double the mixture for her cakes, so that at least once a week, the Bailey family discovered the true taste of good, home cooking.

This pattern continued, eventless, into the summer months, with Meg's sixth birthday imminent. Lizzie had finished baking some scones which she had placed on the rack hoping that they would be cool enough to box up ready for Michael to take home with him, after he'd dropped Meg off. She glanced at the clock and realised that they should have been back some fifteen minutes ago. Then Dorothy started to cry and Lizzie's mind was temporarily filled with patting her baby's back and relieving her discomfort. Suddenly, Michael burst into the kitchen.

"I can't find her, Mrs Udall. We always meet at the school gate and she wasn't there and when I went inside, they said she'd gone, but she wasn't anywhere outside"

Lizzie just looked at him…… it took just a few seconds for it to register what Michael had said…… her other baby was missing.

"No………..no………..not again" she howled.

Michael rushed out to fetch his mother but as he was going through the door, Dr Clayton was coming through the gate, and with him was….Meg! He looked at her and could tell that she'd been crying.

"Where were you Meg" he asked her gently. Meg just looked up at him with her huge tear-filled eyes.

"Let's get her inside to her mother" said the doctor. By this time Lizzie was in the door way, looking as if she was about to faint.

"Meg" she called – and Meg ran into her waiting arms.

"That Tommy Grindey was horrid to me, Mummy" she sobbed. On hearing his special friend's name mentioned Michael took even more interest. He knew Tommy well, and although he loved to tease, there was no malice in the boy.

"What did he do to you, Duck?" asked Lizzie.

"He said that Meg was the name of his sow. What is a sow, Mummy?"

"A sow is a mummy pig" Lizzie explained.

"But I don't want the same name as A PIG" she shouted. "Why? – why did you give me the name of a pig?" She sat down and sobbed.

"Well – Meg's not actually your real name. Your proper name in Margaret and that's what we'll call from now on. Is that better?" asked her mother.

A weak smile was all that Meg could manage but she was pacified and went to tell Bill that she wasn't Meg any more and he must now call her Margaret.

Lizzie turned to Dr Clayton and he started to explain. As he left the vicarage he'd discovered Meg, in a distressed state wandering down Church Lane. After he'd put her in the car, he'd gone back up the lane looking for Michael, but somehow, missed him, so decided to bring her straight back home. In his opinion, she had lost her way, as she was so distressed. He then took his leave, after Lizzie had thanked him profusely for his concern and swift actions.

As he was settling his ample frame into his car, Mrs Bailey, who had been looking out for him, knocked on the window and asked if Lizzie was ok, or did he think she should go and sit with her until Bill returned from work.

Instinctively, Dr Clayton realised that, as a newcomer to the area, Mrs Bailey hadn't been made aware of Lizzie's earlier loss. So, having climbed back out of his car, he cupped her elbow and led her back into her own home. After relating the awful story of what had happened six years ago he left her to make up her own mind about visiting Lizzie and made his way home. Michael came into the house as he saw the doctor leaving and confided in his mother that, after this episode, Lizzie would no longer trust him to take Meg to school. Mrs Bailey felt that he should know what had happened previously and told him the full story, as related to her by Dr Clayton, and if Lizzie decided she wouldn't let him take her again, it would as much to do with the loss of her little boy, as what had happened today. Besides, perhaps they had all expected too much of an eleven year old anyway.

Together, they went in to see Lizzie. Michael was full of remorse and Lizzie hugged him to her.

"It wasn't your fault, Mike" she said." It was that Tommy Grindey – just wait 'til I get my hands on him".

"Oh! Mrs Udall, please don't tell the teachers. He'll get the cane, and when his Mam and Dad hear that he's had the cane, and they will hear, he'll get another walloping off his dad. I know what he said upset Meg, but if he knew how upset she was he'd be upset himself. He is a tease but he's got such a good heart and he's always looking out for Meg when I'm not about. Please………"

What could she say?

CHAPTER THIRTY ONE

Needless to say, the scare had a profound effect on Lizzie, but, she knew that regardless of her own insecurities, she mustn't try to wrap Margaret in cotton wool, or hamper her natural progression into independence.

For this reason, she put aside her own feelings, and allowed Michael to continue taking her to school. True to her word, Lizzie never mentioned to the teachers, Tommy's part in the incident, but she knew that Michael had told him, sparing no details the drastic effect that his teasing had had on the little girl, and also her mother. Tommy went out of his way to be kind and look out for Margaret and to speak to Lizzie with the utmost respect.

Once again, calmness engulfed the little family.

***

As the school summer holidays loomed, Lizzie was determined to see more of Cissie, whilst her demanding schedule relaxed, and also, before the winter began. She realised that travelling on a bus, then a train, with three young children would be no easy task and so Bill insisted on accompanying them on the first trip.

The main problem was the pram – or lack of – as it was far too big to take on the bus. It would have been ok on the train as they could all have sat in the guards van, but they could see no other way but to carry the little girl, who was not yet walking, but getting heavier by the day.

Cissie managed to solve the problem at the other end. She had discovered Marjorie's old pram at the back of the shed and dusted it off and told Lizzie and Bill that she, along with the pram would be waiting at the station for them.

The hot summer days seemed endless. Lizzie tried to see Cissie once a fortnight; they would take turns to visit.

***

CHRISTMAS 1937

Margaret came home from school full of Christmas cheer, singing carols, Christmas songs and telling the younger ones all about the Nativity and Santa Claus.

Excitement filled the little house.

On Christmas morning the entire household was awake by five thirty.

"This is how it's going to be from now on, I'm afraid" Lizzie laughed to Bill.

Bill had made a little desk and chair for Margaret and Lizzie had bought her some crayons and a colouring book. For his son he had made a wooden lorry with an open trailer and Lizzie's contribution was some farm animals, and for Dorothy, Bill had crafted a lovely toy crib and Lizzie had made a little rag doll to fit inside.

They were all delighted with their lovely 'Santa' gifts.

The winter was extremely harsh. And it took its' toll on Bill. He was often late getting in from work, as the snow drifts were too high for him to walk across the fields and when he used the road it was double the distance.

As the snow melted and the sun's warmth became stronger, the hedgerows began to bud and the spring flowers pushed their way through the cold earth. But Bill's energy seemed to diminish. Lizzie was concerned for him and suggested that he should, perhaps, pay a visit to Dr Clayton.

"I was thinking of going to see him tomorrow" he said.

Next morning, Lizzie woke with a start. She leapt out of bed and down the stairs and put the kettle on to boil. She quickly washed and dressed herself, made a pot of tea and pan of steaming porridge. By this time, she could hear Dorothy chortling to herself in her cot, so she hurried to fetch her down before she woke the other two. Lizzie always enjoyed this time of day, just her and her baby, who was now toddling around and getting into everything.

As the clock struck seven, she realised that Bill wasn't up yet. It was so unlike him to oversleep. She sat Dorothy in her pram and gave her a crust of bread to chew on and went to her bedroom to waken him up.

Bill looked dreadful.

"What's up, Duck? She asked.

"I feel so hot".

"You've probably caught a chill" she said. "I'll just waken the Marg and Bill and then I'll bring you a drink".

When she returned, she found him out of bed and climbing into his work clothes.

"Oh no – my man" she said sternly. "No work for you today".

"There's just a couple of things that need attention – I'll see to them and come straight back, I promise".

He called cheerio to the children and to his Lizzie, his voice sounding more and more hoarse, and went off through the door. And fell to the ground.

"Oh Bill, have you slipped, Duck" said Lizzie rushing to help him up.

But he didn't move.

"Bill….. Bill, are you alright? She asked.

There was no reply. Lizzie fell to her knees beside him. He looked terrible.

"Margaret, run and fetch Mrs Bailey – quick".

Mrs Bailey came running into the cottage with Margaret trailing behind. She took one look at Bill's face and rushed back to her own home. They had recently had a telephone installed and although she disliked using the contraption, as she called it, she dialled the doctor's number quickly and explained to Mrs Clayton what had happened. Mrs Clayton sensed the urgency and promised, in her calming voice, that he would be there as soon as he possibly could.

By the time Dr Clayton arrived, Mrs Bailey had helped Lizzie to assist Bill back up the stairs and into his bed where sank into it gratefully.

Mrs Bailey crept quietly down the stairs and immediately started dishing out the porridge for the children and poured milk into their beakers.

They were so quiet.

Dr Clayton thundered down the stairs and bade goodbye to Mrs Bailey and gave a cheery wave and smile to the children.

It was a good ten minutes before Lizzie appeared, and Mrs Bailey guessed that she'd been crying and wanted to compose herself before facing her offspring. She smiled wanly as she crossed the room and took Margaret's coat from behind the door.

"Hurry up, young lady; Michael'll be calling for you any minute. Pick up your butties and put them in your pocket" she said. "Look – here he is, now".

By the time the two of them had left for school, Dorothy was fast asleep and Bill was playing happily with his lorry and animals, he was taking them to market, just like Mr Bailey.

Mrs Bailey mashed another pot of tea and together they sat silently, at the table.

"It's double pneumonia! – do you know what he said when the doctor told him?"

Mrs Bailey shook he head.

"That's ok then – I thought it might be something serious".

Neither of them could raise a smile at this brave quip.

Bill's recuperation was slow.

Lizzie walked up to the Hall most days on his behalf. All of the gardens and greenhouses were planted so just needed watering regularly and a bit of weeding. Lizzie convinced him that she was more than capable of carrying out these simple tasks. Some days she would sit little Bill on the end of Dorothy's pram and take them with her, other days, particularly if it was raining, she would leave Bill in charge, with Mrs Bailey on call if he should need her.

At the Hall, the Duncombes were impressed by Lizzie's commitment and said that Bill must take his time getting well again, and not to come back to work too soon.

Sadly, he was never to return to work again. On her return from the Hall just two weeks after his diagnosis, she discovered he had passed away peacefully, in his chair, next to the fire.

He was seventy-two.

CHAPTER THIRTY TWO

Lizzie had entered the cottage alone, fortunately. The children had been stroking the Baileys' cat which had been sitting on the gate.

She knew, the second she saw his face, that he was dead. She walked straight back out of the cottage and took the children to Mrs Bailey's. Her neighbour could see, at a glance, that something was drastically wrong. She put the kettle on and warmed the tea-pot, then poured a glass of milk for each of the children.

"Take the weight off your feet, Lizzie, Love" she said, pulling out a chair.

Lizzie sat down heavily, letting out an enormous sigh.

"What's happened" asked Mrs Bailey. In hushed tones Lizzie told her what she discovered on her return home.

"I'll bet he's having forty winks" said Mrs Bailey. But Lizzie shook her head.

"No – I just know he's gone" Lizzie replied softly.

"Well – we'll need to inform the doctor, then". She dialled the number and explained quietly what had taken place, but Mrs Clayton said that the doctor was out on his rounds and wasn't sure how long he would be, but the minute he returned she promised he would come straight over.

Lizzie looked so vulnerable. Mrs Bailey decided that they should all stay there for night and she then set about preparing a meal for the seven of them. She said that little Bill could double up with Michael and Lizzie and the girls could sleep in the front parlour where there was a huge sofa, with loads of blankets it would make a lovely comfortable bed.

Lizzie begged her not to go to so much trouble when she went into the parlour to light the fire, but it just fell on deaf ears. Secretly, she was glad that she didn't have to go back into the cottage, but then felt so disloyal when she thought of poor Bill, in there, all alone.

She wished Dr Clayton would hurry up.

Mrs Bailey decided that she would cook bangers and mash with onion gravy for tea. But, she left the sausages frying for far too long and they had a horrid burnt taste all the way through – she had mashed the potatoes before they were cooked through and there were as many lumps in the mash as there were in the gravy. Mr and Mrs Bailey and Michael all seemed to be thoroughly enjoying their meal, but little Bill screwed up his nose at the first mouthful, but one of Lizzie's withering looks stopped him complaining.

By the time the meal was over, Bill and Dorothy were becoming quite fractious as they were getting tired.

"Can we go home now, Mummy" Bill asked.

"How would you like to sleep here, with Michael"? Mrs Bailey said.

Bill shook his head.

"Want to go home to Daddy" he said. Michael could see the little boy was getting upset, so he asked,
"Will you to come and help me feed the calves, please, Bill"?

At this, he leapt to his feet and yelled, "Oh yes" and followed Michael out of the door. Lizzie started to prepare Dorothy for bed, which, tonight, would have to be her pram.

In the lane, they heard the roar of Dr Clayton's car. Lizzie felt a mixture of relief and anxiety.

"You go. I'll see to the little 'uns", said Mrs Bailey. So Lizzie had no choice but to go into her home with the Doctor, who took his time examining the old gentleman.

"I think the pneumonia put too much strain on his heart. To have such a serious illness was just too much for him at this time in his life." He paused. "But, I know this, Lizzie; he died a very happy man". His kind words touched her heart and she burst into floods of tears. Tears that had been threatening to over-spill since the moment she realised that she'd lost him.

"There, there" he said, gently stroking her arm. "Let it all out Lizzie".

She cried.

She cried for her husband

She cried for Margaret, who didn't know any other Daddy.

She cried for Bill, who had his Daddy's gently ways.

She cried for Dorothy, who would never have any memories of her Daddy.

Then she cried for her own loss.

Then, she was spent.

"What happens now, Doctor?" she asked.

"Well, Lizzie, if you had a front parlour, we would put him in there, but as you haven't, we'll have to think of something else. We could take him to the morgue at the Cottage Hospital in Ashtown".

"Then I think that's what we'll have to do" she said.

"It's too late to do anything tonight, but I'll arrange everything first thing in the morning" he promised.

"Mrs Bailey's letting us stay there tonight" she informed him. He nodded.
"That's good. She's a kind soul".

Lizzie then gathered together their nightclothes, before the doctor took his leave, not really wanting to be alone in the cottage with her dear, departed husband.

CHAPTER THIRTY THREE

The following morning, Lizzie was like a coiled spring. She, along with Mrs Bailey, agreed that Margaret should go to school as normal.

When Frank Slater, the undertaker, arrived to collect Bill's body, Mrs Bailey insisted on overseeing the sad task. For this Lizzie was more than grateful. She busied herself with the children and cooked a pan of porridge to take her mind off what was taking place across the road. She knew that her life would never be the same again but, for the children's sake, she had to stay strong – and to stay strong was to keep busy, so, as she completed one job, she moved immediately on to the next. Washing pots, raking out the fire, bringing in the coal, washing and dressing the children – making the sandwiches for Margaret and Michael to take with them to school.

As she was waving them off down the lane, she saw Eva heading towards her cottage – when she saw Lizzie standing at the farmhouse door she quickly changed direction and headed across the road.

"What ya doing here, Liz – is Mrs B poorly?" She enquired.

"Come inside Eva". Eva took a seat at the table – not taking her eyes from her friend's face.

"Oh Eva, it's been awful" she said, fighting back the tears. She then went on to inform her dearest friend all about the terrible tragedy. The only dealings that Eva had had with death and all that goes with it, was Gwen's untimely demise, but, she had a natural empathy and seemed to know exactly the right words to say.

When Mr Bailey came in for his breakfast, after milking, Lizzie said she would get back to her own house. Although she sounded calm and confident, inside she was shaking like a leaf. She couldn't get the picture of Bill, deceased, sitting in his chair, out of her mind.

It was a vision that would live in her memory for the rest of her days.

But, she knew that the longer she put it off, the harder it would be. Mrs Bailey had suggested that Bill and Dorothy should stay with her but Lizzie had declined her kind offer, knowing that having to put on a brave face for the children's sake would make her stronger.

As she and Eva entered the cottage she was overcome by an awful smell. She had heard about the death smell and could only assume that this was it. She asked Eva to keep an eye on the little ones whilst she dashed upstairs, with a kettle of hot water, to have a wash and change her clothes. Dorothy was asleep by this time and Bill was telling his farm animals all about feeding the calves with Michael, so Eva busied herself around the house. Although it was a lovely sunny day, inside the cottage felt chilled, so she lit the fire. She also had noticed the acrid smell so she threw open the little window and the door to get some fresh air in the room.

She knew where Lizzie kept the furniture polish so with a quick flick round with some lavender wax polish on the table and the dresser the room soon smelt as fresh and sweet as it usually did.

When Lizzie came back downstairs, she sniffed the air appreciatively.
"Aw thank so much Eva. I don't know where I'd be without the likes of you and Mrs. B" she said.

"Well, Lizzie, it's no more than you would do for any one of us".
Lizzie was unable to sit still: even as she was drinking her tea, she was up – placing more coal on the fire – sit down – up to check on Dorothy – sit down – up to check on Bill – sit down – Eva felt dizzy just watching her.

"Do you know yet when the funeral will be, you can count on me you know, if there's anything you want me to do"

"Well, Mrs B asked Mr Slater to call back as soon as he could this morning to sort it all out. What time are you at work today?"

"Two 'til ten".

"Right, If you could take the little 'uns out when he comes, that would be a great help. I don't want them to see me getting distressed, as it would upset them" said Lizzie.

"I could take them to Ellswood if you like. Is there anything you need from the shop"? She asked.

"Well – I do need to write a quick note to our Cissie – if I do it now, would you post it for me, please?"

Just then, Frank Slater rapped on the open door and walked in. Eva immediately took hold of the pram and called to little Bill that if he hurried she might treat him to a lollipop.
"I can take Cissie's letter this after, so don't worry, it'll still catch today's post" and off she went.

Lizzie invited Frank to take a seat at the table; she poured him a cup of tea then sat down opposite him.

"First of all I'd just like to offer my sincere condolences, Mrs Udall" he said with sincerity. "Bill was a true gentleman, not much to say for himself, but a very kind man, all the same".

"Yes – indeed he was" said Lizzie, tears immediately filling her eyes, as she thought of Bill.

To lighten the atmosphere, Mr Slater told her a little tale that had taken place in this very room when he and Bill were organising Connie's funeral, a good few years ago.

Frank had asked Bill for Connie's full name and Bill had replied   "Mary Udall" he'd replied.

"I asked him why everyone called her Connie if her name was actually Mary". Bill had laughed a little at that. "Well - she was Mary to me to begin with, then she'd say 'Bill, can you take this lid of this jam jar for me – I conner do it' – every day it would be –'I conner do this' – 'I conner do that '– so, I started to call her Conner and somehow everyone else thought I was saying Connie – so that's how it came about".

Lizzie gave him a weak smile – she hadn't heard that story before.

"You do know that when Connie was buried in Ellswood churchyard, Bill paid for a double plot, so that he could go in with her, don't you Mrs Udall?" Frank asked the question that he had been dreading.

"Oh yes! He told me that even before we got married, and I agree that he should be buried with Connie – they had far more years together than we did......" her voice trailed off into a sad whisper. She shook her head and leapt to her feet and with renewed vigour she pulled open the dresser drawer and took out an old biscuit tin and placed it on the table, taking off the lid before sitting back down. She flicked through the papers until she found the documentation about the burial plot that she was looking for.

"I think this is what you need" she said. At a glance Frank could see that it was, but he also noticed on the top of the box was something else that Lizzie needed to know about. Something, which would make her life a bit easier at this sad time. He picked it up and waited for her to nod her consent.

"This" he said, "Is an insurance policy that will cover the cost of the funeral and there will be a small amount over, so I'll sort that out for you, as well, if you like".

"That would be very kind of you" she replied.

"Now – back to business. I can do Friday, how does that sound to you?"

"Well, perhaps Monday would be better. It's Tuesday now and I have to write and inform Bill's brothers and sisters, he has six, you know, and also, my family" she paused. "On second thoughts, I'll say Friday. If I get the letters written straight away, and in the post by tonight, they should have them by Thursday, at the latest. Yes, Mr Slater, Friday 22nd April. Shall we say eleven o'clock?"

"Are you sure it's not going to be too much of a rush" he asked. She shook her head; there was no point in delaying it.

As soon he was out of the door, Lizzie took out her writing pad and wrote seven identical letters, six to Bill's siblings and one to Cissie. She then placed them in the envelopes, picked up her purse and walked to the post office in Ellswood.

After she had posted her mail she called in at Eva's house where she was greeted by shrieks of delight from Bill and Dorothy. She then walked slowly back to Southwood enabling Eva to have a well deserved rest before starting her shift at the dairy.

CHAPTER THIRTY FOUR

Cissie met the postman as she was going down the road to work.

"You're early today, Charlie" she called.

"Got one for you, Lass. Looks like from your Lizzie. Do yer want it now of shall I drop it off at home for yer?"

"May I have it now, please – if you don't mind?" She wasn't expecting a letter; in fact it was her turn to write to Lizzie, it was a job on her list of things to do tonight.

She tore open the envelope – only one page – 'unusual for our Liz' she thought. Her eyes quickly scanned the brief note.

She stopped in her tracks.

"Oh no" she cried. As the written words sank in, she could feel her legs turning to jelly – she went to lean on the wall. Her breath was coming in gasps, her head spinning. Her instincts took over and she found herself going in the opposite direction to the factory, there was no way she could work today. She went back into the house where Marjorie was still sitting at the table, eating her toast.

"What's up Cis, do ya feel bad" she asked.

"Yes. I feel sick" Cissie whispered.

"Hope ya soon better. See ya after school. Ta-ra", she picked up her school bag and went out of the door, calling 'ta-ra' to her Mam. Fanny watched as she skipped down the road.

"What's all this Cissie – you look dreadful – sit down a minute, duck, before you fall down", she said kindly.

"Look at this". Cissie thrust the brief note into Fanny's hand, as she could trust herself to read out any more bad news.

"I can't believe it" she cried.

"I can't go to work today, Fan, I must go to her – *she* needs me more than that bloody factory does". Fanny had never, ever heard Cissie swear before – in fact, no-one had ever heard Cissie swear before. Fanny could see that she was distraught, just as she herself was. She went upstairs and took a small overnight bag from her wardrobe and set it on

Cissie's bed, and then she went back downstairs and made them both a cup of hot, sweet tea.

"I agree, Cissie, you must go to her. I'll send word to the factory that you'll be away for a few days. I've put my bag on your bed; do you want me to pack it for you?"

"No thanks, I'll do it. I will have to take my clothes for the funeral; I hope I've got something suitable." She didn't have much in her closet as she was saving as much as she could for her bottom drawer, so clothes' buying was way down her list of priorities.

"If you hurry, you could catch the nine thirty train, so drink your tea and get that bag packed" she said. Cissie emptied her cup and went upstairs- by the time she had put in everything that she thought she would need, the little bag was almost bursting at the seams.

"Thanks, Fan" she said as she came back down the stairs. "Will you be attending the funeral?"

"Of course we will. I thought I would ask Dolly and Harry to take me and your Dad in the car, I'm sure they'll want to be there too. So tell her we'll see her tomorrow. Take care, Cis".

She went to the door and watched her step-daughter's figure trundle off down the road, what a desolate little figure she looked. As she turned to go back indoors, out of the corner of her eye, she saw that Cissie had turned round and was heading back up the road as if her pants were on fire.

"Whatever's wrong?" she asked.

"Ted – I need to tell Ted" she gasped. Ted worked for a farmer called Jim Myatt and he'd told Cissie that if she ever needed him in a rush, Mr Myatt had a telephone and it would be alright, in an emergency, to ring and leave a message. The number was written on a bit of paper tucked in a safe place in the drawer in her bedroom. She ran up the stairs and was back down in seconds.

"See you tomorrow, Fanny" she said, giving her a quick hug. "I'll ring Myatt's from the kiosk near the station if I get chance, the sooner he gets the message the better. If not I'll have to ring from Ellswood".

Then, off she went. This time her step was positive and she hurried as she really needed to catch this train or she would have to wait ages for the next one.

At the station, as she was buying her ticket, the guard walked past the office and called to the station-master.
"Bit of an 'old up, George. Dick forgot 'is snap tin so he's at ta run back forrit. He'll be 'ere in five minutes".

Cissie knew that Dick was the train driver, - five minutes was all the time she needed to make her phone call.

She ran to the kiosk and inserted her pennies into the slot, carefully dialled the number and when she heard someone answer at the other end she pressed button A. She hurriedly asked the lady, who she took to be Mrs Myatt, if *she could kindly pass an important message on to Mr Ted Bentley*. The lady said she would, so Cissie asked her to say that *Cissie Plant has had to go to Ellswood and if he went to her home in Livingstone, all would be explained.* She went on to say that *she was sorry to have to trouble Ted's employers* and *thank you so much.*

She then noticed Dick running into the station, snap tin in hand, and knew that she must get her skates on.

She sank into her seat and as she got her breath back it all started to sink in. She thought of the devastating effect Bill's death would have on Lizzie and her way of life. She couldn't begin to imagine how her sister was feeling right now – and how would she manage, with three young children. She couldn't bear to think of the heartache she was about to witness.

***

Back in Endown, Ted received his phone message via Mrs Myatt at lunch time. He asked Jim if he could take a couple of hours off, to go to Livingstone, to discover what the problem was.

"Well Lad – you won't be much use to me, this afternoon if you're mooning about, so you'd better get yourself over there as quick as you can" he said smiling – he added, "hope everything's ok".

Ted caught a bus at the end of the lane almost immediately; then he only had a five minute walk up to the house. When he arrived Fanny was sweeping the front path. When she saw him coming through the gate, she leaned the brush against the house and invited him to go inside.

"What's gone off, Mrs Plant", he asked. Fanny explained the brief note as gently as she could, but said she couldn't give him no more details as she had so little information herself.

"We will be going to the funeral and so will Dolly and Harry. I'm sure we'll be able to squeeze you in, if you want to come with us, that is."

"I need to go this afternoon, thanks all the same. I don't like the thoughts of them being on their own. I can ask our Jack to help with the milking at the farm, tonight. He's leaving school soon and he said he wants to go into farming so he can get a bit of practice in".

He stood up and added "I'll go now; as I said, I don't like to think of them on their own".

"You're a good lad Ted. Our Cissie's lucky to have you. Get off now and we'll see you tomorrow." Fanny said kindly.

***

At the factory, word soon got round that Lizzie Plant's husband had passed away. Reg felt a twinge, but only a small one as he had a lot on his mind, at the moment. Flora had told him this morning that she was going to visit the doctor as she hadn't been feeling at all well; she just hoped it wouldn't be anything serious.

At six o'clock he hurried to his car and drove out of the gates with little regard for anyone or anything that was in his path. He parked the Rolls and rushed indoors to find Flora waiting in the sitting room, a smile on her face.

"We're having a baby – can you believe it? I'd given up all hope – and I'm already five months gone, so well past the danger period. I've never got this far before – isn't it wonderful, Reg". She was glowing with happiness.

Reg felt instant relief that she wasn't going to die – then the relief turned to fury as her words sank in.

"Don't say that Flora" he growled. "Don't forget – you've had David – if you go around saying this is your first child, people are going to get suspicious."

By this time he was red in the face with anger. Flora was shocked.
"Please don't speak to me in that way, Reg", she warned.
"This conversation is just between the two of us. Of course I wouldn't say it to anyone else", she added indignantly.

But, Reg wouldn't be placated.

"You shouldn't even say it to me. For a start, you never know who's listening, so do NOT, EVER, say it again".

Her wonderful news seemed tarnished and Flora was so deflated.

CHAPTER THIRTY FIVE

Cissie leapt from the bus, calling cheerio to the friendly conductor. On the walk up the lane up to Southwood she didn't encounter a soul. In her mind she was preparing a speech for when Lizzie opened the door to her. However, all the most magnificent speeches in the world couldn't say half of what a sister's hug could do. When the door opened, they fell, weeping into each other's arms.

"Thank you for coming, Cis" Lizzie said, between her tears.

"I couldn't get here quick enough" Cissie replied between her tears.

Lizzie related, in detail, the events of the last few days and also the arrangements for the funeral the following day. Cissie, in turn, informed her of Father and Fanny's intentions to attend along with Dolly and Harry. Lizzie was not a little surprised by this news, but extremely pleased to be getting the support of her family, when she most needed it.

They and the children had their lunch and then Cissie suggested that they all went for a short walk. Lizzie looked alarmed.

"The fresh air will do you all the world of good" she said.

"But, won't people talk? – I don't think it's the done thing to go out strolling when I've only just been widowed." She argued.

"Nonsense" Cissie replied. "We're in the 1930's – not the dark ages. Not only do *you* need to get out, but the children do, too: so, go and get wrapped up, it's a bit chilly out there – I'll see to the little ones".

"Bloody bossy boots" thought Lizzie affectionately, thinking her little sister was probably right.

When they arrived back at the cottage with roses in all of their cheeks, Mrs Bailey was waiting for them.

"I've got a glut of eggs. I just don't know what's up with them damned hens – it's all or nothing with them" she said. "I thought they may come in handy for the Wake tomorrow. I mean everybody loves egg butties, don't they?" Lizzie looked at her, blankly, and then at Cissie – they hadn't given the Wake a thought.

"Oh, that's really kind of you, Mrs Bailey" Cissie said, taking over the situation. "I, for one, love egg sandwiches". She took the bowl of eggs and Mrs Bailey went back into her house. They were about to enter the cottage when Cissie saw a man marching up the lane. She looked, and then looked again.

It couldn't be!

But, yes it was……her Ted.

She ran down to meet him, taking great care not to drop the eggs.

"I hope you don't mind me coming, Cissie. I felt I had to come as soon as I got your message and when Fanny explained what had happened, I really didn't like the thoughts of you two having to cope with everything, on your own".
"I'm so pleased you did" she replied. Together, they followed Lizzie and the children into the cottage.

"Thank goodness for Mrs B" Lizzie said, later. "I wouldn't have thought of providing food – but, of course, I need to. People will have travelled here from far and wide to pay their respects to Bill, the least I can do is give them a cup of tea and a bite to eat."

"Well, I'm here to lend a hand" said Ted. "So, just tell me what you want me to do". Lizzie told him he could start by banking up the fire, she needed the oven nice and hot as she had buns and scones to bake, then he could bring in some logs to burn later on, and then chop the sticks to light the fire in the morning. When those tasks were completed, she asked him to go down to the village shop and buy two loaves of bread – thinking, if she sliced it very thinly, they could make quite a lot of sandwiches out of two large loaves. She continued to say that he could use Bill's motor bike, if he knew how to ride it - he gave a nod and a cheeky wink which brought just a glimmer of a smile to her lips.

Lizzie then put the dozen eggs into a pan of water to hard boil, and placed it on the open fire. When Ted returned, exhilarated from the motor bike ride, (with the two loaves intact) he told the girls that he'd seen Eva in the village shop. Eva sent a message to say her parents wouldn't be attending the funeral as they felt they would be more use coming to the cottage to take care of the children, whilst Lizzie was in church.

Once more, Lizzie realised how blessed she was, to be surrounded by such caring people.

***

Friday dawned, downright dismal – in fact, it was pouring with rain. When Lizzie saw the abysmal weather she thought how appropriate it was; just as though the earth was crying with her in her loss. A bright, sunny day would have seemed a mockery.

Lizzie was up early, and went through her usual routine. Once Margaret was on her way to school, they set to work, preparing the sandwiches, arranging them, and the scones and buns on to large plates, and then covering them over with a clean tea-towel. When it was all done they all went to change into their funeral attire.

At ten thirty Mr and Mrs Finney arrived to look after the little ones. It had been their intention to take them out, but as the weather was so inclement it was decided that they would stay in and amuse the children, to the best of their ability.

At ten-fifty, the hearse came slowly up the lane, and was expertly turned around in the gate-way of the Bailey's farmyard, coming to a sedate standstill outside the cottage, with the funeral car directly behind it.

Frank Slater went up to the door and was about to knock when Lizzie opened it. She nodded to the sombre faced undertaker, when he enquired if she was ready. Along with Cissie and Ted, she climbed into the back of the car, and the slow procession began. Lizzie noticed that the curtains in every house, en-route to the church, were drawn as a mark of respect.

On entering the church and following her husband's coffin, Lizzie gasped at the sight that met her. The church was almost full. Mr and Mrs Duncombe, Bill's employers, were there. So were Dr Clayton, Mr Evans, and Dick Ratcliffe along with their wives. All of Bill's siblings and spouses had turned up along with Lizzie's Father, Step-Mother and Dolly and Harry. Mr and Mrs Bailey had squeezed four of the residents of Southwood into their car; Lizzie felt their warmth and love give her comfort and strength.

The service commenced and sad voices were raised together in thanksgiving for the life of William Udall. Dr Clayton gave an uplifting and humorous eulogy, mentioning by name, villagers past and present, lightening the mood for a brief time.

The mourners then followed the coffin to its' final resting place in the churchyard. When everyone else had left the graveside, Lizzie lingered to say her own, last goodbye.
"Dearest Bill – you showed me such love and kindness; and happiness that I had never, ever known. I've been proud to be your wife and I'll keep your memory alive and never let the children forget you. Thank you for everything".

She turned and walked slowly towards her waiting family. Mr Duncombe offered her a lift back home which she gratefully accepted.

On her arrival back at the cottage, she found lots of people waiting, and as Lizzie was wondering where she was going to put them all, Mrs Bailey came out and beckoned to Lizzie that they could use her huge kitchen and sitting room.

"I was just wondering where I could put everyone, thank you, Mrs B. We'll bring the food straight over".

Soon everyone was supplied with a cup of tea, a sandwich and whatever else they required. Lizzie circulated, thanking everyone for coming and, yes, Bill would have been delighted and somewhat amazed by the turn-out – but none of it seemed quite real – it was like a dream, a bad dream.

Cissie and Ted had promised that they would stay over night again, and for this Lizzie was grateful.

The last of the guests had departed by the time Margaret arrived home from school. Lizzie had explained to her and Bill that their Daddy had gone away to live with Jesus, in heaven.

As Bills' solicitor had arranged to come later in the afternoon to read the will, Eva thought it would be a good idea to pop over to Mrs B's with the children, so that Lizzie could give him her undivided attention, also her parents would be able to make their way back home.

When he arrived Lizzie was aware that she had been alone in the cottage for the first time ever. They sat across the table from each other as he removed the official documents from his brief-case.

He read;
To my wife Elizabeth: I leave the contents of the cottage and Fifty Pounds.
To my daughter Margaret: I leave Twenty Pounds.
To my son William: I leave Twenty Pounds.
To my daughter Dorothy: I leave the pair of Staffordshire Dogs.

Once the official statement had been read, the solicitor became more friendly and personal. He offered his condolences and then informed her that

Bill must have had an inkling that he may not recover from his illness, as the last time he was in Ashtown, he had visited the office to put 'everything in order'. He then went on to advise her that she was now entitled to a regular amount of money each week. This was aptly called the Widow's Pension and the act had only been passed by Parliament about three years ago.

"That is such good news" said Lizzie. "I have been beside myself, wondering how on earth I'm going to manage with three children to clothe and feed. Until Dorothy starts school there isn't any way I can get a job. I really appreciate you advising me of this".

"Well I've brought all the necessary forms with me, so if we fill them in now, I can set the wheels in motion and you should be receiving the allowance within the week."

Together they went through the forms, Lizzie giving the information and he, writing it all down.
"Right" he said." That's all completed. I'll post this on to the relevant office as soon as I get back. You have nothing to worry about. Thank you for your time, Mrs Udall, I hope you will contact me if there is anything else that I can help you with. Now, I'll bid you Good day."

"Thank you. You've been so helpful. Good-bye". She shook him by the hand and walked with him to the door.

She watched until his car had disappeared down the lane, then turned and walked across the road to pick up her children, and begin her life as a single parent.

CHAPTER THIRTY SIX

Flora's happiness bubble had been well and truly burst by Reg's initial reaction to her unexpected pregnancy. He had tried unsuccessfully to make amends by saying he thought someone was listening to their conversation, which, even to his own ears sounded rather feeble. Consequently, Flora chose to spend less time in his company. Sadly, she had very few friends; she had attempted to befriend Sarah, the fiancée of Joe Stokes, Reg's right-hand man, but as Reg didn't seem too keen on her, she hadn't really persevered. But, she thought, I need to make a stand. If I want to make a friend of Sarah, surely, it should be *my* choice. She had really liked Cissie Plant, who was such a friendly and caring girl, but any mention of her seemed to get Reg in a really agitated state.

It was Saturday, so David didn't have any lessons to do. Lucille had gone to visit her family for a few hours, and Ellen was tidying the nursery, whilst David was making plasticine models. Flora entered the room and Ellen turned and smiled at her.

"David – how would you like to take a walk with me to the park?"

"Ooo yes" he said excitedly. "And may we feed the ducks, too?"

"Would you like *me* to take David, Mrs Jenkins?" asked Ellen. "Then you could put your feet up for a while".

She knew that pregnant ladies should put their feet up regularly, but she didn't really understand why.

"I can put my feet up later, Ellen, but thank you anyway. Come along with us, if you like".

Ellen looked unsure.

"It'll be quite alright – you can finish your chores when you get back – don't look so worried". Ellen gave her a beaming smile and all together they walked into the village, David clutching his bag of stale bread for the ducks.

David was delighted when the ducks came running to him, and shrieked with laughter as they jostled with each other to get a better position, nearer to the source of the food.

Then, who should come walking by, but Sarah, with Joe. When they stopped to enquire of Floras' health, Flora who was very shy person plucked up courage to ask Sarah if she would like to call at the house for a cup of tea, sometime. She waited for the reply with baited breath – the main reason she was a little off-hand with people was her deep fear of rejection.

"I'd really like to" she replied. "But, as I work during the week it would have to be a Saturday, or, I could come round one evening."

Flora was thrilled that Sarah appeared to genuinely want to spend time in her company, and wasn't prepared to let this opportunity pass.
"How about Monday evening – shall we say six thirty?" Flora suggested.

"Ok. See you Monday." Said Sarah, and they all stood together for a few minutes, watching the ducks performing their comical antics. Then Sarah and Joe said goodbye and went on their way.

***

"Well – what a turn up for the books" said Joe when they were out of ear-shot. "I didn't know you and the Boss's missus were mates".

"You know we're not mates, Joe, don't be daft. But she doesn't seem to have many friends – me and Cissie have said this loads of times. Perhaps she's feeling lonely because her mum's away a lot. She's ok, is Flora – it doesn't hurt to give a bit of your time to someone who needs it" she said generously.

***

"We had better be getting back now, David" called Flora, to her son.

"Five more minutes, Mummy, pleeeeease" he begged.

"Five minutes – and no more" she said, with an indulgent smile. She was feeling very pleased with herself, at being brave enough to approach Sarah, and Sarah's ready acceptance had given a confidence that she had never possessed before.

Time seemed to drag by on Monday. Flora had no engagements that day, but she did have a fund raising event the following day, luncheon with the Mothers Union on Wednesday and a meeting with the committee of the Embroiderers Guild on Friday. She would soon be announcing her retirement from her duties, as her life would be full when the new baby was born. But, today, Monday she was, sensibly, taking it easy.

At six-thirty Sarah arrived – breathless.

"I didn't want to be late" she gasped. Flora invited her into the sitting room where Ellen had already delivered the tray, set with a really pretty china tea set and a plate of garibaldi biscuits. They felt quite uncomfortable in each others company, the conversation was stilted with long silences, and then they would both speak at the same time.

"Oh dear" thought Flora. "She'll never want to come again".

"Oh dear" thought Sarah. "She'll never ask me to come again".

Then Flora dropped a biscuit on the floor, and, as she bent down to retrieve it - she broke wind – so loud that you would have thought they could hear it in the cellar.

Her face was scarlet.

She could hardly bring herself to look at Sarah. But, when she did, she saw that Sarah was in hysterics – in fact, she could hardly breathe for laughing – this set Flora off. Together they laughed until tears ran down their cheeks. Then as the laughter subsided, and Flora tried to apologise for her little 'slip', the laughter started up again. When it subsided a second time and Sarah tried to apologise for laughing, it started them both off, yet again.

And so, a lovely friendship began. Not only had the wind been broken – so had the ice. From that day on, they found they had so much in common and Sarah became a very regular visitor to the big house.

CHAPTER THIRTY SEVEN

Lizzie was up extra early, the day after the funeral. She hadn't expected to sleep well and so it was no surprise that she had tossed and turned all night long. She felt she needed a little time to herself, before her regular routine began. She lit the stove and put the kettle on to boil, for a much needed cup of tea. As she waited for it to boil, she opened the curtains to discover a beautiful spring day. She then quietly raked the dead ash out of the grate, scrunched up some newspaper and placed the chopped sticks on the very top.

She would light the fire shortly – for now, she needed a drink and a think!

"Well, Lizzie – this is your life now" she told herself. "Your happiness was short-lived. But with three young children (and you've got to count your blessings for those three wonderful little souls) it's best foot forward, from now on. Just get on with it".

After this little prep talk from herself, to herself, she finished her tea and began her day.

When Cissie awoke, she was surprised to see that Lizzie had already risen, and not disturbed either her, or the two little girls. She slipped quietly out of bed and into her day clothes, glancing first at Margaret's sleeping form and then peering into the cot where she was greeted by a lovely smile from her youngest niece. She reached into the cot and Dorothy, in turn, held out her arms to be picked up.

Lizzie heard the movement on the stairs and knew who it would be, and was waiting – cup of tea in hand for her sister, and mug of milk for the baby of the family.

"Good morning, Cis – hope you slept well. I just want to say I'm so glad you and Ted stayed over. I know I've got to cope on my own, but today, well, I really need you here."

"It was Ted's idea. He was thinking of the practical help he could give, but I'm glad, too, that we stayed. I'd have been so worried, thinking of you here, coping alone". They shared a sad smile and a hug, then Ted appeared, followed closely by young Bill and Margaret – another day had begun.

They spent a relaxed day together, talking of Bill and playing with the children. Ted busied himself outside, tidying the garden shed, cleaning up the garden tools – little jobs that had been neglected due to Bill's illness.

Mid-afternoon, he went indoors and said the words that the sisters had been secretly dreading.

"We'll have to get going, Cis – there are no buses tomorrow, as its Sunday, so we need to catch the four o'clock, to be in time for the last train. I have to be at work tomorrow – Jim's a good boss, the best, but I wouldn't take advantage of his good nature – and you'll need to be back at work on Monday."

Looking across at Lizzie, he said "Will you be ok, Liz? I wish you'd come back to Livingstone, now that you and your Dad are friends, again. I'll look out for a cottage for you all, shall I"?

Cissie and Ted were both excited by this thought but could tell by the look on Lizzie's face what the answer would be.

"I need to be here" she said softly. They were aware that losing Bill had brought back the memories of her losing baby Bobby, and although she appeared to be coping, they were even more aware that her pain was still very raw, almost seven years on. They realised that she wouldn't ever accept that she would never see him again – whilst there was life in her body, there was hope. They wouldn't ask her ever again to leave this area – now they understood.

They were just about to leave to catch the bus; Lizzie and the children were all togged up in their outdoor clothes, ready to accompany them to the bus stop, as they always did, when there was a soft tap on the door. Cissie- who was closest- opened it to find Mr Duncombe on the step.

"I'm sorry – you're obviously about to go out" he said. "I'll call back in a while".

Lizzie explained what they were about to do and as time was getting on, they would have to hurry. Mr Duncombe quite understood and promised to be back within the hour, as he had another call to make.

It wasn't until she was back in the cottage, after waving Cissie and Ted off, and the slow walk back up the lane, that Lizzie began to wonder why Mr Duncombe had called to see her. She didn't have long to wait – within a few minutes, he was at her door, yet again. She opened the door and he followed her inside, taking off his trilby, as he entered. Without waiting to be asked, he sat his large frame on the couch. He twirled his hat around between his hands – he was obviously feeling uncomfortable.

"I'm just about to make a cup of tea – would you care for one?" she asked.

"I've just come from Mrs Bailey's – so I'm overflowing with tea, as you can imagine" he said, smiling at the thought of her neighbour. "But thank you, all the same".

She sensed his apprehension.

"What can I do for you, Mr Duncombe?" she asked, trying to ease the situation for him.

"I know this is not a good time to be informing you of this, but I don't think there will ever be a 'right' time". She held her breath. This was serious.

"First of all, I want to thank you for all the work you've done for us, during Bill's illness. You really kept things going. However", Lizzie was still standing up and caught hold of the back of the chair, knowing that what was coming next was going to change everything.

"However" he continued, "The time has come for all the heavy work to begin, big lawns to be mown, long hedges to cut; and I can't see that you'll be strong enough to tackle all of that, Mrs Udall". He paused, to give his words time to sink in - and then continued -
"I've been approached by Seth Harrison, from Sidden – he's asked if I'll consider him for Bill's job as Head Gardener". Again he paused, intent on gauging Lizzie's re-action.

But, her pretty face told him nothing.

"Of course……… this cottage is part of the remuneration". Lizzie gave a loud gasp. "You're putting us out of our home" she accused.

"I have another property in Weaverley – Toll Gate Cottage – I offered that to Seth".

"And he's accepted it?" she asked, hopefully.

"Well…no. His mother-in-law is an invalid, and lives in Sidden. Seth's wife needs to be close by, and she can cycle from here in five minutes. Weaverly is too far away for Mrs Harrison".

"Poor Mrs Harrison" said Lizzie with a sarcastic note in her voice.

"I can understand that you're upset, Mrs Udall. I can't tell you how sorry I am" he said sincerely.

"Not as sorry as I am" she snapped, sitting down heavily on the chair, with a sigh of utter defeat.

"Wouldn't you consider going nearer to your family in the Po…."

"No! I would not" she interrupted. "I'll sleep in Mr Bailey's barn, if I have to, but I'm not going back there". Mr Duncombe could see how distressed she was becoming.

"What about the house in Weaverley, would you consider renting the one I offered to Seth?" She had walked up to Weaverley a few times – it seemed a pleasant village, nestling beneath the Sellimore Hills.

"How much is the rent?" she asked.

"Normally, I charge seven and six, as it has three bedrooms, but, if you would like it, you can have it for four and six a week. There's no school in the village, so the children would have to attend Ellswood".

Lizzie didn't reply.

"I could take you now, in the car – just to have a look" he offered.

Lizzie looked at him – he had always been such a kind and caring boss to Bill – and to her – when she stopped to think about it. It must be very difficult for him, having no choice but to tell her to leave. She had known all along that she was living in a tied cottage, after all.

"I'll take it" she said. "And, thank you".

"Do you want me to take you to see it, before you decide?" he said, already on his feet.

"No. Thank you" she replied. "When do you want me out?"

"There's no rush, Mrs Udall" he said gently. "In your own time" He took a huge bunch of keys from his pocket, removed one from the key ring, and placed it on the table, in front of her.

"If you want anything at all, please let me know" He walked towards the door, turned and said "Good afternoon, Mrs Udall". She softened and said, "Thank you – and good afternoon, to you, too".

He closed the door behind him and heaved a huge sigh of relief, as he walked to his car. He hoped he never had to do anything like that, ever again.

CHAPTER THIRTY EIGHT

Sarah became a frequent visitor to the big house, much to Flora's delight. As her pregnancy progressed she relied more and more on her new found friend. Sarah had offered to knit some matinee jackets for the new baby and Flora had provided her with all of the balls of wool. Night after night, when Sarah wasn't meeting up with Joe, they would sit together in the living room and Sarah's needles would click away as the two of them chatted. Sarah had to admit, that although she loved knitting, she hated sewing together all the pieces to create the finished garment. However, this is where Flora came into her own, although she had never mastered the art of knitting, she was an accomplished needlewoman.

Together, they made an excellent and happy team.

Flora's parents had been away for three months, and although there had been plenty of communication between them, Flora had decided not to tell them that she was having 'another' baby – rather let them see for themselves, on their return.

On the said day, Flora could hardly contain her excitement when she saw their car arrive at the Lodge. She immediately picked up the telephone and invited them over for afternoon tea.

She was in the sitting room when they arrived and they were rather bemused as to why she didn't rush to greet them as she usually did.

They went to her chair, in turn, kissing her on the cheek – and still she remained seated, and smiling. When Ellen brought in the tea tray, she thanked her and dismissed her saying "I'll pour it, thank you, Ellen. You may go now."

When Ellen had left the room, Flora rose to her feet, exposing her huge tummy for them both to see. Their mouths dropped open as they looked her up and down.

"Why didn't you tell us" accused Grace.

"I only found out myself shortly after you left and I knew that if I'd told you, you would cut short your holiday, and that wasn't really necessary – I have been so well. I've only got around a month to go and I knew you'd be back in good time for the birth – and that's when I *will* need you with me" she laughed. Her parents were amazed at the change in her. Gone was the timid little mouse; in its place was an assertive, confident, strikingly handsome – but never pretty – self-reliant young woman.

Just then, Reg came into the room, followed by David who bounded over to his grand-parents and threw himself on to them, delighted to be re-united with them. They laughed and hugged and kissed him.

Cuthbert stood up and walked towards Reg with his hand outstretched, "Well done, Old Chap", he said.

"Yes – congratulations to you both" Grace added.

Flora and Reg beamed at each other.

***

Later in the evening, Flora had pains – dreadful pains – she had never known such pain, ever.

Reg insisted on calling the doctor, who said she had gone into early labour and he would contact Nora, the midwife.

By the next afternoon, despite encouragement from Nora, Flora still hadn't produced her offspring. Grace was beside herself and insisted that the doctor be re-called. When he arrived, he agreed that she shouldn't be allowed to go on any longer; the baby's life was now in danger. She needed to be taken into hospital where a Caesarean Section would be performed. When Flora heard these words, through the mists of her pain, she knew that desperate measures were called for.
She pushed, and pushed, and pushed, and pushed harder than she had ever done.

It worked.

Her baby girl was born.

She felt so tired.

Nora started to clean her up, but Flora begged her to go away and let her sleep, but there was a strict procedure for midwives to follow, and Nora was determined to carry it out to the letter. It was whilst she was attempting to pull a clean nightdress over Flora's head that it happened.

Flora started to jerk and shake.

"Take it easy, Mrs Jenkins, I've almost done now she said. "Then I'll bring you a nice cup of tea, and then you can settle down and have a well deserved sleep".

She then realised that Flora was unconscious. She ran to the bedroom door and called, "Get the doctor".

Grace, who was holding the baby girl, sensed the urgency in the midwife's voice, and ran to the door. The doctor was just about to drive away but gave a fleeting glance towards the door, where he saw Grace waving frantically at him. In seconds he'd switched off the engine and was out of the car and taking the stairs two at a time.

He gently laid Flora back into a more comfortable position, before thoroughly examining her.

"Was it an epilepsy attack?" asked Nora. The doctor removed the stethoscope from his ears and let it lie around his neck.

"No – I'm afraid not. An aneurysm in her brain".

"Oh my God"! Nora exclaimed. Barely had the blasphemy left her lips when Flora gave a groan - then silence.

"She's gone" said the doctor, unaware that Grace had been standing in the doorway – watching – and listening.

"No…..no……no……not now" she cried, falling to her knees, weeping, clutching the motherless baby. "Not now……"

CHAPTER THIRTY NINE

The following day, being Sunday, Lizzie decided to walk up to Weaverley and view Toll Gate Cottage, the house that was to be their new home.

It took a good fifty minutes to walk from Southwood with little Margaret; Lizzie guessed it was the best part of two miles. However, when she arrived at the house she was delighted with what she saw. They entered a tiny back yard with a good strong gate, a small and easily maintained vegetable patch, a pump to provide their water, an outdoor lavatory and a good sized rabbit hutch to boot. Cissie and Ted had brought the children a huge rabbit as an Easter present and Margaret had named him Brer Rabbit. Bill had wanted to call him Sid, but Margaret had said that was a silly name for a rabbit and reluctantly Lizzie had to agree.

Inside was just as good – a large living kitchen with a range and beyond that a light and airy sitting room. Upstairs there were two double bedrooms and the single room was as large as the one she was using at the moment.

An ideal house for a growing family, she thought.

After locking up, and placing the key safely in her pocket she ventured down into the heart of the village. She then sensed a change in Margaret and looked down at her little girl.

"What's up Duck – are you tired?" She asked. Then saw that Margaret was watching a young boy peeping round the end of a farm building on the right hand side of the road.

"Do you know him?" she asked gently.

"Yes, he goes to my school" Margaret replied.

"Hello there" called Lizzie. But, the little boy didn't reply, he just bobbed back again, out of sight. The next minute he re-appeared with three more faces alongside. Lizzie had to smile.

"Hello" she said, again. But they all disappeared. Then, a woman of about Lizzie's age peered round the corner, obviously to see what was interesting the boys.

"Hallo!" she said when she saw Lizzie and her family. Lizzie had loved living in Southwood, where everyone had been friendly and made her feel so welcome – once she was married, that is! She hoped the Weaverley residents were as amicable.

"Hello. I'm Lizzie Udall and these are my children, Margaret, Bill and Dorothy" she said proudly. "And we're moving into Toll Gate Cottage just as soon as we can".

"How nice, that cottage has stood empty for far too long. I'm Edie Grindey, by the way, and it's a pleasure to meet you and your family, Lizzie. These little reprobates are my boys, Gordon, Alan, Tommy and Gerald" she said just as proudly. "Would you like to come in, I was just about to put the kettle on".

"That's very kind" said Lizzie. "I'm parched. We've walked from Southwood and its taken ages as its all uphill. It shouldn't take us as long to go back, though", she laughed.

News, in a small community, travels fast. Edie had heard about Bill Udall's demise and knew that, as it was a tied cottage, the family would have to move out, to make way for Bill's successor, but she wasn't expecting them to move to Weaverly.

The two women were at ease with each other and the conversation flowed. Gordon took little Dorothy by the hand and took her to see some baby lambs and Bill went along with them, but Margaret stayed close to her mother's side.

When the children returned, Lizzie, not wanting to outstay her welcome, said they must be getting back. Edie informed her of a short cut through

Nedswood, for which they were very grateful, as within half an hour, they were home.

Lizzie was aware that something was upsetting Margaret, but decided to get the younger ones in bed first, before tackling the problem.

When this was done, she sat down next to the fire. Margaret was sitting at the table, colouring a picture that she had drawn at school.

"Come over here, Duck," she said gently.

Margaret put down her crayon and went obediently to stand by her mother's side. Lizzie wrapped her arms around her little girl and pulled her on to her knee.

"What's the matter, Margie? She asked.

"I don't like Tommy Grindey and I didn't like being in his house" she said, crossly.

It all became clear now to Lizzie – she knew she'd heard the name Grindey before, but then, thought no more of it. Tommy was the boy who had made fun of Margaret, in her early school days.

"He isn't unkind to you now, is he?" Lizzie asked.

"No. But I still don't like him" Margaret pouted.

"Well, I'm afraid we all come across people we don't really like, all of the time, in this life" her mother answered. "We're all different, you see, and like different things. But, if we were all alike, and liked the same things, what a boring world it would be".

Margaret didn't really understand what her mother was saying, but it didn't matter. She didn't like Tommy 'Horrid' Grindey, and, what's more, she never would.

Lizzie was relieved to get to the bottom of her daughter's unusual behaviour and would bear in mind her dislike of the boy.

"Let's get you off to bed, now. It's school in the morning, so, off with you, up the wooden hills", she said, jovially.

As soon as Margaret had left for school, the next morning, trotting alongside Michael, Lizzie started her packing. If she had to go, then go she would, as soon as possible. Mrs Bailey had looked out some tea chests which she found invaluable for housing her crockery. She threw herself into the task in hand with gusto.

By Wednesday, she could see light at the end of the tunnel.

However, her job was hampered when she discovered all of Connie's personal effects, stored in the loft. She couldn't resist searching through the boxes and trunks. There were presents, - possibly twenty first birthday, some wedding – and even her wedding dress – it was like a treasure trove. Bill had left her the contents of this house, in his will, so, legally this was all her property. But no matter how many times she told herself this, it still felt like she was intruding on someone else's life.

By Saturday, it was completed. Mr Bailey was going to take the furniture and heavy stuff on his horse and cart – old Dobbin was a strong old plodder – it would be an easy task for him, particularly through Nedswood. They had agreed to start at eleven o'clock, when Mr B would have finished the milking, had a good breakfast and done his rounds on the farm.

Young Michael worked like a Trojan, helping to load the cart. He was tall for his age and was developing powerful muscles through his chores on the farm. With his help, everything was in place by twelve thirty, so they sat in Mrs Bailey's kitchen, enjoying a 'picnic' of cheese sandwiches and rock buns, provided by Lizzie and tea for the adults and milk for the children, provided by Mrs Bailey.

It was a sad moment for Lizzie, when Dobbin pulled the cart away with all her possessions – she was going to miss Southwood – but most of all, she would miss the Baileys.

Alone, she walked back to empty house and took one last look around. She had scrubbed it from top to bottom and it was shining like a new pin. She closed the door and locked it, placing the key under a plant pot, as requested by Mr Duncombe. As she got to the gate her eyes scanned the garden one last time – and rested on Brer's hutch.

He was still inside.

How on earth was she going to transport a rabbit, along with three children? She looked at the pram and saw the answer to her problem. She lifted out the base, placed Brer into the cavity, replaced the base, and sat Dorothy on the top. Dorothy giggled as she could feel him running backwards and forwards, beneath her.

It was quite a warm day and progress was slow. When they reached the second gate in Nedswood, she was surprised to see that she had caught up with Mr Bailey and the cart.

"Just wanted to give old Dobbin a rest. He's worked up a bit of a sweat" he explained.

Margaret and Bill knew just what he meant, they were tired and their legs were aching.

When Michael suggested that they sit on the cart with him, for the rest of the journey, they were thrilled.

"You're to sit very still" Lizzie warned. They were grinning at her like Cheshire cats as the cart pulled away. Lizzie found that she could go much faster, now that she didn't have to match the children's pace.

Toll Gate Cottage was a welcome sight.

Lizzie's first task was to transfer Brer from the bottom of the pram into his new hutch and give him a much needed drink of water.

They had started unloading the cart when Edie Grindey appeared. With her, were her four boys; one carrying a huge enamel teapot, one carrying a jug of milk, one carrying a basket with the contents covered by a tea-towel, the other, Tommy was bringing up the rear.

After the boys had deposited their loads in the kitchen, Edie suggested that they could all help by taking off the lightest of the boxes, and carry them into the house. With so many willing hands the cart was soon empty. Edie asked Lizzie which box held the cups and she was soon pouring out the tea and they sampled her most famous cherry cake.

Suddenly, everyone was saying goodbye and Lizzie was left alone with her children.

The house seemed big, and quiet.

CHAPTER FORTY

The news of Flora's death was soon all around the factory and the village.

Reg's way of coping wasn't to stay at home, in mourning, but to throw himself into his work – sometimes up to fourteen hours a day.

Cuthbert was inconsolable at the loss of his only child, but Grace found some solace in caring for her grandchildren – in doing so, she felt closer to her daughter. She was at the big house more and more now, more than she was at the Lodge, and suggested to Reg that it would be beneficial to all of them if they (Grace and Bert) moved back permanently, as there was more than enough room. Reg thought this a *bad* idea – if they moved in, he would no longer feel head of the household – **no** -.

"I couldn't let you give up your home, just for me" he said. "Ellen and Lucille are coping really well and you do need some time to yourselves".

Cleverly changing the subject, he came up trumps by asking them to choose the name of his new daughter.

What a thoughtful, generous chap he was!

He and Flora hadn't decided on a name, so he didn't have a clue what to call the little girl, and this ingenious idea was putting him such good favour with the in-laws.

During her holidays in the south of France, Grace had discovered the name Fleur, and thought it a very pretty name. As it was so similar to Flora, what did Reg think?

"I think it's a perfect name for our daughter" he said.

Sarah was devastated by Flora's death and missed her terribly, as they had spent so much time together, over the past months. She confided in Cissie who kindly said that they must spend more time together and Sarah could even accompany her the next time she went to visit Lizzie.

Joe was getting more and more concerned about the state of Sarah's mental health, but he couldn't be with her as often as he wanted, as when Reg was working, so was Joe, his right hand man. It was during one of the long shifts at the factory that Joe decided to confide in Reg, in the hope that he would suggest that he could finish work a bit earlier – Reg should be able to cope alone some of the time – he was the boss, after all!

Sadly, Reg wasn't very sympathetic to Joe's problems.

"The best thing you could do, Joe, is marry her and make a few babies yourselves – that would take her mind off herself."

Joe thought about Reg's words as the evening drew on, his immediate re-action had been "Hard hearted bugger", but then, perhaps it wasn't such a bad idea. They had been seeing each other for around six years now, and they were engaged. There were a couple of vacant cottages close to the factory – in fact – the more he thought about it, the better the idea sounded.

By the end of his shift, his mind was made up, but he had just one more thing to do before he set the date with Sarah.

He and Reg usually left he factory at he same time, and this night was no exception.

They had toured each area together, checking that everything was running smoothly, before handing over responsibility to the night foreman. Then, they both bade him goodnight, and, at the factory gate Joe normally went one way and Reg in the other direction to get into his car. As they were parting, Joe caught hold of Reg's arm and said, "Thanks Reg, for that advice". Reg just looked at him – he'd forgotten all about their earlier conversation.

"That's ok" he said, rather bemused.

"I intend proposing to Sarah at the week-end, but if she has to give up her job, we won't be able to manage on just my wage". Reg could see where this conversation was going.

"So if she's not earning, you'll need more – right?

"Well… yes. That's about it" Joe admitted.

"We'll have to see about that" Reg replied.

CHAPTER FORTY ONE

The summer term was almost over and the children of Weaverley were beginning to anticipate the school holidays and the long hot days ahead of them.

Margaret was now walking the two mile journey to Ellswood School with the rest of the village children. Lizzie had only taken her for the first couple of days. As in Southwood, there were older children who deemed it their duty to take care of the younger ones, both to and from school. The Grindey boys had taken her under their wings. They, like their mother, would have loved to have a little girl in their home. Tommy never put a foot out of place with Margaret, being really careful not to say anything, even in jest, that might upset her – but, even so, Margaret was never totally comfortable in his company.

Lizzie and his mother struck up a lovely friendship. Edie had come from a poor family but when she married Gordon senior, her life had changed so much for the better, but, she had never forgotten her humble beginnings and would help anyone less fortunate than herself.

Each time she saw Lizzie she would have some practical gifts for her – half a dozen eggs, a couple of pints of milk or a rabbit that had been caught in one of their snares. But, she always gave in a way that preserved Lizzies's pride. Lizzie was doing her a favour as they had too many eggs, or the milk or rabbit would 'go off' before Edie could use it. Lizzie treasured this friendship, although there was no way she could reciprocate.

A pretty young widow attracted plenty of attention in the village.

Sid Hambleton, who lived and farmed along with his widowed mother, didn't fail to notice and went out of his way to speak to Lizzie. There was something about this man that Lizzie really didn't like; in fact he made her skin crawl with the lecherous looks he gave her. But, as she was keen to get along with all of her new neighbours, she forced herself to be friendly, even with Sid. So, when a knock came on the door, one evening, she was surprised to see Mrs Hambleton standing on her step.

"Keep away from my boy" she said menacingly. "If you know what's good for you".

Lizzie was dumbstruck – she just looked at her.

"I know your sort" Mrs Hambleton continued. "You snared old Bill, and where's he now? Ay?"

Lizzie's blood started to boil. How dare she? How dare this woman speak to her in this manner?

"You've no worries, there – you daft old bugger. I wouldn't touch your son with a barge pole. So, just tell him that. And tell him to stay away from me".

With that she slammed the door in her face.

When Edie heard of this she laughed and laughed.

"She really does think he's another Errol Flynn, doesn't she"?

"So does he" Lizzie laughed so much she was holding her sides.

However, when she gave the situation a bit of thought later on, she wasn't happy that she had made an enemy.

***

The school closed for six weeks and the hectic, early morning routine at Toll Gate Cottage was now relaxed. The older children's days were spent meandering around the village, sometimes venturing up on the Sellimore Hills and enjoying the panoramic views, or when the sun was bearing down relentlessly, they would take shelter in the leafy glades in the wooded area known locally as 'The Dell'.

Only two of the Grindey boys, Gordon and Tommy, were big enough to help in the fields with the haymaking. This was where Lizzie could help repay her friends' kindness. As Alan and Gerald were only six and four years old, Lizzie insisted on taking care of them whilst Edie helped her husband in the fields: Margaret was secretly relieved that Tommy didn't have to stay.

As with all good things, the summer holidays came to an end. The first couple of days on their own were a novelty to Bill and Dorothy, but then as the weather deteriorated and they had to be indoors, they soon became bored with only each other for company. It was obvious to Lizzie that, although Bill was only four, he was ready to go to school. She decided that the next time she was in Ellswood she would call in and have a word with Mr Walker, the Head Master.

Mr Walker was an amenable person but told Lizzie that the earliest they could take Bill would be Easter, when he reached the ripe old age of four and a half.

Lizzie's mind was racing ahead. With only one child at home, perhaps she could find a little job where she could take Dorothy with her. She was tired of constantly struggling to make ends meet, financially. With three growing children, clothes were always a problem. There were only a few items, like socks, jumpers and pyjamas, that could be passed down from girl, to boy, to girl, and by the time Dorothy inherited, the clothes were becoming quite threadbare. Edie passed on trousers and jackets and shoes where she could.

Christmas and the snow came and went and soon the hedgerows and trees were sprouting their new buds.

Bill started school and, much to Lizzies' delight, she was asked if she would take on the job of school cleaner. She would arrive at the school just as lessons were finishing and her three children would play in the playground whilst she swept and mopped and dusted the classrooms.

So impressed was Mr Walker by her thoroughness, that he asked if she would also clean the school house, where he lived. To do this, she arrived two hours before the end of school, just twice a week, so that when Mr Walker finished teaching, he returned to his home to find it gleaming. This arrangement worked very well and meant that Lizzie was free during the school holidays. It also meant that, not only was she working hard, she was having to walk four miles every day, to and from Ellswood.

Occasionally, someone from the village would come along with a horse and cart and give her and Dorothy a lift, placing the push chair on the back. Lizzie was constantly tired and the only time she managed to see Cissie was during the school holidays. Cissie was concerned that her sister had taken on too much, but Lizzie just laughed and said "Just call me Busy Lizzie".

***

September, 1939

Dorothy had just turned three when war was declared. Apparently, a German named Adolph Hitler was attempting, along with other atrocities, to take over Europe and possibly the world. However, life in Weaverly hardly changed at all.

Occasionally, they would hear a rumble, but they were never completely sure if it was the bombs or thunder.

Edie confided in Lizzie that she was having yet another baby, and Lizzie knew, in her heart that Edie was desperately hoping that her fifth child would be the much longed for, little girl.

When Stephen was born, there was as much rejoicing in the Grindey household, as there had been for their firstborn.

Excitement wasn't just confined to the Grindeys'; the whole village was buzzing with the news that a family of two boys and a little girl, along with their mother, was coming to stay with Dick and Lizzie Salt, farmers in the village and parents of Derek, four, and Janet, two.

The family came from Liverpool, and the father, Arthur Watson, had been to every farm in the vicinity, asking if they would take his family in, as Liverpool, and its' docks, was the prime target for Hitler's bombs. Dick and Lizzie's place was his last port of call and they only agreed that the family could stay for a fortnight. Arthur was stationed at Goatshorn, a couple of miles up the road from the village, where he was in charge of the prisoners of war.

When the village children met the family, they were as intrigued by their accents, as the Liverpudlians were by their Staffordshire dialect.

At the end of the two weeks, Lizzie Salt and Bella Watson had developed a firm friendship, and, although nothing was ever agreed, verbally, they knew that no time factor would be adhered to.

The boys, Arthur Junior and Norman were of school age and they attended Ellswood School, walking together with the other village children, were very soon accepted and even welcomed.

Again, it was almost time for the school to break up for the long holiday. Lizzie could hardly believe that another year had passed.

In fact, she thought, this time next year, Dorothy, her baby, would be starting school.

On the last day of term, Lizzie had cleaned the classrooms, whilst the children played ball outside. They were all hot and tired as they trudged back home.

On the road, they met three workmen, cutting the grass verges with scythes. As the family passed by, they all said 'Good Afternoon' to Lizzie and the children. Their shift was just finishing, so, as two of them walked towards Ellswood, the other caught up with Lizzie and fell into step alongside her.

He introduced himself as Ted Morley and told her that he lived in Hall Lane along with his wife and two sons, Jacob and Phillip. He also confided in Lizzie that his wife suffered poor health and a sad look came over his face. Consequently, the next time they met, she remembered this and enquired of his wife's health. His face clouded as he thought of her, and he replied that she sadly, would never get better.

Lizzie was sorry to have asked and upset him so.

"I wouldn't have asked if I'd known that" she said. "But you know where I am if you need someone to talk to" she added kindly. So, whenever they met up, on the road, they chatted and got to know each other. Lizzie felt terribly sad for the quiet man.

The next letter to arrive from Livingstone came along with an invitation for Lizzie and the children to attend the wedding of Cissie and Ted, in July. The letter told Lizzie how Jim Myatt, Ted's boss, had offered Ted the job of farm manager and a little cottage, alongside his farm, would be available from June. They were busy decorating and furnishing it, and were so thrilled.

Ted's younger brother, Jack, was offered Ted's old job, as farm labourer, and he would also take over Ted's role as head of the household. Jack's wage would soon be supplemented as Charlie would also be working before the end of the year, so Ted was encouraged to start a new life with his beloved Cissie.

Margaret, Bill and Dorothy were so excited, they loved Auntie Cissie and they had never been to a wedding before.

Edie had just passed down a bag of clothes and Lizzie was delighted to find a crisp white shirt, some short grey trousers and a pair of black plimsolls all to fit Bill perfectly.

That was one outfit sorted – only three more to go.

She pulled out a box that was stored beneath her bed. It was full of Connie Udall's clothes, some of them hardly worn. She discovered a lovely, lavender coloured, very full skirt. If she unpicked it, she could make two matching skirts and very simple blouses for Margaret and Dorothy. Then, all she would have to buy would be some white socks and white plimsolls for the two of them, and they didn't cost very much.

Lizzie herself was more than happy to wear the lovely blue outfit that Bill had bought for her to wear at her own wedding. It was, perhaps, a little dated, but, what the heck, there was a war on.

Cissie had told her how everyone was giving her their clothing coupons so that she was able to get enough material for her wedding dress that a friend of Fanny's was making up for her.

As soon as the invitation had arrived, Lizzie had started to put a little bit of money aside to cover the cost of the bus and train fares for the three of them. She wouldn't have to pay for Dorothy as she was under five. She was also hoping to have enough money saved to buy a special present for the happy couple.

When the big day dawned, the children were awake early and soon dressing in their finery. Even Lizzie was caught up in the excitement. They had to walk to Ellswood, catch the bus to Utchester where they would have a wait of forty minutes, before catching the train to Livingstone, where the church was only about five minutes walk from the station.

Lizzie decided to sit Dorothy in the push chair for the journey to Ellswood – there, she would ask Dr. Clayton if she could leave it in his scullery until their return later in the evening. She knew little Dorothy would be worn out by the end of the day, and Lizzie didn't relish the idea of carrying a four year old for two miles, particularly as it was all uphill!

As they left the cottage, they heard the distinctive sound of marching feet. Almost immediately, they were greeted with the sight of the prisoners being marched down to Delbert Farm, under the watchful eye of Arthur Watson. There, they would be given their orders for the day, then sent off in two's and three's to work on all of the farms in the village. Lizzie created much interest within the group. Their smiles and gesticulations told Arthur that the pretty widow and her well turned out family were much appreciated by these hot-blooded, virile, young men. Lizzie was totally unaware of the impact she was having on them, and smiled and said a cheery 'Good Morning'.

When they arrived in Utchester, Lizzie intended putting the forty minute wait to good use. She hadn't had time to buy the wedding present so she marched the children at full speed from the bus station and into Woodissees' shop. The last time she had been into town, she had seen some lovely china two tier cake stands, in their window, and knew this would make a perfect present.

When she had made her purchase, she asked if it could please be wrapped. The assistant very carefully took the stand to pieces and wrapped each bit in tissue paper before placing it all in a box, with even more tissue paper tucked around it. The box was then wrapped in brown paper and secured with a length of string. Then it was a frantic rush down to the railway station.

Bill was so excited with the train and reluctant to leave when they reached Livingstone.

The wedding went without a hitch – Cissie was the perfect blushing bride, Ted the handsome groom, Sarah and Marjorie the pretty bridesmaids and the ladies all discreetly dabbed their eyes with their lacy hankies.

Lizzie enjoyed her time being in the midst of her family – it was as though she had never been away. Cissie looked on fondly, and thought, perhaps, after today, she would see sense and move back to where she belonged.

All too soon, they were heading back for the station. Bill said the best part of the day was riding on the train – in fact – he had decided that he would be a train driver, when he grew up.

The push chair proved to be very necessary, as, by the time they'd reached Utchester, Dorothy's eyes were drooping. Lizzie had managed to carry her from the train station to the bus station, and within minutes of the bus leaving town, she was sound asleep.

As the bus trundled along the familiar route, Lizzie was thinking how glad she was that it was a lovely summer's night – at this time of the year it never went completely dark – she really wouldn't have liked to complete this journey with the children on a cold, dark winter's night.

When they arrived in Ellswood, the bus stopped directly opposite the Abbott's Hotel. Lizzie usually gave her old home a quick glance, but tonight she had to manoeuvre carefully down the aisle of the bus whilst carrying the dead weight of her sleeping daughter, whilst making sure that Margaret and Bill were right behind her. The conductor descended the steps ahead of her and turned to help her down. She in turn held out her free hand to help Bill and Margaret down the last deep step. Thanking the conductor, they then made their way up the lane to the doctors house, where her load would be lightened when Dorothy was placed in the push chair.

It was another hour before they were tucked up in their beds as Bill was struggling to walk the distance.

"I wish there was a train we could catch" he said miserably.

Within six months of the wedding Lizzie received a letter from an excited Cissie, with the inevitable news that she was, at long last, expecting a baby of her own.

CHAPTER FORTY TWO

Cissie loved being in her own little home, at long last. Yes, she missed the camaraderie of the girls in the glazing room, but, being a beloved wife and mother-to-be was really so much nicer. She saw Sarah once a week, and this year, everyone was saving their clothing coupons for Sarah as they had for Cissie the previous year. Sarah and Joe were getting married in June; as Cissie's baby was due in April she was hoping she would be well enough to attend the ceremony with her husband and brand new baby.

Joe had asked Reg if he would return the favour and be his best man. Reg didn't particularly want the job, but felt it would be churlish to refuse. Sarah had sent an invitation by post, inviting Lizzie and the children, but before she sent her acceptance, she received a letter from Cissie, giving a detailed account of the forth coming celebrations, of which she had helped to organise. When Lizzie read that Reg Jenkins was to be best man she knew that she couldn't come face to face with the man who had hurt her so badly, so she wasted no time in writing to decline the invitation, saying she had already made plans and how sorry she was to miss Sarah's special day.

Grace was busy organising Fleurs' christening, on Reg's behalf. She knew all about the strong friendship that had been forged between Flora and Sarah and suggested to Reg that Sarah should be asked to be godmother to the baby.

"I'm sure that's what Flora would have done, had she lived" Grace said – her voice breaking with emotion.

"Yes, I'm sure you're right" Reg agreed. "I'd been thinking along those lines myself".

"I'll ask her" Grace said.

Sarah was honoured to be chosen for this important role, the downside being that Joe would have to go to work that day, and wouldn't be at her side for this special occasion.

She'd already had her 'going away' dress made, and, as clothes and material were so scarce, she decided that she would have to wear this for the christening.

On the day she felt so proud, honoured and sad. Proud of the way she looked, honoured to have been bestowed with this privilege and so sad because her dear friend, Flora would never hold her baby girl or watch her grow up. She was sad, also, for little

Fleur, who would have everything that money could buy, but never know a mothers' love.

After the service, Sarah, along with the other godparents, the godfather was Peter Weston, the son of an ex-colleague of Cuthberts, and the other godmother, Freda Turner was Flora's cousin, all went back to the house, where Grace had supervised the preparation of a pleasant afternoon tea.

Reg didn't fail to notice how pretty Sarah looked, and as she had spent many hours, in Flora's company in the big house, she was comfortable in the familiar surroundings.

She acted as hostess, passing round sandwiches and cakes when Grace was out of the room, and constantly nursing and cooing over baby Fleur.

At the end of the afternoon, Peter offered to give Sarah a lift home, which she gratefully accepted. However, when he dropped her off at her door and drove away, she realised that she'd left her cardigan, either in his car, or at the house. She started to walk back to the house, in the hope that it was there, as it was her only good cardi.

Reg was looking out of the sitting room window and noticed her walking up the drive. He was just enjoying a second glass of port. He leapt to his feet and opened the front door and called to her not to bother going round to the back entrance, as she usually did.

"Lucille's in the nursery with David and Fleur, and there's no-one else on duty, at the moment" he explained as he stood aside to allow her to enter through the front door.

"I think I've left my cardigan" she said "It's either here or in Mr. Weston's car." They went together into the sitting room and saw her cardigan was on the back of the chair on which she'd been sitting.

Reg had always thought Sarah to be a very attractive young lady – and what a lucky bloke Joe Stokes was. Now, after almost two glasses of port, she looked absolutely ravishing!

"Thank you so much for today, Sarah" he said humbly.

"Well, I was just going to thank you, Mr Jenkins" she laughed. "It's been a truly lovely day, and I'm so proud to be Fleurs' godmother".

"Less of the Mr Jenkins – it's Reg. Now, will you have a glass of sherry or a port with me, to end off the day" he asked.

Sarah said she would have a very small sherry and sat down and watched him pour it out. She wasn't used to alcohol and after a few sips it went straight to her head and she became very giggly. Reg found this behaviour so feminine and enthralling, adjectives that could never have described his late wife – he was mesmerised by Sarah.

As he was pouring her a second glass, Lucille knocked on the half open door. Reg turned and, with raised eyebrows, gave her a questioning look.

"May I just pop into the village to post this letter, please, Mr Jenkins. Both of the children are fast asleep, I'll only be about fifteen minutes, or so" she said.

"Certainly, Lucille" Reg replied. No need to rush back".

Sarah was impressed with Reg's demeanour – this was a facet of his personality that she had never seen before.

Shortly after Lucille had left, there was a muffled cry from the nursery.

"May I go and see to her?" asked Sarah. Reg nodded, and Sarah ran up the stairs. Fleur was fast asleep, so must have been having a bad dream. – This made Sarah feel so sad.

She bent over the beautifully draped crib and stroked the baby's forehead, soothing her in a soft gentle voice. A movement in the doorway made her look up. Reg was standing watching her every move – a sad smile on his face. Both knew that the other was thinking of Flora. Sarah walked slowly towards him and into his arms, to comfort him.

Then, they were kissing.

Gently, to begin with, then deeper, more urgent and passionate kisses – then, Reg was leading her across the landing, and down a small flight of stairs, into his bedroom.

Sarah and Joe had kissed passionately, and sometimes he had wanted to take things further, but Sarah was too afraid of becoming pregnant, so convinced him it would be much better to wait until their wedding night, besides which, they were rarely alone in a place where they wouldn't be disturbed or discovered.

But these feelings were something that she had never experienced before. Maybe it was the effects of the two glasses of sherry, but maybe it was the chemistry between the two of them. When Reg kissed her, he aroused feelings that she had never experienced before. She melted into his arms and surrendered herself to him. Reg had forgotten how wonderful it felt, to hold, to kiss and to make love to a beautiful passionate woman. He was amazed to discover that she was a virgin, particularly as Joe had often given the 'nudge' and the 'wink'.

Must just have been wishful thinking on Joe's part.

They explored each others bodies and made love until they were both satiated – then fell asleep in each other's arms.

Next morning, Sarah awoke first. She couldn't think where she could possibly be. Then she turned to see Reg, asleep, alongside her. She was horrified when she brought to mind their night of passion. She blushed to the roots of her hair, thinking of her behaviour – she felt like a harlot.

Reg opened his eyes – he thought the lovemaking must have been a dream – a wonderful dream – but, no. Here was the lovely creature, lying beside him. He wrapped his arms around her and she snuggled up to him.

"You are the most beautiful woman in the world, Sarah" he told her. "I'm never going to let you go, I'm in love with you – please say you love me, too."

"I've never felt this way before, Reg. I thought I was in love with Joe, but I know now it would be a mistake to marry him".

"Oh god, I'd not thought of that. Here I am in bed with the bride-to-be and I'm supposed to be your best man – what on earth are we going to tell him?"

Sarah paled when she thought about the situation. Reg saw the troubled look on her face and couldn't bear to be the cause of her distress. For once in his life, he was thinking of someone else's feelings, before his own.

"We'll go to Gretna Green – get married – then come back and tell the world that we love each other" he said. They knew, beyond the shadow of a doubt, that this was their chance, this was a 'once in a lifetime' love, and they were going to snatch it with both hands.

"First, I'll have to go and see my mother – she'll be out of her mind with worry – I've never stayed out all night before" she told him.

Reg dragged a suitcase from the top of the wardrobe and threw a few clothes inside before going into the nursery and informing Lucille that he would be away for a few days. As it was unexpected, would she mind informing Mrs Wirksworth when she came over later on in the day.

Then they drove to the corner of the road where Sarah's family lived and Reg parked out of sight whilst Sarah ran up the lane. She was back within a few minutes – her eyes glowing when she looked at Reg.

"Mum was out, so I've left a note" she said.

It had been such a relief not to come face to face with her mother. She had left the note on the mantle shelf, in front of the clock. Her mother had obviously just finished a batch of ironing and Sarah freshly laundered clothes were on the table waiting to be put away, so she quickly pushed them into a bag, before snatching her coat from behind the door.

Then she was back in the car, and heading north towards
Gretna Green.

When Sarah's mother returned to her house after just popping across the road, she discovered the note.

Dear Mum,
Hope you weren't too worried about me staying out all night. Have to go away for a few days, but will

be back by Thursday and explain everything to you then.
Love you,
Sarah xxxxxxxx

Her mother was mystified; the letter didn't explain a thing.

***

Reg set off at speed. He wanted to avoid being seen by anyone who knew them. He didn't want his plans thwarted at this late stage. When the deed was done, they would face the music, but then it would be too late for anyone to do anything about it!

What a clever man he was.

***

"Oh oh!" he said. He'd glanced at the petrol gauge and saw that it was getting very low.

"Whatever's wrong"? asked Sarah.

"Petrol" he replied, "Or rather, lack of", he laughed. "Look out for a pump".

They didn't have to travel far before Sarah spied one. Reg drew the car to a standstill and went and knocked on the door.

From the car Sarah watched him, she couldn't believe what was happening – not to her – this was the kind of thing you read about in romantic novels, or watched on the huge screen at the cinema. It didn't happen in the real world.

A man opened the door and although he chatted to Reg, he didn't make any attempt to go anywhere near the petrol pump. Sarah wished they would hurry up as they were still so close to home, and still at risk of being seen.

After what seemed like an age, Reg started to walk back to the car and the man went inside and closed the door. As he climbed in beside her he smiled.

"Some bad news and some good news, Sarah – me darlin'" he said. "The pump is dry – the consignment has been held up, somewhere down south, probably by this damned war. He doesn't have any idea when it'll arrive."

Sarah looked at him, realising that they couldn't go very far, certainly not to Gretna Green, without fuel.

However, Reg was still smiling.

"As well as providing the local community with fuel, that dear gentleman is also a Justice of the Peace. When I explained to him where we wanted to go, and why, he said it would make more sense and also be more convenient just to go to the Register Office in Footly and buy a special licence. We could be Mister and Missus by this afternoon". He slipped his arm around her shoulders and pulled her to him, kissing her passionately. He drew away from her and gazed into her eyes.

Within half an hour they had arrived in Footly and purchased the said Licence. The receptionist said they would have to wait a while, as another marriage was about to take place.

"You wait here, Sarah, I'll be back in fifteen minutes" said Reg. With that, he left Sarah in the company of the sour faced receptionist. True to his word he was soon back, carrying a bunch of deep red roses, which he presented to his bride.

"We can't have a bride without a bouquet" he said. Also, in his hand was a small, black velvet box which he opened to reveal a slim, plain gold band. Sarah looked in awe at her very own wedding ring.

Suddenly, the door opened and a young couple emerged, smiling at each other and tightly holding hands.

"Our turn, I think" said Reg, taking her by the hand.

CHAPTER FORTY THREE

1941

Lizzie watched eagerly for the postman. Cissie was due to have her baby any day now, and she'd promised, that although it wouldn't be her usual lengthy missive, she would write and let Lizzie know, the minute she became an auntie.

Mr Walker, the Head Master, had told Lizzie that there would be a place at school for Dorothy, after the Easter holidays. The little girl was delighted as she got quite lonely when all of the others had gone to school.

The letter was waiting for when she arrived back from Ellswood. Margaret, now almost ten, often had problems with her extra toe-nail. When she was pulling on her socks, sometimes the extra bit would get caught and become infected. Lizzie had stressed the importance of keeping it really short and this had been reiterated by Dr Clayton, as he bathed and dressed it, only this morning.

One day, very soon, Lizzie intended telling Margaret about her twin brother, and that he had also been born with exactly the same rarity. Lizzie was about to sink into a deep sadness, as she always did when she thought of little Bobby, when she saw the letter.

The first piece of new was, of course, that Cissie was now a mother herself; to a little boy they had named David Edward.

How-ever, it wasn't the brief note that had been promised.
Two, well-filled pages, no less. It was all about Sarah *marrying* Reg Jenkins – out of the blue – and his wife barely cold in her grave. Lizzie could just imagine the gossip mongers of Livingstone – suggesting the 'something' had been 'going on' whilst Flora was still alive, with Sarah only pretending to be her best friend. Oh yes – they would be having a hey-day!

***

Meanwhile, in Ellswood, Eva and Jim decided that they could wait no longer, war or no war, they would get married.

So, early in 1944, Lizzie and the children attended the wedding ceremony of their oldest and dearest friend.

Margaret proudly presented the bride with a posy of snowdrops, which Eva carried with pride to the altar to make her marriage vows.

***

1945

Life for Lizzie should have been easier now that all of the children were attending school, but it seemed to get busier.

As her reputation as a first class cleaner spread throughout the area, offers of work flooded in. Lizzie never liked to refuse anyone, but now, even during the school holidays she was working, having to take the children with her. She missed her special time with the children and also her visits to see Cissie.

Her only bit of socialising was when she was walking home from her cleaning jobs in either Ellswood or Siddon, when, more often than not, Ted Morley would be on the same stretch of road. It was as though he was hiding behind the hedge, waiting for her, and then would suddenly appear at her side. They had developed quite a close friendship, as she was always ready to listen to his woes and to sympathize.

In the village, Edie Grindey had just given birth to her sixth son Roy, who soon earned the nickname of Fizzer, and thrilled as she was with the delightful little boy, she realised it was time to stop producing these fine young males, a little girl, obviously not destined to come into their home. Lizzie called to see her whenever she could.

***

The PoW's were now accepted by the villagers, most of the farmers had at least one labouring for them – but language was always a problem. Most of them were German but two of them were Italian. As their route march took them past Lizzie's cottage twice a day, not only had they noticed the attractive widow, but so had her eye been caught by a tall, handsome Italian. She had a friendly smile for all of them, but a special smile and special look for this particular one. When they arrived back at the camp, there was much teasing, fun punching and communication by the international language of laughter.

Pietro Calvo took the teasing in good part. He was a highly respected officer in the Italian army and came from Palermo in Sicily, where everyone in the close knit community, knew everyone else. The Calvo's were locally famous restaurateurs, and had been for several generations.

However, although Pietro loved to cook, he had no desire to carry on the family tradition, – he wanted to be a full- time soldier. Although his father had been disappointed by this decision, he had supported and encouraged his son, as he rose up through the ranks.

With each promotion came a new location, and so forming a lasting relationship with a member of the opposite sex proved to be quite difficult, much to his mother's chagrin. But, he had thought, time enough for that – then came the war, and with that, internment –and he realised that time was the most precious commodity.

The minute he had set eyes on Lizzie, he knew that she was someone very special. Although he had never been in love, he thought that this *must* be what it felt like. He also realised that this was why he had never bothered in the past; it was as though he had been waiting to meet Lizzie. He loved the way she was always rushing around, always busy and clucking around the children like a mother hen – in fact, yes – he loved her, and he wanted to spend the rest of his life with her. He could imagine, as he was drifting off to sleep, taking her and the children back with him to Palermo, and introducing them all to his extensive family......... He also knew that language would be a problem for them so he asked Arthur to help him master the very basics of English to enable him to get by.

CHAPTER FORTY FOUR

In June, Margaret celebrated her fourteenth birthday and was legally allowed to leave full-time education. Mr Walker was aware that higher education would not be an option for her, and when a doctor friend of his told him he was in need of a live-in maid, he had no qualms about recommending her for the post.

Lizzie was delighted for her daughter, also thinking that that would be one less mouth for her to feed. Also, Margaret would, as all good children would, hand over their unopened pay packet, to the parent, at the end of the week.

She left school on the Friday, after her birthday; on the Saturday, they all travelled to Bardy, where the doctor, Dr Dyche, had his home/surgery, settled her in and left her there, and she started work on the Monday.

How she hated it. The patients looked down on her as she opened the door and showed them to the waiting room. She missed her mum and her brother and little sister. She missed Weaverley – she even missed Tommy Grindey. She couldn't wait for Saturday. She caught the earliest bus and almost ran the two miles from Ellswood – and then, there she was, standing in the doorway of Toll Gate Cottage – and nothing had changed.

She had just had time to call into the little shop next to Bardy bus station, to buy Bill and Dorothy a packet of Spangles each, and five Park Drive cigarettes for her mum. Lizzie wasn't best pleased.

"Where's your wage packet, then?" she asked.

"There's only 5/8 left" she said. "The Spangles cost 4d, the fags cost 6d and the bus fare was 1/- return".

"Keep a 1/- for next weeks fare" said Lizzie, holding out her hand for the remaining 4/8.

The day at home passed twice as quickly as the days spent at work and all too soon she was making her way back to catch the bus. Maurice Jennings was stationed at the Bardy barracks and he was heading to Ellswood to catch the same bus, and promised that he would walk back with her to her new home.

The next day her toe was so sore from the trek back home. She didn't have access to any nail scissors and she was aware that her extra nail was far too long. Mrs Dyche noticed that she was limping, and asked what the problem was. Margaret was loathed to tell her about her peculiarity, but Mrs Dyche insisted, and when Dr Dyche had finished his surgery, Margaret was ushered into the room. He was interested to learn of the offending nail and Margaret went on to explain how her twin brother had been born with exactly the same abnormality, as well as a huge dark birthmark on the adjacent big toe. The nail was trimmed back, the toe cleaned and dressed and immediately felt more comfortable.

Although the Dyche's were kindness itself, Margaret was never really happy, being so far away from the rest of her family, at such an early age. Each time she went back home, she stressed to Lizzie how much she disliked living in Bardy. If Maurice wasn't going back on the bus with her, she was terrified as, alone, she made her way from the bus station, back to her 'home'. She passed doorways which were occupied by couples oblivious to anything other than the person they were kissing and groping. She would break into a run for last few yards, relieved to be back safely, but wishing she didn't have to be there at all.

After a few months, Lizzie could see the genuine distress of her first-born, and said
"You've given it a go, but if you really dislike it so much, look for something else. But" she warned

"You mustn't leave until you have another job to go to".

Margaret's heart lifted. She had to wait until the following Saturday before she could enquire about vacancies at the local cotton mill. A few of the mill girls would be on her bus, and as the weeks had gone by, they would chat and pass the time of day with her. As soon as they boarded, she overcame her shyness, and asked who she would need to contact, to secure herself a job – she would love to be a part of this happy group.

"No time like the present, duck" said Edna, the obvious leader of the gang. "Why don't you go now, old Ernie Millward'll be on his break?"

Margaret thought this an excellent idea and was soon walking through the mill gates and asking where Mr Millward could be found.

When she arrived at Toll Gate Cottage, she was looking happier than she had done for weeks, knowing that she would just have to work a week's notice then she could say goodbye to Bardy.

Lizzie thought how nice it would be to have her eldest safely back in the fold – and working in a mill, she would be bringing home much more that 6/6 a week!

***

Christmas was approaching, and a dance was being organised at the Village Hall in Ellswood. The war was finally over and the country would, hopefully, soon be back to normal. Edie and Gordon would be attending the dance and said Lizzie was welcome to go along with them.

Lizzie wasn't too bothered but Edie talked her round, knowing that Gordon wouldn't want to dance. He would be happy standing at the bar, beer in hand, talking to his fellow farmers about the pathetic price of milk, etc. Lizzie, she knew, would be a willing partner for the fun dances – and, of course, now Margaret was living back at home, she could keep an eye on the younger ones.

Lizzie was reluctant to go dancing, as she really had nothing appropriate to wear. Edie had plenty of dance dresses and would willingly have lent something to her friend, but, whilst Lizzie had always remained slim, Edie had carried extra weight even before giving birth to six children. So, although they were of a similar height, Edie's clothes would have drowned Lizzie's slender frame. There was only one thing for it – out would come the wedding outfit, yet again. The only shoes that she possessed were some black lace ups that Margaret had been given, by Mrs Dyche; they had belonged to her son, who had long since grown out of them. Margaret hadn't liked to say that they were too small for her, so Lizzie, who was a shoe size smaller than her daughter, had claimed them for herself.

When Edie saw what Lizzie intended wearing on her feet, she knew this was where she *could* be of help. She had a pair of pretty, silver dancing shoes, but no matter how hard she tried, she could no longer squeeze her podgy little feet into them. So, on the day of the dance she popped into the cottage with them. Lizzie's face was a picture.

She sat down and tried one on.

Perfect fit!

"You shall go to the Ball, Cinders" laughed Edie. Lizzie, usually so undemonstrative, leapt to her feet and hugged her friend.

"What time are we going, then, Ugly Sister?" They both exploded into fits of laughter.

Lizzie put on the other shoe and they had a practice dance around her sitting room.

"We'll call for you about half seven" she said. Gordon had just acquired a small van, which was a bit smelly, but there would room in the front for the three of them.

***

That morning, Lizzie had been up extra early and had had a good stripped wash and washed her hair, which badly needed cutting – she remembered how she'd cut it herself, before her wedding, and how Eva had kindly re-cut and permed it, for her. Eva, although not a trained hairdresser, had cut Lizzie's hair ever since.

Jim and Eva would be missed at the dance as she was due, any day, to give birth to their first baby.

Thinking of the curl, Lizzie knew she had some little metal curlers, somewhere. She rooted around in the drawer and found five. She placed them around the ends of her hair and left them in place all day. Only when she was dressed and ready to go did she remove them, and the effect was stunning. Soft shiny curls framed her face. She even found a sliver of lipstick and put a dot on both cheeks and blended it in, before outlining her lips. When the children saw her, they gasped in amazement.

"You look lovely, Mum" said Bill sincerely.

"You all be good, or else" she warned. They all nodded.

***

The band was already playing when they entered the packed Village Hall. Gordon went over to the bar and bought them all a glass of shandy.

The band leader announced that the first dance was to be Progressive Barn Dance, and he wanted to see everyone on the floor, but not everyone took notice.

"I'll be the bloke" Edie insisted, so Lizzie danced the first couple of minutes with her friend and then was whisked away, first by Maurice Jennings, then Joe Finnikin, then his brother, Bill. Then Dick Salt, then Mr Bailey spun her round and Arthur Watson and then…..a pair of dark brown, laughing eyes was looking down into hers. It was her Italian prisoner of war – but they only danced for a couple of minutes before she was passed on to Fred Goodhall.

When the dance came to an end, her breath was coming in gasps, and not necessarily from exertion.

She made her way back to where Edie was sitting. Her eyes aglow and her cheeks flushed. She watched as *he* made his way back to the corner where all of the POW's were sitting, under the watchful eye of Arthur.

The next dance was the Gay Gordons, then non-progressive Barn Dance, Bowling-the-Jack, the Hokey-Cokey and a Quick Step which Edie and Lizzie tackled with gusto.

The band took a short break and the band leader said a few words, thanking the locals for supporting this effort, etc. He then went on to say,
"When I passed Fred Goodhall's farm earlier in the evening, I saw three ducks sitting on the fence. I went to the first duck and said 'Hello little duck. What is your name and what do you do?' The duck replied, 'Hello. My name's Donald and I like messing around in puddles.' So, then I went to the second duck and said 'Hello little duck. What is your name and what do you like to do?' The duck replied, 'Hello my name is Daffy and like messing around in puddles.' Then I went to the third little duck and said, 'Hello little duck. What is your name and what do you like to do?'
The third little duck replied, 'Hello. My name is Puddles.' " The entire audience roared with laughter.

During this interval, Mr and Mrs Bailey came over and introduced Michael's new girl friend, Pat, and quickly brought Lizzie up to date with the happenings in Southwood.

Then the band struck up again. After another Hokey-Cokey, the Conga, interspersed with another Quick Step and Fox Trot, they were soon announcing the Last Waltz. Edie managed to get Gordon on to the floor, but, although their steps matched it looked nothing like a waltz. Lizzie saw *him* coming over to her and she slid happily, into his arms, as though that was where she belonged. When the music stopped they stayed locked in each others arms. All around, people were shouting, "More, - more", so, obligingly, the band struck up yet another, Last Waltz.

As the music died, the revellers tried once again, to have 'just one more' but the Band Master directed the musicians to end the evening in the usual way. As the first notes of the National Anthem sounded, everyone became silent, and then sang together, the poignant lyrics. Even the POW's stood to attention, but with their heads bowed in respect.

Maurice Jennings then leapt on to the stage and shouted,
"Three cheers for England. Hip Hip…"

"Hooray" chanted the crowd. As the cheering continued, Lizzie noticed that Arthur was leading his charges through the door. Her admirer turned and saw her looking – he gave just a little wave, which she returned.

Then Edie was at her side and the three of them were clambering into the little van.

"First stop, Toll Gate Cottage" said Gordon.

"It's been a grand night – don't you think, Liz" asked Edie.

"Grand" said Lizzie, dreamily.

At her gate, she leapt from the van, calling good night along with her thanks. In the house, a low lamp was still lit, making the room look peaceful and cosy. She crept up the stairs to find all three of her children fast asleep. She walked slowly back downstairs; there was no way she could go to sleep, just yet. She placed a couple of thin logs on to the dying embers and then placed the kettle on top, thinking she would have a nice mug of cocoa. That would help her get to sleep. She went into the kitchen to fetch a mug – and almost jumped out of her skin. A face appeared at the window. It was her handsome Italian dance partner. She opened the door and put her finger to her lips, then led him into the sitting room.

In limited English he told her that Arthur had allowed him a couple of hours to come and see her and to tell her of his feelings for her. He spoke in little more than a whisper as he informed her that they were being moved on, the following day, but – he would be back to her – no matter what. He would come and live here or she and the children could go with him to Sicily. Wherever they were, they were meant to be together. Then he took her in his arms, and held her tight, told her that he loved her, kissed her, and then he made love to her. She now knew she had never been in love before, she told him of *her* love for *him* and that she would happily follow him to the ends of the earth.

Then he said he would have to go. "But you will wait for me, cara?" he asked.

Neither of them slept a wink that night.

***

The next morning, Pietro sought out Arthur. He wanted to thank the kind guard for the part he'd played in allowing him the time he needed to tell Lizzie of his feelings. He had already known, in his heart, that she mirrored his feelings, but just to hear her say the words would keep him sane, until he returned to her. He had no idea as to where he was being transferred – even Arthur hadn't been informed.

"I want to thank you from the bottom of my 'eart" he told Arthur. "I will never forget your kindness".

"It went well then?"

"Ooh yes, it did. It went very, very well. She is the woman I 'ave been seeking all my life. And – she feels the same as me. I'm a lucky man – Yes?"

"Yes – you are. You're a very lucky man, Pietro. But, enough talk for now. We have to leave the camp, today. Check the lorry first; I think there's a rear brake light not working"

"The bulb 'as died" said Pietro. "I do it right away, Boss". Arthur then called out instructions for the rest of the POW's to clear their billets and leave everything ship-shape and bristol fashion.

When he returned to the lorry, the POW's, having carried out all of his orders, were standing in line, carrying their few personal effects wrapped in a blanket and tucked underneath theirs arms. Arthur had just come from the Mess and noticed that Pietro's belongings were still on his bunk.

"Either the jobs taking longer than it should, or he's done a runner", Arthur said to himself.

Arthur sensed that something was wrong. The lorry had moved! He ran to the rear of the vehicle and found the Italian – trapped between the lorry and the wall.

Death had been instantaneous. The heavy vehicle had crushed Pietro's ribs, which, in turn had punctured his lungs. Lizzie's face had flashed before him, as he departed this world.

CHAPTER FORTY FIVE

CHRISTMAS 1945

Lizzie was up early the next morning and starting her tasks for the day. She was still on cloud nine after her wonderful evening and was humming to herself when a quiet knock came on the door.

She was surprised to see Arthur on her doorstep, but any friend of Pietro's was a friend of hers, so she gave him a dazzling smile, and invited him inside. In the sitting room, she asked him to take a seat but he just shook his head. He moved towards her and took her hands in his.
"Mrs Udall – Lizzie – there's no easy way to tell you this – but, there's been a dreadful accident" he paused to let his words sink in.

"Pietro was crushed by a lorry" he continued. Lizzie nodded to let him know she had understood what he was saying.

"But he's going to be alright" she asked.

"No Lizzie – he died…… about half an hour ago – I came here as soon as I could. I'm so sorry".

"I need to see him" she said.

"That wouldn't be a good idea, Love" he said. Then she started to shake, her teeth began to chatter as the finality of the situation penetrated her brain, and then she began to cry silent tears, not just for herself but for her lost love.

Upstairs, Margaret was awake, and wondered what was happening. She could hear muted voices and ran down the stairs, but when she saw Arthur, she stopped in her tracks – she was only wearing her nightgown. She rushed back to her bedroom and threw on her day clothes, aware that something dreadful had happened that concerned her mum. In seconds she was back in the sitting room, asking Arthur to explain what was wrong.

"Make your Mam a cup of tea – there's a love" he said kindly. "I have to go now, but I'll be back to see you later on," he promised Lizzie.

Margaret made a pot of tea and placed a cup in her mother's trembling hands.

"What's happened, Mam?" she asked.

"A friend of mine's died" she said, matter-of factly. "It happens – It's sad, but – it happens".

Margaret assumed it was someone elderly from the village. Her mother had drunk her tea and was on her feet busying herself, with her chores. Margaret assumed that all was well again.

When Arthur left the cottage, he knew he needed to inform PC Stanway of the accident, who, in turn, advised him to fetch the doctor, who would need to see the body and certify that he was, indeed, dead.

A full investigation was carried out later that day, but tests proved inconclusive. Either, the hand brake was not applied correctly, meaning that Arthur (he was the only driver of the vehicle) was at fault, or, it wasn't maintained correctly, meaning that Pietro (as the only mechanic) was at fault.

Lizzie couldn't settle in the cottage. She smoked one cigarette after another, then called to the children that she was just going down to Granny Waring's to get even more Park Drive. Ted Morley was in the shop, buying paraffin. He smiled when he saw Lizzie come through the door, but she barely glanced at him. He left the shop, but waited outside for her.

"Have I upset you, Lizzie?" he asked.

"No. Why?" she demanded.

"You don't seem yourself. You're usually so kind and caring towards me" he said, rather pathetically.

"So – I'm not having a good day, today, so perhaps *I* could do with some kindness, and someone to care for me, for a change" she snapped.

Then she walked away.

He watched her retreating frame. He would go and see her tonight, he decided. He would make sure his wife was comfortable, and then he would go and show Lizzie Udall how kind and caring he could be.

When Lizzie arrived back at the cottage, all of the children were up. They sensed that she was in a bad mood, and knew it was best if they kept out of her way for the rest of the day. They even took themselves off to bed early that night, so she was left alone; and it was only eight o'clock.

"So much for finding true love" she thought. "Last night was the happiest of my life – I thought everything was about to change..... for the better.....that didn't last long, did it?"

She went into the kitchen to fetch her cigarettes out of her coat pocket and saw Ted coming through the gate. She'd never invited him to her home and thought he had a bit of a cheek, just turning up without being invited.

She met him at the open door with her hands on her hips. He looked terrified.

"What do *you* want" she demanded.

"Well, I think I must have over-stepped the mark" he said. "I'm always complaining about my life, and never ask you if you're alright. You looked a bit peaky this morning, so I've come to listen, not to talk……if that's ok with you?"

"You'd better come inside – you're letting all the cold air in, but not for long, mind. And you'll have to be quiet, the children are all asleep."

They sat down on opposite sides of the fireplace and he produced a bottle of brandy, from a paper bag.

"Get a couple of cups, this'll make you feel better" he said. said.

The brandy burned her throat, but when he offered to re-fill her cup, she didn't object. After the second one, she felt comfortably warm and relaxed. She lit yet another cigarette and held out her cup for another top-up.

"It's a bit strong, is this" he explained. "Best take it easy. We don't want you with a hang-over tomorrow now, do we?"

"Just one more little one, pleeeeeease" she said in a silly voice. As he was still trying to make up with her, he didn't like to refuse. She gulped it down and patted the cushion, next to her.

"Come and sit over here, next to me" she invited. The brandy had taken away all her inhibitions, - he now looked… just like.. Pietro – and she pulled him towards her kissing him passionately on the lips. Ted's mind was also befuddled with the alcohol; he had never, ever drunk it before. But, he wasn't going to by-pass a chance like this! He kissed her back and let his hands roam over her body. When she didn't object he took things a stage further, expecting her, at any minute, to slap his face – but, it didn't happen! Soon, they were both naked – and past the point of no return……..

It was over in seconds. It had been such a long time since he had seen any sexual activity. He didn't know what to do next. Lizzie appeared to have fallen fast asleep.

Perhaps he'd better go. He didn't like to leave her exposing herself in all her naked glory so, he took her coat from the back of the door and draped it carefully over her and quietly left the cottage.

CHAPTER FORTY SIX

Reg and Sarah knew that they would have a lot of explaining to do as they travelled back to Livingstone the day after their marriage. They had spent their wedding night in the Savoy Hotel in Footly where Reg had requested that a breakfast of champagne and strawberries be delivered to their room the following morning. Then they spent the rest of the morning in bed.

At lunch time he said "Gather your things together, Mrs Jenkins; it's time to face the music".

Their first port of call was Sarah's mother's house. Although she was quaking at the knees,

Sarah walked in with her head held high, and holding on tightly to Reg's hand.

"What on earth is going on, Our Sarah" her mother demanded.

"We were married yesterday" Reg informed her.

"Married? You two – to each other"?

"Yes, Mum"

"But what about Joe"?

"That's where we're going next" Sarah said, looking at Reg for confirmation. He nodded in agreement. None of this was going to be as easy as he expected it to be.

"Well, you'd better get back here straight after, and explain to your father just what you've been up to," her mother warned.

Sarah thought it best to see Joe on her own but Reg was concerned for her, in case he became violent, so stayed close by, but just out of sight.

Joe couldn't believe what he was hearing. He was aware that Sarah had been away from home for the last two nights, and she hadn't been with him!

The woman he intended to marry in a couple of weeks was now informing him that she had just married his best man – his boss – the man he looked up to.

But, he had been sure that there would be a simple reason for her absence – he never expected anything like this.

He was speechless.

He gave her a look that made her blood run cold. Then he turned and walked out of the factory, back to his home, where most of his belongings were packed in a trunk, ready to be transferred to their new home. He packed a bag with as few possessions as possible, and disappeared.

Rumour had it that he had joined the Merchant Navy, but his mother never, ever forgave Sarah for making a fool of her son and being the cause of him leaving the area. She also made it very plain that if Lucille expected to become a member of her family, by marrying Matt, she should look for employment elsewhere.

Avoiding Joe's mum was easy for Sarah, as, if any business needed attending to in the village, she would order Ellen to go. When she did go out it was in the car, with Reg.

Lucille dutifully left their employ, but wasn't too sure that she wanted Mrs Stokes for a mother-in-law, so she found another position in Warwickshire. Close enough for Matt to visit, if he so desired, but far enough away from his dictatorial mother.

Sarah thought that David would benefit from going to the local school, now that he was ten years old, so they didn't bother replacing the Governess.

"He needs to be in the company of children of his own age" Sarah said, wisely, and Grace totally agreed with her as she hadn't really approved of him being tutored at home.

Reg was, indeed, a happy man. Sarah already loved little Fleur and David had really taken to the happy pretty lady who had been a familiar face around the house and a special friend to his mummy.

Sarah was intrigued by the young boy's toe. Within a couple of days of moving in, David had come to her straight after his bath (he was a big boy now, and didn't need 'women' in the bathroom with him, *when he had no clothes on*) and asked her to trim his special nail. He, too, had experienced discomfort when it had grown too long, so he knew it was necessary to keep it short. Sarah trimmed it back for him and asked him about the huge black freckle that was on the adjacent toe, and growing with him.

"Daddy says it's my special mark and he'll never, ever, lose me, because of it," he replied.

Although Reg was quite close to his son, he was looking for a boarding school for him to attend. He thought, to put his son amidst the 'right' sort of people, (although his career was a foregone conclusion, he would, of course, inherit the factory) and mixing with gentry and the like from an early age could only stand him in good stead.

Sarah didn't agree with her husband. She said the young boy should be given more time at home, chance for her to become close to him – he had – after all, suffered a great loss in his young life.

Reg had to admit that, in this case, she was probably correct, and agreed to defer the move for a couple more years; secretly, he was glad that she took her role as step-mother so seriously. He had made a good choice, yet again.

What a clever man he was!

CHAPTER FORTY SEVEN

Lizzie woke up very, very, very slowly. For a minute, she couldn't think where she was. She sat up, even more slowly. Why was she not in her bed? Why was she naked? Her head felt like a drum was being beaten inside it. It was coming back to her now. Ted had been to see her.....

She started to pull her clothes on, and then changed her mind – she needed to wash herself. She rose slowly, and lit the primus stove and placed the kettle over the hissing flame.

When it came to the boil, she poured the water into the bowl and, with a bar of carbolic soap, scrubbed and scrubbed every inch of her body. She then went into the sitting room and gathered together all of her clothes from where they'd lain, strewn around the floor. Then she made herself a cup of strong, sweet tea, took two aspros and lit her first cigarette of the day. She didn't want to think about what might have happened.

"Don't try to kid yourself, Lizzie Udall – you mean - what *did* happen" she thought. "How could I? How could I behave like that? - And on the very day that my only love was taken away from me. How can I mourn for him when I've behaved like a trollop?"

She was filled with self-pity and allowed herself to cry – but only for a minute – she didn't even deserve the relief that crying brought.

The she heard movement above her. The children were awake and if they saw she'd been crying, they'd want to know the reason why. She went back into the kitchen and splashed her face with icy cold water, and lit another Park Drive.

"Mornin' Mam" Bill was up first.

"Do ya want a cuppa?" Lizzie asked; now back in control of her emotions.

"Sounds like a good idea to me" replied her son." But I'll make you one. You sit down." Lizzie ignored his kind gesture and filled the kettle yet again, before returning to the sitting room and starting to clean out the grate. Her head pounded even more when she bent over, so when Bill offered to take over whilst she made the tea, she readily agreed. Both of the girls were, by now, downstairs and being very careful not to say the wrong thing to their mother, aware that she had been really agitated the previous day.

Tomorrow was Christmas Day, and Lizzie was so glad that she had organised everything early, this year. When she took the rent money to Mr Duncombe, he was waiting with the usual goodies. A large capon had replaced the small goose that they'd been given in the early years; this easily fed the four of them on Christmas Day, and the meat from the legs made sandwiches to see them through Boxing Day, too. Also in the hamper was a tin of ham, a tin of salmon, a chocolate log and last, but by no means least, a box of festive crackers. They had provided the Christmas fare every year since they moved to Weaverley, plus all the years in South wood, and Lizzie realised how well respected and appreciated Bill had been by his employers.

The children's presents were wrapped and under a small tree that Bill had brought back from the Dell. Dorothy had made some paper decorations at school and had taken great pains to place them carefully on the tree. The sitting room was looking quite festive, particularly now Bill had finally got the fire going.

The children all had a bowl of bread and warm milk for their breakfast, then donned their coats and went off together. They had decided to pool their money and walk down to the village shop in Ellswood, to buy a present for their mother.

No sooner had they left the house, when Arthur Watson knocked on the door. Lizzie invited him in but couldn't bring herself to look him in the face – so great was her shame.

"How ya doin, Gal" he asked kindly.

"I'm alright, thank you" she replied.

"I've just come to tell you that Pietro's body has been taken to Frank Slater's. I wondered if you'd like me to take you to see him, I'm sure I can arrange…"

"No! Thank you" she interrupted. "Nothing could be gained by me going to see a dead body. I appreciate what you're trying to do, Arthur. But nothing can bring him back – so, I've got to get over it".

Arthur was shocked at her callous attitude, and turned to go.

"Ta-ra, Arthur"

"Ta-ra to you, too, Lizzie"

As he walked away, he shook his head. He couldn't believe how unfeeling Lizzie seemed to be. He had thought she was a caring and gentle soul who had loved Pietro as much as he'd loved her, but he was obviously mistaken. Again, he shook his head in disbelief – he would never understand the female mind.

CHAPTER FORTY EIGHT

David enjoyed going to the village school and was popular with his peers. Sarah hoped that Reg had changed his mind about sending him off to boarding school.

Reg, however, had other things on his mind. His new foreman, Robert Gibbs, had informed him that a man had been asking about the owner of the factory – a man, who Robert had said, looked vaguely familiar, but he couldn't think where he had seen him before. The man had been around for a few days, but Reg had yet to see him. He was unnerved by this man's presence – he wondered if it was Joe Stokes come to seek his revenge for stealing his bride. He ordered Robert to bring him straight to the office, the very next time he saw him, thinking that, if it was Joe, he would be comparatively safe within his own domain. When a knock came on the door of his office, later in the day, he didn't even bother to look up; he just called 'come in'. He felt a presence across the desk and raised his eyes from his work to look into a pair of piercing blue eyes – identical to his own.

"Charlie" he whispered.

"Hello Reg. No point in asking how *you* are. Done alright for yourself, I see". His sarcasm, obvious.

"What do you want, Charlie"? Reg asked. A million things were going through his mind. He walked over to the door to where he could see Janet, his secretary busy with her typing. He asked her to bring them in some coffee. In those few seconds as he was regaining his composure, Charlie had sat down on his captain's chair on the other side of the desk, and was smirking at his twin brother.

"I suppose you're the bloke that my foreman's told me about; he said someone had been asking questions about me".

"Could be" said the wily Charlie.

"No wonder he said you looked familiar" said Reg, warming slightly to the mirror image of himself. He decided that 'friendly' was his best option when dealing with this rogue of a brother; a different tactic to what he would be expecting.

"It's good to see you, Mate" said Reg. "What's been happening in your life, then"?

"Not as much as in yours, by the look of things" replied Charlie.
"Well, I've worked really hard to get where I am" said Reg, with as much honesty as he could muster.

"So you could give me a bit of help, then"? His twin asked, rubbing his thumb across the ends of his fingertips. Quick as a flash Reg replied, "I could give you a job". He saw the disappointment flash across Charlie's face.

"An honest days' pay for an honest days' work is the only help I'll give. I need a delivery driver, to start as soon as possible" then raised his brows in askance.

"I've nowhere to live" Charlie whined. Reg quickly wrote down his butlers address, knowing that his daughter had just got married and there was sure to be vacant room in the house. Pushing the piece of paper into Charlie's hand, he said, "Just tell them Mr Jenkins sent you". As was usual, Reg was one step ahead of Charlie, but he said he would give the job a go and then went on his way.

When he had left, Reg sat with his head in his hands. What if…? What if Charlie had turned up whilst Flora was still alive?

Sweat appeared on his upper lip at the very thought. Flora would then have known that he'd lied about the accident, she would then have found out that David was *his* son, she would have told her father, and then… Reg would have been out on his ear.

CHAPTER FORTY NINE

Lizzie kept well out of Ted's way – more out of shame than any other reason. She was grieving for Pietro and constantly felt tired and listless.

Margaret's fifteenth birthday was approaching and she seemed so much happier at the mill than she'd been at the doctor's house, in Bardy – she enjoyed the banter and camaraderie with the other girls, and occasionally had a night out in Utchester with them.

Bill was rarely at home these days; he roamed the countryside with the Grindey boys after he had helped them complete their chores on the farm.

Dorothy had developed a close friendship with Janet Salt. Although Janet was a few years younger,

Dorothy seemed to enjoy taking care of her and also, Jean, the little girl from Liverpool. Together, they would all take turns in riding and grooming Janet's pony, Bonnie.

As the seasons changed, once again, and the weather became warmer, Lizzie was still in the doldrums. But, was it any wonder, she thought to herself. To be given a taste of happiness and to have it snatched away, after such a brief time – she sighed – life could be so cruel. Then there was the guilt. It was now five months since she had lost Pietro – and the episode with Ted - and up to now, she still hadn't spoke to him. Oh, he was around, she was well aware of that; but she had always managed to evade him, even if it meant jumping into a field and hiding behind the hedge, until he had gone by.

She was still working hard; cleaning the school, the schoolmaster's house and also two private houses in Sitton. As she was returning from her final job of the day, she met up with Bill and his mates. They were 'nutting' in Wild Hay but said they were just about to go home, so they fell into step with her. The weather was particularly warm and Lizzie hadn't had anything to eat or drink since breakfast. As they reached the last cattle grid, she stumbled. The boys managed to reach out and break her fall and carry her slight frame to the side of the road, sitting her lifeless body against the wall. Bill ran round the corner to a well and filled his cupped hands with the lovely, sweet clear water. On his return, he raised his hands to her lips; the cool water seemed to revive her immediately. Embarrassed by the young boy's attention, she leapt to her feet, and almost collapsed again.

"Sit still for a bit, Mam" Bill advised, wisely.

"Aye lad, I think I will". Bill went back to the well for more water, wishing he had a cup, or any sort of container, to take back to her. After resting for a few minutes she then said that she felt well enough to continue her journey home.

The route they were on took them directly past Ted's home in Hall Lane, but Lizzie was unconcerned when she saw him working in his garden. She knew he wouldn't try to approach her whilst she was with the boys. He just stood and watched, as she walked by.

Dorothy was in the house when they arrive home, and Bill told her to put the kettle on.

"Put it on yourself, Bossy Boots" she retaliated.

"Mam's not very well" he whispered. So, immediately she put the kettle on and cut some slices of bread which she then buttered and took into the sitting room, to her mother.

"Thanks, duck". Lizzie gave her youngest daughter a weak smile.

The next minute, Edie came rushing through the door, baby Roy ledged on her hip.

"Whatever's up? The lads have just told me you're not very well". Lizzie tried to make light of the incident but Edie could see how pale her friend was.

"I *am* coming up for forty, you know. It could be the 'change'" she said.

"I've heard it makes you feel a bit peculiar".

"Well, I don't think it would hurt to see Dr Clayton, for all that" Edie told her.

"I think I will" Lizzie relented. "I haven't felt right for a while".

Dr Clayton listened to her heart, her chest; he looked into her ears, her eyes; took her temperature, her pulse; everything seemed to be normal.

"What about your monthlies" he asked. "Are they regular?"

"No. Not for a while now – well, I can't really remember –I haven't been too regular since I had Dorothy. I was thinking….. Could I be on the 'change'? I am almost forty".

"Get on the couch and lift up your skirt" he instructed. He felt her stomach, and pressed and prodded.

"Could you be pregnant, Lizzie?" he asked. When she didn't reply, his suspicions were confirmed. She was speechless – why, why hadn't she realised.

"I don't know what I'm going to do" she cried. It's a job to feed and clothe myself and the three I've got, without another one in the house".

She sobbed and sobbed.

"Don't worry, Lizzie. If you really can't cope with another child, and I don't think you can, I can arrange things for you. There are lots of couples unable to have their own children, and would be happy to give this one a good life", he said, not unkindly. Lizzie was, by now, too distraught to argue.

The doctor then went on to explain that he knew of a 'home' in Stafford, where she could stay for six weeks, before her baby was adopted.

"Six weeks" she screamed. "How can I stay anywhere for six weeks – what about my other children?"

"Well – Margaret's fifteen, she'll be alright on her own – but she wouldn't be able to look after the young ones, as she would be at work. What I can suggest is, for them to go into 'care'. I do know of a place not far from the 'home'. Would you like me to sort it all out for you?" he asked kindly. Lizzie knew that she had little choice, so she just nodded her head, unable to speak for fear of bursting into tears.

"You know, this war has left a lot of ladies in the same predicament, Lizzie, so the longer we leave it, the less likely we are to secure places for you all." She thanked him and walked very slowly back to

Weaverly, and had almost reached the village when she heard a familiar voice behind her.

"Have you been avoiding me?" Ted accused. She didn't bother to reply, she just kept walking. She had intended going straight home but changed her mind and went to Edie, instead.

"I'll put the kettle on" said Edie when she saw Lizzie's strained face. "Do you want to tell me what's wrong or shall I just mind my own business".

"I'll tell you, because it'll be all over the village, very soon" Lizzie sighed. "I'm in the family way". Edie really didn't know how to re-act to the news. Edie, the natural mother, was delighted that another little miracle was soon to take place, but Edie, Lizzie's best friend and confidant, who knew Lizzie's circumstances better than most, was deeply worried by the news.

"Are you sure?" she asked.

"Just back from seeing the doctor – I thought he'd tell me I was on the change".

"Oh, Liz. What are you going to do?"

"Dr Clayton said he can sort everything out for me". She went on to explain about going into the home, the children into care and the baby being adopted. By the time she had finished speaking, they both had tears streaming down their faces.

"Is this what you really want?" Edie asked her.

"I don't know what I want – it's all such a shock"

"I wish I could help…."

"Edie, you're such a good friend, but I think you've got more than enough on your hands, with your own six." she said.

"But I thought your first question would be, 'Who is the father'".

"That's nothing to do with me" Edie said, emphatically. So Lizzie said……nothing!

How could she, when she didn't know herself. She said she would have to go as the children would be home and wondering where she was.

***

By mid-August, it was obvious to all that she was pregnant. She was alone in the house when Ted knocked on the door.

"What do you want"? She snapped.

"I want to accept my responsibilities" he replied. "I'll take care of you and the baby, financially, but, you know that I can't leave Mary, she's too ill to live on her own". Then he walked away, without waiting for her re-action.

The next day, the postman delivered two letters to Toll Gate Cottage. One, a newsy one, from Cissie, the other from the 'home' confirming that she had been allocated a place, commencing…the next day.

She started to panic.

She hadn't even told the children.

She had nothing ready.

Then, there was another knock on the door. Oh! No! Not Ted again. No, it wasn't Ted, it was Dr. Clayton.

"I've just called to tell you that I can take you and the children to Stafford, tomorrow. I'll be here about 10.30, straight after surgery" he said coldly. Lizzie was concerned as she had never seen him like this before. In all the years that she had known him, he had always been very kindly towards her.

"What's wrong, Doctor?" she asked softly.

"I've just come from Hall Lane. Mary Morley has had a bad turn, brought on, I believe, by a confession from her husband – do I need to go on?" She lowered her head in shame.

"Will she be alright?" she whispered.

"Time will tell – aye, - only time will tell". With that, he left the house.

By the time the children had returned home, she had prepared a pot of rabbit stew. After they had eaten, Lizzie began to tell them what was about to happen.

"Tomorrow, Dr Clayton is taking us three to Stafford. I have to go into hospital and you two will go to boarding school, not very far away from me". Before she could say more, Dorothy started to cry.

"I don't want to go to boarding school" she howled.

"Oh, shut up, Our Dot, stop blarting – and listen to what Mam's saying" ordered Bill.

"Well, it should only be for six weeks….."

"Six weeks" screamed Dorothy. "That's forever". And cried louder than ever.

"It'll soon go, and at least you'll be together" Lizzie comforted.

"You must be really bad, Mam," Bill said, thinking of his late father.

"No duck, not really – they'll soon sort me out, don't you worry" Lizzie replied honestly.

"Marg, you'll be alright on your own, won't you? – Edie's just down the road if you need her". As Margaret was nodding her head in agreement, Bill butted in, saying
"Why can't *we* stay here, with our Marg – she can look after us".

"Because you can't" Lizzie snapped. "No more talk now, go and put your clothes in a bag". They knew that they must do as she instructed, with no more arguing and went obediently up the stairs, knowing that life was going to be very, very different, after today.

***

When Dr Clayton arrived the next morning, they were all ready and waiting. He stayed in the car and waited for them to go out to him.

Lizzie and both the children clambered in the back together and he set off. Conversation was stilted – Lizzie tried to keep the children's interest by pointing to things and places of interest, en-route, but they hardly noticed anything; they were too wrapped up in their own private misery.

The car pulled into the grounds of the 'boarding school' first and as it came to a halt, Lizzie moved towards the door, ready to get out, but the doctor shook his head.

"You stay there" he ordered, and escorted Bill and Dorothy, both clutching their belongings, to the main door, where a stout woman, wearing a nurse's uniform was waiting to greet them. The nurse bent and said something to the children - they turned and waved to Lizzie, then disappeared behind the huge door. Lizzie's hand was still raised when Dr Clayton climbed back into the car. Lizzie couldn't trust herself to speak; her tears were just a breath away.

Ten minutes later Dr Clayton expertly manoeuvred the car up yet another drive, and parked outside yet another front door. This time the doctor didn't get out.

"Thank you Doctor" Lizzie said sincerely, "For everything".

"Off you go, Lizzie – and good luck" he replied. "By the way, Mary Morley passed away, this morning".

CHAPTER FIFTY

Dorothy clung to Bill's hand as the nurse led them down the long corridor. Her Mam had looked so little, sat in the back of the doctor's car.

"I'm Nurse Hartley – the girl's dormitory is this way, Dorothy. Bill, you go with Nurse Keane". Bill followed Nurse Keane, as instructed while Dorothy was led up the stairs. She had never felt so alone in her short life. The nurse was explaining that this was her bed and was placing clean bedding on top of the mattress.

"It's your responsibility to make your own bed each day, and change the sheets and pillow slips each Saturday, and to keep the area around your bed clean and tidy. But, I'll give you a hand and show you how it's done, just today" she said kindly.

Together, they spread out the bottom sheet and Nurse Hartley explained how to form the neat 'hospital corners' and tuck everything in. Dorothy was in desperate need of the lavatory and kept looking at the Nurse, in the hope she would notice that there was a problem, but she just kept on about the importance of neatness and tidiness, until Dorothy could no longer control her bladder. She felt the warmth run down both of her legs – oh – the shame.

"You naughty girl" shouted Nurse Hartley. "I'll show you where the mops and buckets are kept and you can clean this mess up yourself, then perhaps you'll use the lavatory, in future. Dorothy started to cry, but this only made the Nurse even angrier.

"For goodness sake, Child, stop that noise". When she came back with the mop and bucket, Dorothy made even more mess as her hands were too small to wring the water out of the mop properly, and there was water, everywhere. Nurse Hartley snatched it from her and expertly dried the area in a flash. She took the mop and bucket back to the sluice room and when she returned she was carrying a huge pair of navy blue knickers.

"Put these on, then go into the sluice room and wash your wet ones and put them on the line, they'll be dry by morning" her demeanour was much kinder now, so Dorothy whispered her thanks and gave her a glimmer of a grateful smile. Then they walked together to the canteen where she ran straight to Bill's side.

"Are you alright"? He asked and she just nodded.

"We *will* see Weaverley again, don't you worry. If Mam doesn't come back for us in six weeks, we'll run away". They sat together at the table, but neither had much of an appetite. Six weeks is such a long time, when you're only ten years old.

***

At the 'home', Lizzie's first impression was the cleanliness of the place.

Cold, unfriendly, austere, but clean.

She walked the length of the gleaming corridor until she came to a door marked 'Matron Stone'. She gave a little knock and waited. The door was flung open by a tall, huge chested woman wearing a crisp white uniform.

"Udall?" she asked.

"Yes" Lizzie replied.

"Yes, Ma'am."

"Yes, Ma'am."

"That what I like. A quick learner, follow me" They went up a flight of stairs and into a huge room, containing about a dozen beds, all evenly spaced out on either side.

The windows were so high you would have to stand on a chair to look out of them and, consequently, the light around the beds was muted, making the cold room look quite ghostly.

"Leave your belongings on your bed, and follow me". Lizzie was taken into a large bathroom, where she was told to remove all of her clothes and get into the bath, which was filled with Luke-warm, disinfected water. Then she was given a small piece of carbolic soap and told to wash her hair, and every inch of her body. Privacy wasn't a word in Matron Stone's vocabulary; she watched Lizzie's every move, her eyes constantly straying to the swollen breasts and belly. Then she handed her a rough towel and a shapeless serge dress.

"You all dress the same, whilst you're here" she was told. When Lizzie was dried and dressed, she was taken back down the stairs and into yet another huge room, which was obviously the dining room. Seated at the long table were nine, very young, very silent girls – all very pregnant. Matron gestured for Lizzie to take her place at the table, and then proceeded to say grace. Before they had even said 'amen' they were rising from their seats, bowls in hand, heading towards another table where two more residents were serving soup and handing out a chunk of bread. Lizzie followed suit, aware that all eyes were on her, as she was more than old enough to be mother to each and every one of these girls. She took the bowl back to the table and tasted the watery contents. All it really tasted of was salt – and the bread was hard and stale.

When they had finished eating, they were all assigned to different tasks. Some washed and wiped the pots, while others prepared vegetables for the evening meal. Lizzie was given the job of cleaning the huge dining room, alone. She had to wash down the walls, clean the windows, scrub the table and all of the chairs, and finally, the floor.
"Hard work never killed anyone" said Matron Stone. "The devil finds work for idle hands". In fact, she had a different simile for every day of the week.

"Thought you would have known better - at your age" she said to Lizzie. But Lizzie just ignored her disparaging remark, and carried on with the scrubbing, although her back felt like it was breaking.

That night she fell into the uncomfortable bed and pulled the rough blanket over her exhausted body. However, sleep eluded her, as most of the other residents sobbed themselves, noisily, to sleep.

The pattern of every day was, up with the lark, pray, eat, pray, scrub, pray and early to bed. The monotony was only broken when one by one they went into labour and were taken to the infirmary, never to be seen again.

***

Cissie hardly heard a thing from Lizzie, these days. No news is good news, she told herself. David was growing up fast and was a joy to his parents. She saw Dolly, Mary and Florrie most weeks and was a frequent visitor to her father and stepmother's house. Jim had met a lovely girl, whilst he was in the army, and had moved to her home town of Barton, so she rarely saw him.

She was often invited, by Sarah to visit her at the big house, but Cissie preferred it when Sarah came to her little cottage, as, if Reg was at the house, he seemed as uncomfortable in her company, as she did, in his.

Reg had his way and his son, David, was now attending Repton boarding school. During the school holidays, he spent more and more time with his father at the factory and had a natural talent for sculpting the clay. Reg was so proud of his first-born. Since Flora's demise, Grace and Cuthbert had begun to think of Reg as their own son, and shared his pride in David. What a competent pair of hands to leave the factory in – when the time came.

At sixteen, David left school with first class grades. Reg took him to the factory and showed him which was to be his own office, and gave him a brief outline of the duties expected of him. David gently said, "Father, I thank you for all of this, but, I really don't want to follow in yours and Grandpa's footsteps. I thought you would realise, that with my high grades, I wish to go on to University. My desire is to study medicine, become a doctor – that is my dream".

Reg was taken aback. He had no idea his son's mind was so set on this career path, he'd just assumed David would want to take over from him, when the time came. Now, his lifetime's work seemed rather futile.

CHAPTER FIFTY ONE

The 'boarding school' was quite a friendly place, the other girls tried hard to make friends with Dorothy, as they felt sorry for the little girl who cried herself to sleep every night. But all Dorothy was interested in was break and lunch times, when she could be with her big brother. He would assure her that they would see Mam again, very soon. By Christmas, he said we'll all be back in Weaverley. Christmas? It was only September. Christmas was a lifetime away, thought poor Dorothy.

Meanwhile, just a very few miles away, their mother was constantly thinking of her children. She couldn't wait to see them again. She knew that

Margaret would be alright, back at home with all her factory friends and Bill, also, would be coping, but it was Dorothy that filled her with concern, she was such a home-bird.

The heavy cleaning was taking its toll on her aging, pregnant body. Every week, they were forced to clean the entire building, from top to bottom. Scrubbing walls, floors, tables and chairs until their hands bled and their backs felt they were breaking.

The date was 21st September. Lizzie had felt tired all day, but today it had been her turn to scrub down the stairs – job they all dreaded and hated. Later, she fell into her bed and was saying a special prayer for her children, when the first pain started. Bearable, to begin with, but as the night wore on; they became more and more intense, making her gasp. By daybreak she was having the pains every five minutes, each one lasting longer than the last. Rita, the girl in the next bed was woken by her groans and gasps. She heaved her own cumbersome body from its resting place and stroked Lizzie's hair back off her face.

"Do you want me to fetch Matron" she asked.

"No. Not yet" moaned Lizzie. The bell then rang to inform them that another day had begun. Lizzie managed to crawl out of bed, and wash and dress herself between contractions. On her way down stairs another pain overtook her body, causing her to drape herself over the banister.

At breakfast, she suffered only a couple of minor pains, and so Matron was unaware of the progress of Lizzie's confinement.

"You – Udall – that staircase is a disgrace – you'd better clean it again and make a decent job of it, this time, or you'll find yourself cleaning again tomorrow".

"Alright, alright" said Lizzie, through gritted teeth "Keep your flipping hair on".

The other girls were silent. Matron walked over to Lizzie and stood as close as Lizzie's large tummy would allow.

"What did you say, Udall?" Matron was seething.

"I said, alright, alright, keep your flipping hair on, Ma'am" There were little titters from around the room.

"Quiet" yelled the livid Matron Stone. "You lot – get to your tasks. Udall, you wait here".

When the room was empty, Matron stood in front of Lizzie with a look of pure hatred on her face.

"Don't you try to put one over on me – Lady".

At that moment Lizzie was struck by the worst contraction that she had ever experienced. She gasped and held her protruding stomach.

"And, please, don't try that one, - you don't fool me – go and scrub those stairs down, now".

Lizzie could barely walk, but fetched her bucket of water and scrubbing brush and struggled back up the staircase, with Matron Stone right behind her. She struggled to get down on her knees and started to scrub the already immaculate stairs. Another pain took over her body, but she had no sympathy from the matron, who stuck her foot in Lizzie's back.

"Get on with it, Whore", she spat. Lizzie couldn't see what she was scrubbing – a red mist filled her eyes – the pain was now unbearable. Her waters broke as she lost consciousness.

When she opened her eyes, she had no recollection of what had taken place – she was just aware of her intense need to push. The nurse saw that she was now fully conscious and almost ready to bring her baby into the world.

"Push, now, Lizzie, push" she encouraged. "Now, relax, my love, and wait for your next pain" Pain was coming thick and fast now, with very little time to relax, in between. She let out a scream as she bore the worst pain she had ever known.

"Well done. Almost there now, you've just delivered the head. One more push and you'll be holding your little one." Lizzie grunted and groaned and pushed. Then, - it was over.

The baby was cleaned and swaddled and placed in its mother's arms.

"Clever girl – you have a lovely little daughter" Lizzie looked at the baby and saw the dark hair and the dark eyes of Pietro.

o-o-o-o-o-o-o-o-o-o-o

In Weaverley, Ted and his sons returned from Mary's funeral. Ted knew that his confession had hastened her death and he would always feel responsible. The boys were unaware of what had taken place, but were distraught to have lost their mother, so early in their lives.

Edie had been at the funeral, along with almost everyone else in the village, such was the close knit community. The way Edie looked at him made Ted think that Lizzie had told her, and he wondered if he dared ask if she had heard from her friend. But, not today. Today was about Mary, - the mother of his children.

CHAPTER FIFTY TWO

Like all new mothers, Lizzie was confined to her bed for two weeks, following the birth of her third daughter, Kathleen.

After her confinement, she was taken, along with her baby, to yet another institution, and was informed that her baby's prospective adoptive parents would be visiting later in the day. Her mind was racing, her heart heavy. Could she give away the product of her one true love? She looked at the baby and again, all she saw was Pietro's face.

Then came the dreaded knock on the door – she was led into an adjacent room where a friendly couple watched as she entered, with her baby. The man leapt to his feet and stuck out his hand to Lizzie.

"Hello. I'm John Walton, and this is my wife Bella" he was pumping Lizzie's spare hand up and down as he spoke. Bella was very beautiful, with long curly black hair, and eyes to match, and lovely ready smile.

"Bella is Italian" John said proudly, when he noticed Lizzie scrutinizing her.

"Pleased to meet you" she said.
This couple could have been hand picked to raise her baby, and she could feel the love between the two of them. If she was going to give her baby away, there would be no-one else, on this earth that she would rather give her to, than John and Bella Walton.

But, she knew, before she even entered the room that, no matter what, she was keeping her child – her lasting link with Pietro.

"Mr Walton – Mrs Walton – I can see what good people you are, and I'm sure you would love and care for my little girl, as if she were your own. But, I've changed my mind. She will stay with me – she is not going to be adopted – by anyone.

Bella began to cry, softly. John slid his arm around her and pulled her towards him. Lizzie walked out of the room, whispering "I'm so sorry", as she left.

She went straight to the Principle, Mrs Palmer's office and gushed,
"I've change my mind. Can you ask Dr Clayton to come and fetch me?"

"Sit down, Udall. Do you realise what you're letting yourself in for? Times are hard, as it is, and as you well know. You have to think of the other three children. This one will have a wonderful life with the Waltons – it'll want for nothing. They are so wealthy, and so loving – the only thing missing in their lives, is a child, to love and cherish – think of your baby, Lizzie and what a favour you'll be doing for it. What can you give it, compared to the Walton's?"

"I agree with all you say, Mrs Palmer, but, she is my baby, and she is not an IT. I'm keeping her, and nothing you say will make me change my mind. Now, will you contact Dr Clayton for me, please"?

"You are a stupid woman, Udall; let them have it, for goodness sake".

"Don't you call me stupid. She is my baby, and she belongs with me. For the last time, contact Dr Clayton, please".

She turned and walked away. Mrs Palmer knew she had lost the Walton's battle.

***

To Bill and Dorothy, it felt like they hadn't seen their mother for months, although it was just six weeks. The magic time. Six weeks was the length of time that Mam had said they would be apart. When they met at lunch time, Dorothy's eyes were filled tears.

"Its six weeks, and we're still here, and we'll still be here at Christmas" she cried. Bill placed his arm loosely on her shoulder and said, "We'll run away, tonight. We'll find our way back home, don't worry – so stop blarting, will you?" Comforted by his positivity, she managed a weak smile.

"What time are we going?"

"When everyone's gone to bed, I'll wait for you by the front door – I know where the key is kept. But don't tell anyone, and don't make a sound when you're getting dressed" he ordered. Dorothy was now, not only pacified, but excited at the thoughts of running away, in the dead of the night. She ate her lunch with gusto.

So, when lessons were finished for the day, and she was summoned to the Matron's office, she was sure it was because they had been over-heard, and it was with trepidation that she entered the room.
She wasn't at all surprised to see Bill already there – but what she was amazed to see was – dear old Dr Clayton. Bill's eyes were shining. "We're going home" he sang.

It only took a matter of minutes for them to gather together their meagre belongings, and soon they were in the back of the car – and heading towards – Mam!

Lizzie was waiting at the end of the drive; she couldn't stay in the presence of that Mrs Palmer for one minute longer. She had the baby on one arm and her brown paper carrier bag on the other.

Dr Clayton stopped the car and leapt out to help Lizzie and the baby on board.

"Thank you so much, Doctor" she said. Bill and Dorothy hugged their mother over the back of the seat, then settled down to enjoy the journey home.

"Do you think you've made the right decision, Lizzie?

"Yes…yes, I do. I'll manage, don't worry".

The children then started chattering excitedly, saying they knew that they would be going home today, and then looked knowingly at each other. Lizzie had no more opportunity, during the rest of the journey, for further conversation.

***

At Toll Gate Cottage, the doctor dropped them off at the gate and said he must hurry back for evening surgery.

Lizzie entered the house first, and was struck by the dank, neglected air. She placed the baby on the sofa and looked around her home. It was so good to be back. Bill and Dorothy thought so, too.

Lizzie soon had the fire lit and the kettle on the boil.

"Pop down to Mrs Grindey's for me, you two, and ask her for some milk and half a dozen eggs. You'd better go and get some bread and some paraffin from Granny Waring's, while you at it. Tell her I'll pay her tomorrow – and, be quick". She hadn't drawn her widow's pension in the six weeks she'd been away, so she knew a nice little sum had amassed.

"And bring me five Park Drive, as well" she called after them.

When the children came back with the provisions, Margaret was also back in the house. She explained to her mother that she hadn't been at home very much, as the mother of one of her workmates had taken pity on her and said she was welcome t
o stay with them. As she hated coming back to an empty house she had jumped at the chance, but, consequently, their home had been neglected.

They were all delighted to meet their new baby sister and took it in turns nursing her whilst Lizzie prepared scrambled egg on toast and cups of tea for the four of them.

Bill and Dorothy were washing the pots when they saw Edie hurrying up the road, towards their house, pushing her pram. Bill opened the door to her and she parked the pram in the yard. The two friends greeted each other and Lizzie poured her a cup of tea. Edie brought Lizzie up to date with village happenings, including Mary's funeral. She noticed that Lizzie had gone very quiet.

"Tell me to mind my own business, if you like, but, is she (nodding her head towards the baby) his? There's been a bit of talk".

"It's true" Lizzie replied.

There, she'd done it, now. But, as she knew she would be blamed for Mary's death, and as Ted had already accepted responsibility for the baby, she thought she might as well take advantage of the situation. Edie looked at her friend but remained non-judgemental – these things happened, particularly during a war.

"Can you make use of my pram?" she offered. Lizzie was thrilled. Years ago, the wheels from her old pram had been fastened to an old wooden box, and made Bill the proud owner of one of the few go-karts in the village. Edie pushed the pram through the kitchen and into the sitting room. In it, was a lovely soft mattress and matching pillow, soft white blankets and a bag containing fluffy white towelling nappies, tiny vests and nightgowns.

"All of this?" she asked.

"Well, I don't think I'll be needing any of it again, do you"? She laughed. Lizzie realised that she had almost forgotten what a laugh sounded like. Edie noticed the pained look on her friends face and said.

"You've gone through hell, haven't you, Liz".

"Well, it's not been all sunshine, and that's for sure" Lizzie replied. But, it's all in the past, now".

Edie stayed a while, and brought Lizzie up to date with the village news. Joe Finnikin's wife had produced their first child, a daughter, just the day before Lizzie's travail, so that would be nice, the little girls would start school together and would probably become best friends.

The Watson family, who had returned home to Liverpool at the beginning of the year, shortly after the war had ended, had themselves been blessed with another child – a little boy they had named Leonard. Lizzie's thoughts wandered to that fateful night; no wonder Arthur had been so accommodating – letting Pietro visit her – he had been away from the camp himself, procreating with the lovely Bella.

Edie then said she must return home, but didn't realise that she had brought some normality back into Lizzie's life, in that short time.

Lizzie knew she would soon recover from her shocking ordeal – she had managed to overcome worse things than this, after all!

***

Word soon got round the village that Lizzie Udall was back and with yet another child in tow. When the news arrived at Hall Lane, Ted wasted no time in visiting her.

"You can move into my house as soon as you like" he told her. Lizzie went to look around and, whilst the garden was huge, with an enormous orchard at the bottom, the house itself was tiny. Just two up and two down.

However, Lizzie had little choice; she gave notice on the tenancy of Toll Gate Cottage and moved after their marriage in December, 1946.

Christmas was quite a merry time for them all in Hall Lane, although a bit cramped and crowded. The three boys were in one bed, in the small bedroom, two at the top and one at the bottom, the girls shared a single bed in the same room, whilst Lizzie and Ted and the baby, in her cot, shared the larger room.

Water had to be carried by bucket, from a gated well in the adjacent field, but they always had to remember to secure the gate, as the cows thought this water was much sweeter than theirs, in the nearby trough. The only lavatory was situated in the orchard, just about as far away from the house as was possible.

Lizzie had been a lone parent for all of nine years, and in that time had become very independent. She was having great difficulty adjusting to married life.

When she discovered Ted had savings stashed away, she pleaded poverty and he quieted her with whatever amount she requested, and consequently, his savings soon dwindled away. Although Lizzie liked to smoke her cigarettes, she said the smell of his pipe tobacco nauseated her, so she made him either go outside, or smoke it in the shed.

Life wasn't good for Ted, but he so wanted to make this marriage work. It was a rare occasion for them to be alone in the house, so when Bill went out with the Grindey boys, his own sons were walking in the Dell and Dorothy and Margaret had taken Kathleen out in her pram, he began to tell her of his unhappiness. Lizzie's quick temper had begun to show itself, more and more.

"If you don't like it, you know what you can do" she blazed. Ted now felt angrier than he had ever done, and all of his resentment came pouring forth.

"I've given you all I can, Lizzie. I've let you bleed me dry, mentally and financially, but nothing I do seems to make you happy. I did the right thing by you; I acknowledged that the baby was mine......"

"Ahhh.....but, she's not yours Ted Morley. You acknowledged her, yes. But, only *I* know who the father of my baby is, and *I know* that it's *not you*.

He looked at her – shocked.... disbelieving.... hurt – how could she – how could he have thought he loved this bitter woman.

Lizzie just sat there, unrepentant, smoking her cigarette.

He went up the stairs and quietly packed all of his belongings, then went into the little bedroom and gathered his son's things together. He took the bags with him into the field. As it was going dusk, the children were all returning home. He called

Jacob to his side and when Phillip arrived, soon after, the three of them walked away together, in the direction of Sitton, and never looked back. Ted and Lizzie never spoke to each other, ever again.

Once more, Lizzie was a lone parent.

CHAPTER FIFTY THREE

Margaret and her friends either went to Utchester, to the picture house or to a dance together, when they had saved up enough money. Lizzie still took Margaret's wage packet from her and gave her back a meagre allowance plus her bus fares. It was during one of these outings, to a dance, that she first encountered a young man who really caught her eye. His name was Tom Peaty and thought he was so handsome. They danced together all evening and then he walked with her to catch the last bus, with the rest of her friends.

"Can I take you to the pictures next week?" he asked.

"I'd better ask my Mam. I'll let you know" she replied. Lizzie thought, at twenty one, he was too old for her unworldly and innocent daughter, but in the end she agreed to let her go, just this once. But, she would have to meet him if he ever wanted to take her out again.

The Saturday after their first date, he arrived at the door.

"Hello, Mrs Morley." He said confidently. "I'm Tom, and I'd like your permission to take Marje out, regularly". Lizzie took an instant dislike to this arrogant young man, who couldn't even call her daughter by her proper name. But, Lizzie thought that if she refused permission, 'Marje' would probably go out with him behind her back, so she reluctantly agreed.

Bill left school and was offered a job by a village farmer, Joe Finnikin. Now Lizzie had two small wages coming in, but was still constantly short of money. The old Lizzie would have found herself a couple of jobs to help make ends meet, but Kathleen's birth had left her weak and lethargic. Besides who would look after the little one?

In March, Margaret had been seeing Tom for ten months, when Lizzie sensed there was a problem. She hoped and prayed that she was wrong, but when Marg informed her that Tom was coming to see her on Saturday, Lizzie knew that her worst fears were coming true.

"I want your permission to marry Marje" he said.

"She's in the family way, isn't she?" Lizzie demanded.

Tom was shocked.

"Has she told you?"

"She doesn't have to. Mothers know these things".

"Well – are you giving your permission – or not?"

"You're an impudent bugger, Tom Peaty" she was so angry at his attitude. "Yes, I'm giving my 'permission', because if you don't marry her, now, I'll be after you with a shot gun, believe me."

"That's good, because it's all arranged for the 23rd April – you can come if you like".

"Just get out – now – you cheeky sod" Lizzie was furious – she was afraid if he didn't go, she would throw something at him. Together, he and Marg walked up the road, deep in conversation.

At times, Lizzie was her own worst enemy. She was always so tired and didn't have much patience with anyone, so, when Margaret spoke excitedly of her forthcoming marriage, Lizzie told her,

"For goodness sake, give it a rest. I'm sick of hearing about this damned wedding – it'll end in tears – mark my words".

"Oh Mam – don't say that. Tom's a smashing bloke, when you get to know him. You've not given him a chance".

"Not given him a chance, he came here, full of his own importance, begging to take you out and in no time he's got you – in the family way – and you, no more than a child yourself. I don't like him……. and…… I never will".

"But you'll come to the wedding, surely"? Margaret pleaded. Lizzie had such a stubborn streak, and sometimes it caused her to cut her nose to spite her face – and this was one of the occasions. She wanted to be with her daughter, of course she did, on what should be the happiest day of a girl's life; but she detested the bridegroom so much, that she replied,
"If you were marrying anyone else, of course I would – but, Tom Peaty? – no, I won't be there".

Margaret knew that all the pleading in the world wouldn't change her mothers' mind. When she told Tom he comforted her by saying,

"She'll be there, you'll see. She won't miss our special day".

But, miss it she did. She desperately wanted to see her daughter wed, but after all she'd said, her silly pride prevented her from going. Bill didn't attend either, as one of the other farm hands had broken his wrist and Bill was needed on the farm.

"I don't like weddings very much, but I'll be thinking about you, Our Marg" he told her affectionately. So, of the family, just Dorothy attended, taking her younger sister with her.

The legal union didn't really change Margaret's situation very much, as she continued to live in Weaverley, and Tom continued to live in Utchester. He lived with his invalid father (his mother had been dead for years) and his brother, George and sister-in-law, Doris, in a two bed-roomed house, sleeping on the couch in the living room. Margaret could see for herself that was no room for her – and very soon the two of them would become three.

Because she was so upset about missing the wedding, Lizzie kept up her tirade. At every opportunity, she decried Tom Peaty.

"But Mam, he married me – he's done the right thing – and I know he'll look after me – and the baby."

"And where is he now?" Lizzie demanded.

"He's looking for somewhere for us to live".

"That's what he tells you – you fool. He's out womanising, not looking for a house...." She stopped when Margaret burst into tears.
"How can you say that? You don't even know him – you've never given him a chance".

She stormed out of the house and sat herself on the wall, in the orchard. From this vantage point, she would be able to see Tom, when he came down the road. The warm, early summer sun did little to soothe her troubled mind – Mam's constant jibes about her husband really got to her. In her total misery, she failed to notice the beauty of the day. The birds were at their most eloquent, the cloudless sky a beautiful azure blue, with the tiny stream rippling past her feet. Then she saw him – her heart skipped a beat. She pushed herself off the wall and ran up the field, over the milk stand, on to the road and into his arms. All was well. What a lovely day, she noticed.

Tom could see through her smiles that something – or someone – had upset his pretty young wife.

"What's wrong?" he asked.

"It's Mam".

'Now there's a surprise', he thought. As Margaret repeated their earlier conversation, she could see that Tom was getting very angry.

"Go and get your things together. You're not staying here another day" he ordered.

She went indoors and up to the room she shared with her mother and two sisters, gathering her few belongings and wrapping them in a piece of brown paper. On her way out she looked at her mother, silently begging her to have a change of heart and accept Tom. Lizzie was sat next to the fire, puffing on her Park Drive.

"I'm going with Tom, Mam" she said.

"Go then" Lizzie replied, nonchalantly.

Outside, Kathleen was playing in the soil and looked up as Margaret and came out of the house and walked up the path, not glancing in her small sister's direction. She'd gone.

Kathleen ran into the house and said, "Mummy – Margie's gone"

"I know" replied her mother, not letting the little one see the tears in her eyes. How could she have been so cruel to her first born?

She'd lost her now.

CHAPTER FIFTY FOUR

Regs' vigour and enthusiasm for the factory had waned, since David had informed him of his intentions. Fleur was now fourteen and quite a beauty. The local boys were very interested in the young heiress, but Reg watched her like a hawk. He didn't want some fortune hunter getting his grubby hands on *his* daughter and inheriting *his* factory (little thinking that this was precisely what *he* had done, almost twenty years ago). Tonight, he would talk to Sarah – he was aware that she longed to have a child of her own, although she had been a lovely step-mum to David and Fleur. It wasn't too late – she was younger than Flora was when Fleur had been conceived. Maybe she would need a bit of help from the professionals, but, they could afford it, for goodness sake. Yes, he needed another son, a boy who *would* want to take over from him – that was the answer!

Sarah was thrilled at the suggestion, and said she would see her doctor the following day and set the wheels in motion for a consultation with a specialist.

Cissie was in the waiting room when Sarah arrived for her appointment. Cissie's David had a severe chest infection and Cissie had been without sleep for the last couple of nights. Sarah was so excited that she confided in her friend.

"I didn't realise that you wanted a baby" Cissie told her. "I thought you were more than happy with your ready made family." Cissie also knew how she enjoyed the lifestyle; attending the Hunt Ball and other society functions, being dressed to the nines in all the latest fashions, expensive hairdos, as well as being driven around in a smart car, and other people keeping her house clean and doing her laundry. But, when she thought about it, a baby wouldn't interfere with her lifestyle. Like Flora, she would have a nurse maid and so *she* wouldn't have *her* nights disturbed. Immediately she'd had this unkind thought, she regretted it. Sarah was her friend, and Cissie was happy for her, and she wouldn't swap her gentle Ted for a million Reg Jenkins', for all his money and status, but she just hoped David's chest would soon be better so that she could get good night's sleep.

How money talks! Within a couple of days Sarah had an appointment with consultant gynaecologist, who soon discovered her problem: a small blockage in her fallopian tubes was preventing her from conceiving. A simple operation rectified this and she was told to 'go forth and multiply' by the humorous old man. Within three months she was pregnant – with twins!

Reg was ecstatic when Sarah returned with the news. In his excitement, he almost let himself down. It was on the tip of his tongue to brag that now; he had fathered two sets of twins, but stopped himself, just in time! But, it didn't stop him thinking 'What a clever man I am'.

***

Sarah was visiting Cissie's home and discussing her delight at finally having her own babies, when a letter arrived - from Lizzie. The last Cissie had heard of her erring sister was that she had married again and had yet another baby. What she didn't tell her was that it didn't happen in that order. This letter was informing Cissie that, once again, Lizzie was on her own, as her husband had walked out on her. Cissie felt exasperated with her sister's woes. She seemed to attract 'bad luck'.

However, Sarah's talk of twins reminded Cissie of Lizzie's loss. She knew that the course of Lizzie's life was changed, the day she lost little Bobby. So Cissie decided that this was one piece of local news that she would keep to herself, for as long as possible – to tell Lizzie of Sarah's news, would be the pinnacle of insensitivity. Not that she felt like writing to anyone today, she just wanted a good night's sleep.

***

David Wirksworth-Jenkins always came home during the University holidays and continued to show an avid interest in the factory, helping his father in any way he could. He was also a natural when dealing with the work-force. He saw their point of view, and listened to any suggestions they had to make. Reg constantly hoped that he would get this doctor malarkey out of his system and join the family business, where he so obviously belonged. Everyone could see what a good leader he would be.

Reg soon had a change of heart. Sarah was around six weeks off giving birth and David was due to return to his studies the following day, so was spending time with his 'mother' and finishing his packing – which he always insisted on doing for himself. They had just finished a leisurely lunch together, when Sarah rose from the table and promptly fell to the floor in a dead faint. In seconds, David had her in the recovery position, made sure that nothing was in her mouth, and loosened the clothing around her throat. He noticed that her ankles were swollen, like balloons – why had he not noticed this before. He telephoned the ambulance, who arrived within minutes. He explained that he was a student doctor, and, in his opinion, his step mother was suffering from toxaemia.

At the hospital they discovered that her blood pressure was at a dangerously high level, and, left any longer could have proved fatal to the babies, as well as Sarah. The early diagnosis and prompt action from David had, without a doubt, saved all of their lives. From that day on, Reg encouraged his son, every step of the way on his journey to become a respected member of the medical profession.

Sarah was hospitalized until her babies were ready to be born, with David a very regular visitor.

Towards the end of the pregnancy, Sarah's blood pressure once again went beyond the danger level, and it was necessary for her to undergo an emergency caesarean section. The twin boys were very tiny, and were immediately transferred to incubators. The local vicar was called to the hospital to baptize them – Colin and Christopher – as Sarah fought her way back to good health. The doctors advised her to be satisfied with her two little boys and not to even think of having any more babies.

Whilst Colin thrived, Christopher struggled. He was a pale and sickly baby, taking an age to drink his formula milk, only to bring the majority of it back again, within minutes. Sarah was beside herself with worry. David returned home as often as he could, and Sarah was comforted and re-assured by his presence. On one occasion, the tiny boy had stopped breathing, but David calmly revived him with mouth to mouth resuscitation – much to the gratitude and admiration of his father and step-mother.

The concern for Christopher brought home to Reg how important *both* of his sons were. He was consumed with guilt for the pain he must have caused Lizzie, all those years ago, when he felt it his right to transfer one of their babies from her care, to his own. He could do nothing about it now – it was too late – but at last he had some understanding of what he had put her through.

What a clever man he was??

CHAPTER FIFTY FIVE

In August, 1949, at the age of forty three, Lizzie became a granny for the first time, to a pretty little girl that Marg and Tom christened Rosemary Anne. Her birth helped heal the rift between Margaret and her mother, as Lizzie realised that Tom was now part of her family – whether she approved or not. The young couple now had a home of their own and Lizzie was a frequent visitor, when she could afford the bus fare, that is.

Rosemary was only two years old when Marg gave birth to a bouncing baby boy they named William Thomas, after her brother. Two years later, another baby boy was produced. They called him Michael James, and he was followed two years on by Margaret's younger sister's namesake, Kathleen Mary.

Bill was called up for his National Service in 1952, leaving his youngest sister laid up with Chicken Pox!

He was terrified at the thoughts of leaving the village, never mind leaving the county – but even more scary was the thought that he may even have to leave the country – on his own.

He was taken first to Aldershot and then on to Blandford for his early training, but he made the journey back to Weaverley just as often as he could, sometimes arriving home in the middle of the night, waking up the family with the sound of his heavy army boots echoing down the whole of Hall Lane, causing great excitement.

He was with the Catering Corps and practised his new-found culinary skills during each leave, much to the delight of his mother and younger sisters.

In 1953, Lizzie's dear friend and confidante Edie, along with husband Gordie and all of their brood, left the village for pastures new, leaving Lizzie virtually friendless in the village.

At the end of his conscription, Bill felt the need to spread his wings and soon passed his driving test, taking up lorry driving as his chosen profession. This job brought him in close contact with his new boss's daughter, Pamela, with whom he fell deeply in love, and soon begged her to marry him. Although Lizzie liked the girl, she was pretty and very kind-hearted, she still thought that he could have done better for himself – in other words – no-one would have been good enough for her blue-eyed-boy!

Dorothy was never short of a boyfriend. She enjoyed shop-work, and was employed in a fruit and green grocery shop in Ashtown, before moving across the road to good old Woollies, where she caught the eye of a young Ashtown fellow.

She loved clothes and make up, but as she was still giving Lizzie most of her wages, she was constantly short of money, and on one occasion, when she was absolutely skint, Bill took unfair advantage of this. He offered to buy her Staffordshire Dogs, the only things of value that she possessed. Dorothy was undecided as they were all she had to connect her with the father she had never known. But, in that moment of weakness, she agreed and the deed was done. So, when she married her love, George Handley, and moved to Ashtown, her dogs remained in Hall Lane.

For all of her disapproving and strict ways, Lizzie was a far better Granny than she had been a mother. Margaret's children all loved to go and stay with her, enjoying the way they all had to sleep together, in one bed, with only one bed-spread over them – if they got cold she would throw a couple of coats over them. But they were never ready to go home when the time came.

Another baby boy was born to Marg and Tom in 1958. He was a beautiful but frail little soul they called Paul Geoffrey. Lizzie said he was the 'scrapings of the barrel', another old saying from her own childhood, possibly.

Paul wasn't the only one that was frail. Lizzie had always been slim, but she was now quite thin and looked much older than her years.

Money was always tight; she had to rely on Bill for so many things, as her maintenance from her ex-husband was sporadic, he only sent it, if, and when he felt like it. She was still smoking her Park Drive, often substituting a cigarette for a meal, and at times her cough racked her poor body.

Early in 1959, her health caused grave concern. Her legs swelled and caused her much pain. Margaret visited when she could, but with five young children it wasn't easy. Dorothy, too, visited as much as she could, but she was working full time, so it was left to twelve year old Kathleen to sit with her mother overnight and ensure she didn't lie down – as, if she did, the fluid in her legs would flood her heart and she would die. Kathleen took the nursing of her mother very seriously and would scold her, if she sank down in her bed.

By Easter, Lizzie could be seen to be deteriorating and was taken into hospital. Tests were carried out and she was found to have numerous ailments, the most serious was as serious as it gets – cancer.

Within days of being admitted, it was obvious to the doctors that she would never go back home to Weaverley.

On Wednesday 22nd April, 1959, the nurse had just given Lizzie a drink of water and noticed that her breathing was becoming laboured. She called the doctor who came immediately, and drew the curtains around her bed. Her breathing became more and more shallow. The doctor realised that the end was near and sat down at her bedside, taking her hand in his. He stroked it gently, and told her that all was well – it was now time for her to stop fighting and she should let herself go and meet her Maker – it was time for her to go. Her eyelids fluttered. Her eyes opened and she looked into a pair of piercing blue eyes.

"Bobby" she whispered. He continued to stroke her hand, re-assuring her.

She sighed……….. And then took her last breath.

The doctor sat for a moment, saddened that no member of her family had been with her, for her passing. But, it had been so peaceful. He rose from his chair and gently closed her eyes and pulled the sheet up and covered her face, then quietly left her bedside. He informed the Sister, and then went for a much needed cup of tea after signing the death certificate.

Dr David Wirksworth -Jenkins